HOT TALES OF GAY LUST

More titles from Xcite Books

9781907016097
£7.99 $11.99

9781907761522
£7.99 $11.99

9781907761638
£7.99 $11.99

Xcite Books are also available as ebook downloads on
iTunes, Kindle and www.xcitebooks.com

HOT TALES OF GAY LUST

LANDON DIXON

Published by Accent Press Ltd – 2011
Paperback ISBN 9781907761454
eBook ISBN 9781907761461

Printed and bound in the UK

Cover design by Adam Walker

Contents

Raining Men

RAYMOND SEARLES SAT AT his desk, working late, as usual. He was poring over some briefs he wanted to have ready for a court date tomorrow morning, his dedication to his job directly related to his ambition, inversely impacting on his personal life.

He looked up, out at the darkened, deserted outer office. All of the other firm's lawyers had long since gone home to their families. Raymond's hand dropped down onto the telephone, thinking of Jess. He really should give him a call, tell him he'd be coming home ... soon. What was this, the third, fourth night in a row he'd worked late already this week?

Raymond shook his head. He couldn't remember when he *hadn't* worked late. There was just so much to do and so little time to do it in, so few partner openings coming up next month. His hand slid off the phone.

He'd only get another lecture from Jess, anyway. The guy was great, but he'd been harping more and more, lately, on how little time they'd been spending together. Raymond could do without that hassle right now. He'd make it up to Jess at the weekend. They'd go to the beach, make love on the sand ... How long *had* it been since they'd last made love?

Raymond shook his head with a rueful grin and went back to his work, forgetting all about Jess.

He didn't raise his head out of the law books and

paperwork again for another two hours. And only then when he heard something splattering against his third floor window. He spun around in his chair and stared at the window.

It was raining, coming down hard. The wind was gusting water against the glass, sheeting down in torrents out in the street.

Raymond rose out of his chair and stretched his legs, looking down into the rain-washed night. He glanced at his watch – 1 a.m. The street was deserted, the pavement glistening like oil with the moisture, the air misted with it.

No, the street wasn't quite deserted. A couple came running down the sidewalk, hand in hand, their other hands up over their heads, trying to shield themselves from the rain. They quickly gave that up and jogged to a stop. One of the men pushed the other up against the wall of the building opposite, and kissed him.

Ah, lovers in the rain, Raymond thought. He reached over and snapped the light off on his desk, to give himself a better view from the dark.

They were two men, all right. One was tall and lean and blond, the other shorter, smaller, with dark hair. They were haloed in the yellow, shimmering light of a streetlamp, the dark-haired man pinning the blond up against the wall and working the man's mouth over with his mouth.

Raymond couldn't see faces, but he could see the action clear enough; the only one who was seeing it, judging by the emptiness of the street and the buildings all around. The men probably thought they had the stormy night all to themselves, because the brunette pulled the blond's T-shirt out of his jeans, baring the man's chest to the rain, then to his mouth. The smaller man began vigorously kissing all over the taller man's chest, raining his lips down like water.

Raymond could see now that this might develop into something. He could remember a time when he and Jess didn't have a place of their own to make love, so they had to

2

improvise with whatever was available. That was also a time when the passion flared so hot and bright they had to improvise as fast as they could. Like those lovers down in the street below.

Raymond felt his balls tingle, his cock surge in his pants, watching the one man ravage the other man's chest. That chest was smooth and slick and no doubt hot, getting felt up, the nipples getting tongued and sucked, no doubt hardening, expanding with erotic sensations thanks to the one man's hungry mouth. Raymond slowly unzipped the fly on his dark-blue business suit and reached inside.

He shivered when he clutched his cock. He was even harder than he'd expected, pulsing with excitement, and need. It *had* been a long time, too long; since he'd done anything so sexually spontaneous. He glanced behind him at his open door. The outside offices were still dark, quiet, no one around to disturb him. He drew his erection fully out into the open, let it beat hotly in his warm, gripping hand.

The lovers were kissing again, arms around one another, heads moving, bobbing. Raymond took a tentative stroke of his cock, and shuddered with pleasure. It was a hot night, despite the downpour, and the pair below were wearing just jeans and T-shirts. And those were coming off fast now, the shorter man stripping off his tee, the blond pulling his the rest of the way off. Their skin shone in the light from the streetlamp.

Raymond stroked slow and sure, tugging on his erection with a practised hand. Then he groaned, when the men suddenly dashed off down the sidewalk, grasping their wet T-shirts in their hands. Raymond's hand froze on his cock. Was this the end of the show?

No! He blew out his cheeks in relief, and amazement, when the men darted into an alley, began seriously stripping off their clothes, taking their lovemaking to a whole new level that rated at least some measure of privacy. Or so they thought.

3

Because now Raymond actually had an even better view of the sexy goings-on. The alley was almost directly across from his window, the men turned sideways now, one no longer partially blocking out the other, the streetlight still illuminating their activities, silhouetting things even more dramatically and erotically.

Jeans came off, were discarded on top of the damp T-shirts already lying on the slick alley floor. The men were just in their briefs, their soaking wet briefs. Raymond could see the prominent bulges at groin level. He licked his lips and swallowed, gliding his hand along his own straining erection just a little faster, a little harder.

The dark-haired man pressed the blond up against the alley wall, their naked flesh melding together, thinly-clad cocks squeezing together. Raymond groaned, mentally experiencing the wicked pleasure of two men's cocks jamming, sliding against one another's. For the shorter man was pumping his hips, pumping his cock into the other man's cock, as they kissed, frenched, their outstretched tongues dancing together under the onslaught of water and desire.

Raymond loosened his tie and unbuttoned his shirt with his free hand. He slid his hand onto his chest, quivering when his searching fingers found a buzzing nipple. He cupped one pec, pinched one nipple, did the same to the other aroused pec and nipple, glaring down at the men in the alley, pumping his cock.

The dark-haired one pulled his tongue out of the blond's mouth and began kissing and licking his way down the blond's chest. He swirled his tongue around nipples, sealed his lips to one and sucked on it, did the same to the other nipple, the blond man writhing against the dripping wall. The brunette went lower, his hair plastered to his head, his tongue flicking out and tasting, basting hot, taut skin. He gripped the blond's thin hips and swarmed his mouth-organ all over the tightened muscles of the man's heaving

4

stomach.

'Jesus, yes!' Raymond breathed, taking it all in, mesmerized by it all. He pumped his cock and rolled his nipples, watching with unblinking eyes as the man speared his tongue into the other's bellybutton and squirmed it around.

The blond's cock bulged his sodden briefs to bursting, right in front of the squatting man's face. 'Suck it! Suck his cock!' Raymond hissed, his mind briefly flashing onto Jess, how that lovely man could suck so hard and so hot.

And that mind's eye picture of Jess, squatting down on his knees with his delicious mouth and throat full of Raymond's cock, caused Raymond to temporarily halt the heated hand motion on his prick. Was he cheating on Jess? Jerking off while he watched two men make love in an alley?

He grinned, stroking again. It would never stand up in court, he thought, only half humorously. Masturbating wasn't cheating, no matter what triggered it. And what had triggered it was now burning wetly incandescent before Raymond's very glaring eyes, a stunning scene he just couldn't look away from, not get off on.

The kneeling man had his fingers in the waistband of the blond's briefs, was slowly pulling them down. The blond arched his back and his groin out, urging his lover on. The briefs slid lower, tangling over the top of the man's erection, which was now pulled straight out, at a tremendous length.

'Yes! Pull them off! Suck him off!' Raymond urged, twisting a nipple so hard he wanted to scream.

The brunette gave a final yank, and the water-logged briefs popped off the blond's penis and fell down his legs. Hot, bare, long cock jutted out, twitching in the rain, cap and shaft shining.

The kneeling man grasped the standing man's cock, lacing his fingers around pulsating shaft. And Raymond swore he could hear the howl of the blond, as the man felt

5

the impact of that hand.

The brunette stroked, pumping the thrust-out cock, motions oiled by the falling rain. Raymond tugged on his own prick in rhythm, his mouth broken open like the blond's. The brunette cupped the man's balls, squeezed. Raymond dove his hand down off his chest and clutched his own sex-tightened sac, and squeezed, twisted, stroking and stroking and stroking.

Lightning split the sky wide open, bathing the ultra-erotic scene in pure white light. Just as the brunette opened his mouth up wide and swallowed the blond's cap.

'Yes!' Raymond grunted, swirling his fingers all over his hood.

The kneeling man pulled on his lover's bloated knob with his plush lips, pulling the blond off the wall, then pushing him back. He dodged his head closer, taking shaft into his mouth, and sucking on it. And then he pressed his advantage all the way home, consuming the blond's entire cock in one breathtaking swallow.

'Fuck, yeah!' Raymond growled, marvelling at the oral skills of the man on his knees.

The brunette's face pressed right up against the blond's abdomen, cock disappeared, buried in the other man's mouth and throat. The blond grabbed onto his lover's hair, his body vibrating out of control, overwhelmed by the exquisite sensations he was feeling.

The brunette abruptly pulled back. Cock burst out of his mouth, huge and hard and even wetter still. He gripped the base of it, mouthed the hood and shaft, sucking tight and hard and almost full-length.

'Give it to him! Suck him!' Raymond hissed, torquing up the pressure on his own prick, matching the frenetic pace of the talented cocksucker below.

Lightning flashed and rain slashed down, the brunette urgently wet-vaccing the blond's cock, the blond bending with the savage sensuality of it all. And then a peel of thunder ripped the heavens, and the brunette yanked dick out of his bottomless throat and mouth and sprang to his feet. He spun the blond around, spread him up against the wall.

Raymond grinned through gritted teeth, his cock gone numb-hard in his urgently pumping hand. He twisted and pulled on his balls, his body bowing now just like the blond's had earlier.

The blond planted his hands on the wall, his long legs slightly apart, up on his toes. As he felt the sharp slap of the brunette's cock against his butt cheeks. He knew he was going to be fucked, up the ass, in the rain, out in the open.

One more brisk bash of granite cock on trembling cheek and the brunette gripped the blond's hip with one hand, plunged his dick in between the blond's water-dappled buttocks with the other. Both men shuddered, cockhead hitting manhole. Then driving home.

Raymond fisted his prick, watching the one man sink into the other, cock penetrating anus and plunging chute. Until the brunette took his hand away and squeezed the final few inches of turgid meat inside his lover with a hard thrust of his hips, his thighs touching up against the other man's quivering cheeks.

The street lit up with lightning, thunder shaking the buildings, as the brunette rocked back and forth, fucking the blond.

Raymond groaned and fisted harder, faster, his face and body burning. The brunette clutched the blond's hips and vigorously pumped his. Raymond could see silver cock gliding back and forth, plundering ass, almost hear the crack of wet flesh against wet flesh, even over the raging storm. He'd fucked Jess many a time just like this, though not in a long time, and not so publicly.

The brunette moved faster, pumping rhythmically, rippling the blond's cheeks, ploughing the blond's ass. Raymond fisted in a frenzy, his breath coming in gasps. He wanted to time it just right, get off just as the rain-soaked

7

men got off, making the spectacle complete.

The blond had his own cock in his hand and was furiously tugging on it, as he got cocked up the ass. They were all coming closer, driving forward, the pressure piling up to the blow-off point.

Raymond couldn't control himself. 'Fuck, yes!' he howled, snapping up straight and jetting out of the end of his overhandled dong. Rope after rope of heated sperm blasted out and splashed against the rain-washed window.

Just as the brunette reared back his head and roared out his ecstasy. As the blond jerked and spurted sperm against the cement wall. The men were jolted almost to pieces by their unrestrained joy, the brunette blazing liquid fire into the blond's ass, the blond adding to the unrelenting torrent of liquid already coating the streets. Raymond couldn't remember the last time he'd come so hard and so long.

When he finally arrived home, he was surprised to find Jess still awake. The man was in the bathroom, rubbing his hair with a towel.

'What's the matter?' Raymond asked good-naturedly, still feeling slightly guilty about what he'd been a part of. 'Did you get caught out in the rain?'

Jess grinned, lowering the towel down to his shoulders. His brown hair gleamed wetly under the bathroom lights. 'You could say that,' he responded.

Raymond smiled back, relieved that the man wasn't mad at him for working so late again, ignoring their home life again. But then he heard the dryer rumbling in the background and, as he looked at the small, smiling brunette, he began to get a cold, sinking feeling in the pit of his stomach.

His worst fears were confirmed, when Jess added, 'I went to see you in your office tonight. But I got sort of waylaid by the rain. Will you be working late again tomorrow night?'

Field of Reams

THE SUN WAS BEATING down on me hammer and tongs. A car approached, moving fast up the lonely highway. I stuck out my thumb half-heartedly like I had two dozen times before that day, wondering idly which ditch I was going to sleep in that night – the one on the north side of the road or the south.

The car zoomed past me. I watched it go by.

Then, suddenly, I saw the brake lights flash, and the vehicle slewed to the side of the road, kicking up a dust cloud on the shoulder. My heels kicked up a couple more dust clouds, running for the car.

A big, busty redhead was parked behind the steering wheel. 'Get in, stranger,' she said with a slur and a wink.

I dumped my backpack in the backseat, my ass in the front. The woman hauled ass, spitting gravel and chewing up pavement again. Before we'd marked our first mile together, her hand was down in between my legs, rubbing my crotch.

The car was a convertible. The sun beat down on me hammer and tongs.

'Where you headed, big boy?' she asked. Even in the wind, I could smell the liquor on her breath.

'Anywhere,' I replied, trying to close up my legs.

She kept her hand down there, rubbing, stroking my dick to stunning unresponsiveness in my thin jeans. I hated to break it to the lady that I didn't play her game, so I didn't. My limp interest in her handling spoke volumes for me.

By mile ten, she spoke what I'd been dreading to hear, 'Get out!' She jerked the big convertible off the road, skidding to a stop. 'There ain't no free rides in my car.'

She left me in the dust by the side of the road.

The sun was starting its long slant into oblivion, so I walked off the highway and into a wheat field, headed for a stand of trees far off in the distance, some shade and maybe a barn to spend the night in.

I made the trees in an hour, walked through the thin line of them, into another big field neatly planted with radishes. There were people here, Mexican vegetable pickers come up north to make some money for their families down south. They were just leaving the land after a hard day's work, headed for a cluster of buildings off in the distance.

I followed them, keeping to the treeline that ran alongside the field. They were all men, short and copper-skinned, with gleaming black hair and eyes. They were dressed in jeans and plaid workshirts, spoke to one another in Spanish, making with the hand gestures. I followed them to a dusty compound that contained a bunkhouse, a shower facility, a barn, and a large, white farmhouse where the bossman and his family must live.

The men started stripping off their clothes even before they reached the shower building, showing off their tight, muscled bodies to one astonished voyeur. I followed their taut little lighter-bronze buttocks right into the facility with my unblinking eyes. Then I took a quick glance around and dashed out of the trees, over to the side of the building, hugging one wall with my head down.

The shower building had a peaked, green-plastic roof, four white-plastic walls that didn't quite go up to the roof, leaving open space all around, top and bottom. I poked my eyes up above the wall, using that open space to look into the already steaming facility.

There was a stainless steel partition in the middle of the interior, eight showerheads hooking off the partition on either side, a cement floor with drains underneath. Nothing fancy, but it got the job done, allowing the 12 men to wash the day's toil off their hard bodies.

I licked my field-dry lips, peering over the wall and watching the men soap up their arms and chests and legs and groins, let the hot needle-spray water wash over those very same body parts. For a man like me, queer as most of these guys' passports in all probability, it was a picture worth a thousand hard-ons.

Their muscled bodies shone, glistening, their strong, agile hands running all over their torsos and appendages, along with my eyes, rubbing, caressing, stroking – each other!

I gave my sunbaked head a shake, my hands gone damp as the shower floor on the top of the wall. Was I suffering from heatstroke, or were these field studs actually soaping each other up, feeling each other up?

They were; they sure as the steel in my jeans were! They'd taken their hands off their individual bodies and were helping themselves to one another's shoulders and arms and chests and groins and buttocks, sudsing and rubbing like it was the most natural thing in the world to help get your buddy get clean while you got dirty.

I watched in shock and awe, pressing my emblazoned groin tight against the thin, corrugated wall, vibrating with excitement. The men were rubbing all over each other, helpfully scrubbing one another's skin to burnished cleanliness. Guys' asses cracked delightfully pale open, as they squatted down and ran their hands up and down sturdy legs, squeezed those same hands up and along handsome, hardening cocks, flowed them around mounded butt cheeks.

I undulated against the wall, voyeuring the steamy show. And then I almost busted a cap right then and there, as the men rose up and into each other's arms, started kissing one another.

'Workers' paradise!' I mouthed, amazed.

The job of soaping and rinsing done, the guys were going to work on each other's mouths and tongues, kissing, frenching; in pairs and threesomes. Full, tan lips smacked together and thick, red tongues coiled together, over and over, all over the place, the wet, wicked sounds of lovemaking rising up above the drum of the water on the floor and bodies, beating against my ears, my cock beating against the wall of the sultry steam room.

Dicks rose up and filled hands, men cranking each other as they kissed tongues and lips. One guy went down on his knees and easily inhaled an upthrust prong into his hungry mouth, as I visually urged him on. Another guy grabbed onto the top of the metal partition and bent his back, arched his bottom, a man in behind doing a man's job, sticking the guy's ass with his hard-on.

I'd stumbled onto nirvana. This was no farmer's daughter and son experimenting with one another in the hayloft, while the old man gave his old lady a good ploughing in the farmhouse. This was mano a mano a mano action of the most glorious kind, involving rugged men who knew exactly how to handle the tools and equipment involved. I tore a hand off the wall and ripped my zipper down, pulled my own throbbing scythe out of my jeans and polished for all I was worth.

'Lookin' for work? Or jest lookin'?' somebody thundered.

I spun around, clutching my cock in a stranglehold.

A huge man stood there, black as the good earth itself. His thick arms were folded across his broad chest, his thick lips twisted into a scowl. He was wearing a white T-shirt under a pair of blue overalls, tan workboots, his bare arms gleaming in the sun like his shaven head. The big bossman, no doubt.

'Uh, I was just, um ...'

There was no way to rationally explain it, what with my cock shooting out in my hand like that. Just like there was no way to rationally explain what was going on in that shower facility right behind me. But the big guy tried.

'Name's Kenton,' he said. 'I run this here farm. Using workers of a "special kind". Men who might have a tough time getting work, being accepted in other places.'

The guy was a humanitarian, as well as a hunk. 'I want a job!' I gulped.

He grinned, showing off teeth as white as that house of his. 'We got a special kind of interview. Think you can cut it?'

'I'll cut anything you want – fruit, vegetable or man!'

He nodded, took my arm and led me through the swinging door and into the shower building proper. The men inside had stopped making out, were staring at me, their eyes shining. Kenton said something in Spanish, and their eyes lit up even more, their tongues flicking out to bathe their lips, their hard cocks quivering in between their legs.

'I told 'em we got a new one, wants to be interviewed,' Kenton informed me. Then added, 'Take off your clothes. We do it kind of informal 'round here.'

He unfastened his overalls and let the straps drop, pulled off his T-shirt. I quickly followed his lead, stripping off my shirt and undershirt and jeans and underwear; admiring Kenton's powerful, muscle-ripped body and hanging, snake-like cock every inch of the way.

A small wooden table was brought into the building, pushed up against the metal partition. I was pushed up against the table, bent over top of it so that my ass stuck out in back and my cock stuck out down below the edge. The taps were still on, and I gripped the table, my arms and legs trembling, taking hot spray in the face and body. Then I almost went head-first through the partition, as a Mexican hit me up the ass, driving his soapy cock deep into my chute. The interview had begun.

The guy plugged me full-length, filling my anus with heat and cock. Then he gripped my hips and pumped his, fucking my ass. I bit my lip and dug my fingernails into the smooth varnished wood, taking it up the ass and loving it, the wicked man-loving coming in short, powerful thrusts. Then coming in hot, powerful bursts, the guy spraying into my bung after only 20 strokes or so.

The next man filled my chute, letting the water wash away some of his coworker's jizz, before he took his turn working my ass. These guys were good – the man banging me hard and rhythmic – and fast – the man grunting and blowing his load inside me.

I felt a warm, wet mouth inhale my cock and tug on it under the table. One of the other men, squatting down and sucking me off, as yet another man plunged his dick into my ass. I was getting it at both ends, the best job interview I'd ever had.

I was bathed in sweat and water, ass crammed full of cock and come, own cock thrusting into some guy's sucking mouth. My head spun and my body shimmered, my butt on fire, chute getting churned, spermed relentlessly. Man after man mounted me, fucked me, blasted my ass with their cocks and their jizz.

It went on and on, guys gripping and ripping me, driving me wild. Until the squatting guy finally pulled my iron-hard dong out of his mouth and got to his feet, took his turn at my hole, banging against my butt cheeks, blowing against my bowels.

I clung to the shuddering table, gasping for air.

'Just one more question to satisfactorily answer,' a familiar voice growled. 'See if you'll really fit in.'

I jerked my head around and stared at Kenton. The Nubian monster was standing in behind me, gripping his huge, ebony cock and stroking, staring at my dripping, reamed-out ass. I'd been fucked six ways from Sunday, but nowhere to the width and depth this big man's dong promised. He had to be ten solid inches of throbbing onyx.

He placed a huge hand on one of my quivering butt

14

cheeks and let it sink in, branding me with his heat. 'Ready?'

I stared at his gleaming dome and chiselled face, his pumped pecs and ribbed stomach, that unbending rod in between his legs in his hand. 'R–ready!' I gulped.

I turned back to face the metal, gripping the table so hard I almost popped splinters. Blue-black hood squished against my asshole, making me jump. Night-shaded, vein-ribboned shaft squeezed into my anus, making me shiver.

I'd been plumbed and pumped by 12 cocks, but that was just tillage for what was ploughing my ass now. Kenton's tool swelled my bum to new heights of tingling sensation, his cap, his shaft, slowly, slowly widening my channel, sinking into my chute. I full-body trembled, dancing around on my tip-toes, feeling that mammoth erection bulge my bung with every fibre of my being.

The other men were lined up alongside me, some stroking their cocks, some stroking their buddies' cocks, watching Kenton drive home his brutal, benevolent point of worker unity. He grasped my waist with both hands and thrust his dong the last few inches into my anus, bloating me to bursting.

'Yes!' I groaned, fully impaled on the man's stake.

He grunted his approval, blunt fingernails biting into my flesh, cock embedded in my ass. 'You got the job,' he confirmed, pumping his hips, plugging my chute.

'Yes!' I exulted a second time.

Kenton stretched my anus in long, languorous thrusts of his dong, pulling almost all the way out, my rim desperately clinging to his hood, then plunging all the way back in again, delving depths my butt had never experience before. I closed my eyes and grit my teeth, feeling every swollen, pulsating inch of the man's cock.

He pumped faster, and faster, pushing me up onto my toes again. His muscled thighs smacked against my rippling cheeks, cock pistoning. The hot-velvet friction was incredible, stoking me to inferno, making me blaze with emotion.

He thrust harder and even deeper. The wet, cracking tattoo of his body against my butt echoed obscenely in that lust chamber, the other men gone silent and wide-eyed. I was rocked back and forth by the pounding of his cock, my own cock flapping numbly. His balls slapped my ass, my own balls boiling, as if ...

'Oh, God!' I cried, going off hands-free.

The sawing pressure in my chute had overwhelmed me. I flooded with waves of searing wet heat, my cock spraying all on its own, in frantic rhythm to Kenton's cock pounding my ass.

'Yeah, you'll do fine!' the big man growled, thrusting, shooting.

Hot semen splashed my bowels like never before, Kenton pumping, pouring. I bleated and blew out my own ecstasy, just about folding that table up like an accordion in my crushing hands.

My wanderings were over. I'd finally found a place to call home, a harvest of bounty to call my own. Hard cocks make happy workers, that's Kenton's motto.

Body Guard

I WAS HIRED TO be one of Countess Trollop's bodyguards in April, and by May I was reaping the whirlwind of the pop tart's wild backstage scene. Sex, sex, and more sex, all a gay man and a bevy of gay back-up dancers, singers, designers and roadies could handle. Countess Trollop was the latest sensation, and she knew she had to live up to the debauched lifestyle her fans expected of her.

It was late, after a show one night, and I was in Countess Trollop's boudoir-style dressing room, two guys sucking my cock and another sucking my tongue, while the Countess watched stretched out on a satin four-poster bed. She was elegantly and outrageously attired in her latest 18th-century, French-inspired get-up and popping bon-bons into her lush, petulant mouth. As the man next to me on the blood-red sofa tugged on my outstretched tongue as hard and soft and succulent as the two men on their knees were tugging on my towering prick.

All three were back-up dancers, blowing off some steam and me after another successful, standing-room-only show. The guy next to me on the sofa was sleek and black, eager and giggly as a schoolgirl. He liked tongues, in his mouth, on his balls, up his ass. He was doing one hell of a job pulling on mine, plush lips sealed tight, head bobbing away, big brown eyes shining with glee.

The man on the left of my cock on his knees was a small, fine-featured Hispanic, smooth as caramel and just as tasty. He was licking up and down one side of my straining hard-on, the athletic, redheaded white guy with the sky-blue eyes licking the other side. Together they were playing my skinflute better than any of the musicians in Countess Trollop's travelling freakshow.

'Feels good, Rodney?' she cooed from her bed of feathers and lace.

'Yeah,' I grunted, no denying it. This gig came with some awesome fringe benefits, if you could stomach the obscene excesses.

Countess Trollop herself I'd never seen having sex, or getting sexed, so far. She was as delicate as a hot house flower, a tiny, pretty thing who painted her face like an Eighth Avenue whore, costumed herself more flamboyantly than Marie Antoinette. But she had a voice of pure gold, a seduction factor off the charts, and that's exactly where her first CD had landed.

She teased a chocolate-covered pecan with the tip of her scarlet tongue, as the Hispanic guy pulled my dick away from his friend and mouthed it all for himself. He went deep, down to the balls, making me hit the high notes in my black friend's mouth.

The redhead contented himself with my balls, sucking the hairy, heavy sac into his mouth and playing billiards with his tongue. The black guy let go of my tongue when I blasted another groan in his face. He ripped open my shirt, ran his hands all over my chest, his thick, moist mouth-organ all over my nipples.

It was crazy, insane, nuttier even than one of Countess Trollop's concerts. But I wasn't complaining; I was fully on-board for the ride. Plus, I was still doing my job; I had the Countess in clear view, guarded from any harm. She'd curled up in a silky ball, blinking her inch-long purple lashes at me, as I got cock-sucked and tea-bagged and nipple-licked.

The guys had all the right moves, on-stage and off. I was getting close to blowing a few hot, sticky licks of my own. The redhead disgorged my balls and sucked on my prick, pulling it out of his colleague's mouth and popping it into his own. As the over-excited boy-toy on my chest sunk his gleaming white teeth into first one buzzing nipple and then the other, making me buck. The Hispanic guy licked at my balls, tonguing my pouch hard and wet with his wide, strong tongue.

'Fuck!' I growled, jerking.

'Heads up, boys!' Countess Trollop peeped.

The redhead yanked my surging dong out of his mouth and it was all hands on deck, all three guys urgently pumping me. I spasmed, blowing my top, seed leaping out of my prick and into the air, raining down on the faces and tongues of my three backstage lovers. I shot burst after burst, shimmering with raw lust, popping off something fierce as the pop tart smiled and sighed.

New York, one week later. The show was a spectacular success, the largest and most outlandish spectacle yet. Countess Trollop had wowed the Big Apple, making the young girls scream and the old men cry. I'd kept her safe all that week, and now the post-performance party was going full-blast deep in the bowels of the stadium.

The room was huge, furnished with couches and loveseats and divans all of the Countess's choosing. Full of men getting it on, kissing and sucking and fucking in a cacophony of sexy, fleshy, moaning and groaning sounds, the room reeking of sweat and perfume and semen.

There was a three-stack in progress on a black velvet futon – three guys piled up in one another's laps, two cocks in two assholes, other hard dick flapping around as the men underneath pumped in unison. There was a huge black stud nailing a tiny white guy up the ass on a purple sofa, the ebony giant looming over top of the little man, almost crushing him, pummelling his asshole apart with his pile-driving dong. Whitey was getting stretched to the tearing

19

point, and he screamed for more, digging his painted fingernails into the black man's churning butt cheeks and urging him on.

There was a foursome going on the crimson-carpeted floor, one man doing another doggy-style, while that man sucked off another laid out on the floor, while that man sucked off another man straddling his head and pumping his mouth. It was a well-oiled fucking and sucking machine, sweat glistening off the nude, oversexed men in the sparkling light of three disco balls.

And I was the caboose in a five-man train, pulling up the rear literally and figuratively. Five of us were standing humped close together, naked, linked by hard cocks and soft assholes. I was the tallest in the crowd, so I got the last link in the chain, drilling into Aaron's sweet, pink chute, while he pumped the man in front of him, who pumped the man in front of him, etc ...

Aaron was Countess Trollop's choreographer, a thin, supple, glossy-haired guy with a body and mannerisms almost as feminine as the Countess herself. I prefer my men gay as possible, and this guy was absolutely flaming.

He dressed in puffy, big-cuffed blouses and skin-tight leather pants, dabbed on the make-up and body-spray with a trowel. He was smooth-shaven all over, his creamy-white skin like silk, his limbs shapely, butt sumptuously mounded, anus ripe and warm and flowered as a well-tended orchid. I was plumbing that luscious bung with my cock, bouncing off those lovely cheeks with my thighs. As Aaron churned the man in front of him at the same pace, my fucking setting the rhythm for the whole five-man chain.

I had an arm around Aaron's chest, the other around his neck, licking in behind his ears, pistoning my cock back and forth in his sucking ass slow and sure and sensual.

Someone slapped one of my bare cheeks and squeaked, 'Having fun, big boy?'

Countess Trollop. She was parading around in a blood-red satin ballgown dotted with golden fleurs-de-lis, a towering white wig on her head, two red dots painted into her pancake-made-up cheeks. She winked at me, surveying the roiling sea of male flesh, a martini glass in one of her lace-gloved hands.

I grinned back at her, torquing up the pressure on Aaron's ass. And she tottered away on her six-inch spike heels, queen of all she surveyed, but not an active participant at all in the rampant orgy. I know there were about six bisexuals and five gay guys in the funky crowd who would've given their left testicle for the right to do Countess Trollop. But she was above all that.

I dropped my hands down onto Aaron's narrow hips, really ramming the guy now, rocking the whole train. They shunted faster, harder, cornholing the chute in front of them. The crack of sweaty flesh filled the humid air along with the smutty scent of come, the grunting and groaning of our train and the other configurations of fucking and sucking men.

My cock seized come-hard in Aaron's ass, and I pumped my hips in a frenzy, firing that runaway train. 'Fuck, yeah!' I howled, jolted by orgasm, exploding inside Aaron's anus and dousing his bowels with sizzling sperm.

He shook out of control on the end of my spurting, spearing cock, spunking the guy in front of him, and on down the line. Just another typical night on the road as a member of Countess Trollop's travelling circus.

London was our next stop on the tour, and the wildest, most wonderful night of my life.

Countess Trollop took the old town by storm, the tabloids full of her exploits, unfounded rumours about her background. Her past was deliberately shrouded in mystery, and she lived her singing life like she was afraid that past could catch up with her at almost any moment.

We were alone in the bedroom of her penthouse hotel room. The party was still raging a floor below, but the

21

Countess had asked me to escort her upstairs, saying she was feeling a little ill.

But now she was showing no signs of ill health, as she crawled up behind me sitting on the edge of her bed and suddenly wrapped her slim arms around my neck and kissed me on the cheek. 'I'd like you to make love to me, Rodney,' she breathed in my ear. 'Would you?'

I cranked my head around, stared into her big violet eyes. 'What?! But–but ... you know I'm gay!'

She smiled, her plush lips glossy with chartreuse lipstick. She was wearing one of her French royal court wigs, and she took it off, revealing short, slick, brown hair, her adorable, shell-like ears.

Then, as I watched with popping eyes and cock, she stood up to her full five-foot-five height on the bed and unfastened her outlandish hoop dress. She wriggled out of the garment, revealing her smooth, delicate, naked body beneath – the semi-erect cock hanging down from her shaven loins.

'You're a–a ... man?!' I gasped, hardly believing it, despite the dangling evidence presented right before me.

She ran a white satin-gloved hand over her boyish chest, picked up my hand and placed it on her cock. The appendage jumped in my mitt, the "man" quivering.

'It'll be our little secret,' he purred in his falsetto voice. 'I just had to let you in on it.' He smiled shyly, his cock swelling with blood, filling my hand.

'But why? I mean, why do you put on this whole ... female act? Look at Prince.'

'Because I am feminine, my voice and most of the rest of me.' He looked down at his cock, which had poled out six inches of manhood in my gripping hand. 'But I didn't just want to be some sort of transvestite Las Vegas sideshow. I wanted to be a star.'

He tiptoed closer on the bed, his cock bobbing up higher and harder. 'Please.'

I gave my head a shake. Then exhaled, 'Yes, ma'am – sir.'

I pulled the gorgeous creature's cock closer and sucked his mushroomed cap into my mouth. He moaned, grabbing onto my hair, thrusting his girlish hips forward so that his cock poured into my mouth.

I grasped one of his slender legs and planted it on my thigh, so that the man's groin was directly in my face, his cock fully consumed in my mouth. I moved my head back and forth, sucking on the hardened sweetmeat.

'Oh, God!' he whimpered, his little body trembling as I wet-vacced his cock.

I gripped his taut butt cheeks and pressed him even closer, kissing his balls each and every time I plunged my mouth down the length of his prick. I tasted pre-come, salty and rubbery as any man's, all right. He shuddered, his cock jumping in my mouth.

'Please, Rodney, make love to me!' he gasped.

I thought I had been, but I knew just what he meant. Still clutching his butt cheeks, still keeping his cock buried in my mouth, I lifted the man up and climbed fully onto the bed myself. Then set him down on his back on the opulent sheets.

I slowly disgorged his cock and sat up on my knees above him, loosening my belt, unfastening my pants. His eyes glittered with tears, his body shaking beneath me, his cock shining with my saliva.

'Please, don't be gentle,' he said with a faint, almost frightened grin.

I pulled out my huge slab of meat and greased it thoroughly with the lube that's standard travelling equipment on tour. Then I lifted the man's cute little bum up off the bed, slid a pair of slickened fingers in between his cheeks and along his ultra-smooth crack. He bit his lip and moaned, cock vibrating.

'Ready?' I asked. He looked so small and tender and

23

vulnerable in the shadow of my dong.

'Fuck me!' he breathed.

I lifted his bum with one hand, steered my gleaming cockhead in between his heated cheeks with the other. I touched asshole. He gulped, gripping the sheets on either side. I pressed forward, squishing huge and thick against his resisting rosebud. Then oozing in, filling, stretching his ring, sinking into his tunnel.

It was the hottest, tightest, most sensuous entrance I'd ever made in an anus, stretching the writhing man, bloating his chute and bum with my cock. Until I was two-thirds deep inside of him, and I leaned my big body against his smooth legs, looking down at him, and started pumping his ass.

He clutched my hands on the sheet and stuck out his tongue, urgently slapping the bleached pink appendage against my tongue, as I churned his chute, bouncing into him on the bed. His ass was a gripping, sucking delight. I thrust harder, quicker, rocking the bed and the man. If his fans could see him now, I briefly thought, staring down at his cock jumping in rhythm to my cock in his ass.

He grabbed onto his dick and started stroking, staring up at me with glazed eyes. His mouth gaped open, and I filled it with my swarming tongue, like I was filling his anus with my pounding cock.

It was almost painfully honest, raw, wicked. My thighs thumped against his shuddering butt cheeks, my cock sawing back and forth in his chute.

'Oh ... Rodney!' he cried, satin hand flying up and down his prick.

Sperm shot out the tip of his dick, splashing his ecstatic face and striping his heaving chest. I grunted and fucked. Then spasmed, blowing out my own balls, coming in hot, brutal bursts in his ass, searing his bowels.

We lay in each other's arms afterwards, me and Countess Trollop. And when he sucked my cock as I sucked

24

his, I determined to let the good times roll for as long as they would, his secret safe with me.

The Fucking Edge

I DROVE MY COCK deep into his hole, swelling his ass. He groaned and grabbed onto his chest, spinning his nipples between his fingers, as I gripped his ankles and started rocking him back and forth on top of the pool table.

He was hot, tight. I stretched his chute with my club, slamming all the way in, pulling almost all the way back out. His ring clutched at my hood. I drove my entire eight inches into his bowels.

He rolled his head from side to side on the green felt, his blond hair getting tangled in his pleading blue eyes. He'd never been reamed like this before, never this ruthlessly, and he didn't know himself whether he wanted me to stop, or to go even harder. I didn't give a fuck what he wanted. I drove him harder, spreading his legs wide and cleaving his anus with my axe. He was a hot piece of ass, and I liked the ride.

Footsteps sounded on the stairs, above the smack of my thighs against the blond's ass cheeks, his tortured squeals of pain and pleasure; footsteps rushing down into the basement. 'What the hell's going on?!' Kris bleated.

I turned my head, still cornholing the blond. 'Fucks it look like?' I grunted. 'I'm stretching this slut.'

Kris staggered down the last couple of steps, his brown eyes bulging. 'But–but ... we're married! You can't ... you promised ...'

'Can't teach an old horndog new tricks, huh?' I grinned, pumping rhythmically into the blond. We were both naked, his little body and my big one shining under the lights.

'C'mon over and grab a piece. Guy's got a nice cock.' I reached in between the man's trembling legs and grabbed onto his dick, jerked it upright. It surged in my hand, my cock surging in his ass.

Kris went ape-shit. 'You cheating ... asshole!' the little redhead screamed. 'I'm going to kill you!'

He ran back up the stairs.

'Maybe I should get out of here?' the blond yelped on the end of my cock.

'You're not going anywhere, pretty boy. I'm not finished with you yet. Here, play with this.' I yanked his cock almost right off his body, grabbed back onto his other ankle, fucking him even harder.

His frightened eyes got that glazed look they'd had when I'd first rammed my meat into his ass. He grasped his bouncing cock, stroked as I pumped.

Kris came flying down the stairs, a kitchen knife clutched in his hand. He ran up to me and pressed the tip of the blade against my throat.

'Oh, Jesus!' the blond groaned, his eyes going all scared again. His neat, trim, tanned body glistened with sweat, his shaven balls bounding to my thumping beat.

I didn't miss a beat. I kept right on fucking the blond, as Kris pressed the knife into my throat. 'Either use it or lose it,' I growled. 'I'm not pulling out of this hot stuff until I've christened his bowels with my jizz.'

Kris glared at me, his eyes shining madly, the knife shaking in his little hand. I like them small in body and big in cock, and Kris had a dong. My own hammer squished back and forth in the blond's anus. I even corkscrewed a bit, getting even deeper penetration, meeting Kris' eyes and laughing.

He dropped the knife, and it clattered to the tiled floor. He buried his face in his hands and started sobbing. I grabbed his thin neck and shoved him up against the pool table. 'Do something useful. Suck this guy's cock.'

I let go of him and picked up the pace on the blond's ass, stroking faster, harder. Kris blinked his tears away and climbed up onto the pool table. He straddled the blond's head, afraid to look at me, undid his pants and pushed them down. His cock sprang out into the open almost as hard and big as mine.

I laughed. 'Thought so, you fucking drama queen.'

He bent over the blond's groin and grabbed his cock and stuffed the bloated tip into his mouth, staring at me now. His head went straight down, consuming the guy's prick in one gulp. The blond moaned from under Kris' dangling dick.

'Suck him, Blondie!' I grunted. I couldn't even remember the guy's name. He'd looked a nice piece of ass in the sporting goods store, and I'd taken him home. I hammered my cock into his anus.

Kris sucked, Blondie sucked, the pair sixty-nining each other as I shunted chute. The blond couldn't take it, all the domestic drama, the cock sawing his ass, his cock in Kris' mouth, driving him wild. His body bucked on the table, his ass walls squeezing down on my prick, coming.

Kris' throat worked overtime, jizz leaking out of the corners of his mouth. Then he trembled and gasped with his mouth full of meat and come. I knew that gasp, had heard it enough times before. He unloaded his steaming load in the blond's mouth, right down the guy's throat.

I watched it all with a grin on my face, never breaking stride in the blond's ass. 'OK, get his dick out of your mouth,' I told Kris. 'I'm going to come all over his cock and you're going to suck it clean.'

Kris popped the blond's prong out of his mouth in a gush of come and saliva, looking expectantly up at me, feeling me torque the blond. I clutched Blondie's ankles in twin death grips and hammered into his ass, rattling the pool table and the pair of men on top of it.

'Here it comes, lovers!' I rasped. Then grinned, and shot into the blond's ass, shuddering with ecstasy, creaming the guy's chute to overflowing.

Teaching them both a valuable lesson – about who's boss.

A week later, I was in the shallow end of the pool in our backyard, up to my thighs, two guys kneeling in the water in front of me, taking my meat into their mouths as I fed it to them.

It was a hot, humid day, the sun burning down. We were all nude. Maybe the neighbours could see over their back fences, maybe they couldn't. Made no fucking difference to me.

The guy on the left of my dick was Rene, a smooth-built brunette with sparkling blue eyes and a red-lipped mouth. The guy on the other side was Lester, a lean black man with a shaved head and a gold earring studding his right ear. His ebony skin gleamed under the sun like his deep brown eyes, as he watched me feed my snake into Rene's mouth, right down the guy's throat.

Rene gagged, clawing at my left thigh. I smacked his hands away, drove home more of my cock. His cheeks bulged obscenely, and you could see his throat bloat with the progress my prong was making going down. Lester played with my hanging balls, watching, waiting eagerly for his turn.

'Oh my God, no!' someone cried.

I looked up. Lester looked around.

It was Kris, back from work and changed into his swimsuit, wanting to cool down after a hard day at the office. Now he was hot, blowing another gasket. 'That's it! I've had all I can take!' He plunged back inside the sliding doors.

Rene stared up at me with enquiring eyes, his gag reflex forgotten, my balls pressing into his chin. Lester got up to leave. I pressed the man back down into the water with a hand on his shoulder. 'No one's going anywhere until I've blasted your mouths full,' I stated.

I gripped what little was left showing of my prick and pulled it out of Rene's mouth, nice and slow, spit shining all over the engorged member. I popped out, turned slightly, rammed into Lester's neon-pink mouth.

His nostrils flared as he struggled to suck air into his lungs, as I relentlessly drove my dick into his mouth and down his throat. He didn't gag like Rene, but snot bubbled out of his nose and spit strung down from the sides of his stretched lips. His mouth and throat were as wet and hot as any man's. I plugged him full, held it there.

Kris came running out of the house with my nickel-plated .38 in his hands. He dashed around the side of the pool and jumped in, jammed the muzzle of the gun up against the side of my head.

'Holy fuck!' Rene yelped.

I held him down with a heavy hand, keeping my cock buried full-length inside Lester's maw. 'I thought we were through with this shit, Kris?' I growled.

The gun barrel trembled against my temple. 'You thought?' Kris screamed. 'I thought *you* were through with this shit – having sex with other men with no consideration for me or our marriage!'

I laughed, gently undulating my dong back and forth in Lester's mouth and throat. 'I considered you. Get down on your knees. There's room for one more, lots of cock to go around.'

'You goddamn asshole!'

Lester's eyes bugged almost all white. Rene's shoulders trembled. I pumped Lester's face, shifting my hips, fucking his throat.

Kris cried out and the gun fell out of his hand and into the pool. I steered him in front of me, pushed him down, alongside the other two kneeling men. Then I slowly pulled my gleaming cock out of Lester's mouth and filled Kris' with it.

30

That stopped his sobbing. He looked up at me with tear-brimmed eyes, as I pushed into the back of his throat and down. The redhead could deep-throat with the best of them, his gag reflex long gone thanks to my repeated mouth-fuckings.

The other two men watched me plunge Kris' kisser. I'd picked them up at a bar I used to cruise all the time when I was single, still went to on a regular basis now that I was married. I was supposed to be at work, but the cop's union is a good one, and the day was just too nice to waste it on a beat.

Kris grabbed onto my ass, his fingernails biting into my cheeks. He bobbed his head vigorously back and forth, wet-vaccing out an apology. I crushed a clump of his red hair in my one fist, Rene's brown hair on the opposite end in the other. Then I jerked my hips back, pulling my slab out of Kris' maw.

'Everyone have a taste,' I said, sticking my dick at Lester in the middle.

He swallowed the meaty crown, chewed on it, while Rene and Kris paired up on either side of my vein-ribboned shaft, sucking up and down the sides. It felt good, and I grunted, tilting my head back into the sun, getting sucked and licked three ways.

Kris and Rene hummered my swollen tube-steak between them, tongues caressing, lips cushioning, as Lester tugged on my hood with his thick, black lips. Then Kris dipped his head down to my balls and gobbled up my sac and sucked on it.

My legs buckled a bit. Lester inhaled more of my prong, his diving lips meeting up with Rene's sucking lips on the side of my shaft. Kris juggled my balls around with his tongue, my entire pouch in his mouth.

It was hot, it was wet, it was wild and wide-open. I got a firm grip on the base of my dong and force-fed each of the men in turn. I slammed it into Kris' mouth and pumped back

31

and forth. I pulled out and drove full-length into Lester, plumbing the depths of his throat, fucking it. Then I yanked free and plundered Rene's mouth and throat, pinching the red-faced man's nostrils closed as I sawed back and forth inside him.

I went up and down the line, stuffing hungry mouths, stretching bulging throats. Until I felt the seed start to pop in my tightened sac. 'Get closer, all together. I'm going to come.'

They flung their arms around each other's shoulders and crowded in close like I was taking a group snapshot. I stroked my shining meat, bucked.

Semen blasted out the tip of my surging cock and splashed against the junction of the three men's mouths, their outstretched tongues. I striped each of their eager faces in turn, sprayed their tongues all together. It was like feeding time at the zoo, and I fed them a huge, hot load. They fought with their tongues and mouths to get all of the sizzling sperm I had to deliver.

It was a couple of weeks later, and I was heading out to my car in the grocery store parking lot. I could see the car was rocking even before I got to it.

When I got to it, I looked in. Kris was on top of some guy I'd never seen before, in the backseat. The guy's feet were up around Kris' ears, Kris' bare, tanned ass clenching and unclenching. He was butt-fucking the guy, in the back of my car.

I opened the door, and Kris turned his head and looked at me, a grin splitting his pretty face like he was splitting that laid-out man's ass. 'Three can play at this game,' he cracked.

The car smelt of sex. I dropped into the seat and cranked the engine.

'Oooh, sex on the move,' Kris cooed, pumping into the other guy.

I could hear the smack of thighs against ass cheeks, the grunts and groans of the two men, as I gripped the steering wheel with whitened knuckles and hit the road out of town.

'Pull over and come join the fun!' Kris yelled over the backseat, leering at me in the rearview mirror. He was pounding into the other guy, leaning against the man's legs and really thrusting his hips, pumping his buttocks, cock going in and in and into the man's asshole.

I jerked the wheel over to the right when I came to the park, pressed the accelerator down hard. The moans and squeals from the back, the crack of bare flesh against bare flesh filled my head.

I came to a fence, drove through, across a field, the car bouncing. The fucking in back stopped. Kris popped his head up in between the seats. 'What are you doing?! Where are you going?!'

I pressed the accelerator all the way to the floor, and the car rocketed across the field. When we were 30 feet away from the wooden guard rail that signalled the edge of the cliff, and the 500-foot drop beyond, I shouldered the door open and tumbled out of the car.

I hit the ground hard, rolling. The car flew over the cliff and into the great beyond.

I don't put up with the shit Kris was trying to get away with it. I fuck them, I own them.

End of story.

Some Like it Rough

DECKER STEPPED OFF THE elevator, saw the two men fighting with each other in the hall; not really fighting, more like slapping. He grinned and advanced on the pair of lovers.

He'd seen them move in a month before, heard them yelling shrilly at each other for the past couple of weeks, even where he lived at the end of the hall. They were both small, blond, tanned, a pair of sweet-looking, tight-assed pixies who fought like pumas with one another. Decker could only imagine what their lovemaking was like.

'Hey, what's going on?' he barked.

The two men turned and stared at him, their blues eyes flashing. They could've been twins – sweet, succulent twins – only one was slightly taller and slimmer, Connor. He seemed to enjoy picking on the other, Billy.

'What business is it of yours?' Connor flared, planting his small hands on his narrow hips.

Decker cuffed him across the face, knocking the man backwards. 'I make it my business, when I have to hear it and see it – you fairies fighting with each other.'

Billy's eyes were wide, and his mouth hung open. Connor held a trembling hand up to his cheek.

Decker was a big man, broad-shouldered, wasp-waisted, with dark brown hair and eyes, a ruggedly handsome face complete with a dimpled chin built into a square jaw. He looked tough, capable of handling any trouble, or starting it.

'Hey, you can't ... you can't just ... hit Connor like that!' Billy squealed.

Decker gave him the back of his hand, knocking him against the door of his apartment. 'I'll do whatever I want ... to get some peace and quiet around here.' He glared at the two blonds. 'And don't tell me you pansies didn't like it.'

Connor lowered his hand from his face, quivering red lips forming a grin. Billy looked at his lover, at Decker, squirming around like he had to pee – or do something with his cock.

'Let me in,' Decker growled. 'We're going to settle this right now.'

Billy could barely fit the key into the lock. Connor couldn't get into the apartment fast enough.

Decker shoved the pair into the living room, took a look around. The place was done up almost entirely in white – white, overstuffed furniture, thick white carpeting, white walls, a sparkling clean white kitchen leading off from the living room. 'Pretty posh,' the big man commented, rubbing his dick in his jeans.

'We like it,' Connor said. 'We've still got some more work to–'

'Yeah,' Decker grunted, cutting him off. He planted his two hands on Connor's rounded shoulders, planted the man down onto his knees in the shag. 'I've heard enough out of your mouths. Now I'm going to stick something in.'

Billy fell to his knees alongside Connor. The two men started at the massive bulge in Decker's jeans, the expanding outline of his cock. Decker rubbed it, looking down at the men. 'Who wants it first?' he said.

Billy's little hands scrambled all over the front of Decker's pants, fumbling the button open, tugging the fly down. The zipper rose up and along the length of Decker's cock, dropping down inches and inches later at his balls. Billy pulled the jeans apart, and Decker's cock flopped out into the open, long and hard and getting longer and harder, swelling up into the air. Billy tried to wrap his hands around

35

it. Decker cuffed him upside the head.

'Don't get greedy, little man. I'll dish out the meat around here.'

Both men watched from their knees, as Decker's cock rose higher, engorging, smooth-curved hood bloating and sniffing at the air, smooth-skinned shaft filling up and out, jutting from Decker's loins. Until the man's cock was mammoth full-length, right in front of Billy and Connor's shining faces.

Decker gripped his dick, smacked Connor's face with it.

'Ooh!' Billy murmured.

Decker slapped Billy's face with the huge appendage, the hard-soft impact heating up both men even more. 'Stick out your tongues, you pair of cock-sluts!' Decker ordered.

Pink tongues leaped out of red mouths, glistening, trembling, stretching as far as they'd go. Decker smacked the flat of Connor's tongue with his heavy hood, Billy's tongue. 'You use your mouths for sucking my dick from now on, not yelling and screaming at one another. Understand?'

The men eagerly nodded, tongues hanging out like a couple of blond puppies.

Decker smacked Connor's right cheek with his wettened dong, whacked Billy's left. 'Understand?!'

'Yes! Yes!' the men gulped.

Decker drove his cock into Connor's open mouth, almost right down to the balls. Connor didn't even gag, his mouth and throat like a drain, like Decker had suspected. His lips sealed around shaft, both men thrilling at the feel of cock stuffing mouth.

Decker dug his big hands into his Connor's soft blond hair, his long, powerful fingers clutching tight. Then he pumped his hips, hard, fucking Connor's mouth.

Decker's cock plunged down the blond's hot, wet, tight throat, pulled all the way out to the point of bulbing Connor's straining lips, then ploughed all the way back in again. Over and over.

Connor's wide blue eyes went watery. His nostrils flared, gasping for air. His cheeks billowed, throat bulging. Billy watched Decker's cock dive down his lover's throat, engorge his mouth, anxiously holding his own mouth gaping open.

Decker fast-fucked Connor's face, jerking the man's head back and forth, smacking his balls against Connor's chin. Until he abruptly let go of the one blond's head and yanked his cock out, speared it into the other blond's mouth.

Billy took it just as deep, just as delighted. He tried to grab onto Decker's pumping hips, to steady himself. But Decker smacked his hands away, grabbed onto Billy's head and pistoned his face. Drool surged out of the corners of Billy's mouth, the man's plush lips stretched wide, like his mouth and throat to accommodate all that thick, juicy cock.

Connor barely had time to get his breath back, before Decker hit his mouth again, stuffed him full of cock. Decker fucked Connor's mouth, Billy's, plunging deep and pumping hard. The men were dizzy, rocked with sensation. Decker's balls tightened, his gleaming dong coursing come-hard.

He pulled his dick free and shoved the two men's heads together, stuck his cock in between. So that he was gliding shaft along both sets of lips, both tongues, a man on either side of his thrusting prick.

'Yeah! I'm going to come all over you sluts' faces!' Decker rasped, poling fast and hard in between Connor and Billy, the two men's tongues and lips cushioning, stroking the churning cock. 'And you sluts are going to lick each other clean!'

It wasn't a request, it was a command. Connor and Billy urgently bobbed their heads in agreement, never losing mouth contact with Decker's pistoning cock.

Decker grunted, grabbed onto his dick. He twisted Billy's head around, jerked, jetting hot come into the man's open mouth. He grabbed onto Connor's head, blasted a thick rope of sticky jizz into that man's mouth.

Decker went back and forth, rocked back on his heels by the force of his brutal orgasm, striping Billy's tongue, splattering Connor's nose. The men's faces were coated with come, their mouths full, and gulping.

They threw their arms around one another and excitedly licked each other off, tonguing simmering come between them. As Decker dripped the last few drops out of his cock down onto the carpet with a squeeze of his hand, watching with a hard grin on his face.

'Wanna take a ride on my bike?'

Decker turned his head, looked at the man leaning up against the bar. He was huge, leather-clad arms and legs thick with muscle, head a block of granite atop cinder block shoulders, face heavy with beard. He had a red rag tied around the top of his head, a pair of gold nose studs. 'Won't your friends mind?' Decker asked, nodding at the table of equally tough-looking bikers ten paces away.

'Fuck 'em,' the man grunted, voice guttural as the roar of a Harley. 'I ride solo when I wanna. Haul ass with whoever I want.'

Decker set his drink down on the chipped counter of the stripper bar. 'You aren't too rough, are you?'

The biker grinned gold-plated teeth. He tucked a strand of Decker's soft, brown hair in behind the man's left ear with a sausage-like digit. 'Not too rough,' he rumbled. 'Name's Torrance. Let's get to know each other, huh?'

There was barely room on the back of the chopper for Decker, what with Torrance's massive body filling the leather seat. Decker gripped the sissy bar in behind, as Torrance revved the machine to thunder, released the brake and let the bike leap forward. They roared out of the gravel parking lot and onto the highway, the howl of the engine tearing the night apart.

It was little more than a shack by the edge of the river. Torrance skidded the big bike to a stop on the clay and dumped Decker off the back. Then he kicked out the stand, dismounted, pulled Decker off the ground and pushed him through the slatted door of the shack. 'Ain't much, but the road's my home,' he said, lighting a kerosene lamp, hanging it on a nail.

Decker glanced around at the sunken cot, the rickety wooden table and pair of chairs and couple of cupboards, the junk strewn all over the dirt floor. 'You got that right,' he commented.

Torrance strode up from behind, clutched Decker by the back of the head and twisted his face around. He slammed his mouth down onto Decker's open mouth, thrusting his tongue inside and thrashing it around.

Decker had taken all he was going to take. He jarred his palms into Torrance's chest, knocking the bear of a man backwards.

Torrance licked his thick lips, grinning. 'You wanna get rough, huh?' He advanced on Decker, raised a paw, swung it.

Decker easily blocked the blow with his arm, landed one of his own, smacking Torrance across the face with the flat of his hand. Torrance's head jerked back, his grey eyes gone wide. Decker smacked him again, and those eyes welled with tears.

'Yeah, I thought so,' Decker growled, shoving Torrance back against the wall. The whole shack shook. 'Not so tough without a big bike strapped to your crotch. You want it up the ass, you're going to do it my way, pussy.'

Torrance wiped his mouth with the back of his hand, staring at Decker. He charged. Decker easily side-stepped, shot out a leg, tripping Torrance, sending the big man sprawling head-first to the ground. Decker strolled over, went down, sinking a knee into the small of Torrance's back, then crashing his hand down onto the biker's wide, mounded ass.

The crack of palm against leather went off like a gunshot. Torrance shuddered, whimpered. Decker whacked Torrance's ass again with the flat of his right hand. The man's broad cheeks rippled beneath the well-worn black leather, the man's body trembling. 'Just a big, overgrown baby with his loud toy bike, huh?' Decker gritted.

Torrance shifted, squirmed, but Decker held him pinned down; not that the biker was really trying to escape anyway. Decker hit his ass again, right cheek, then left. Then both at once, whistling his hand down onto Torrance's butt.

He flailed the man's leather-clad ass, turning his hand into a blade that knifed through the air, the hardened palm striking sharply, repeatedly, blazing into the biker's cheeks, shivering the man full of shimmering heat. Torrance jumped with every blow, groaning, thrusting his big bottom up to meet the crushing hand.

'Not hurting you enough, huh?' Decker rasped. 'You want it harder, skin-on-skin! You want me to spank your bare ass, don't you, you big, tough biker pussy?!'

He didn't wait for a reply, wedging his burning fingers into the waistband of Torrance's pants and yanking down. As Torrance arched up off the dirt. The leather pants skinned down, butt cheeks popping out into the open, rounded hills trembling with need, pale skin streaked with red where heavy blows had already landed.

'Fuck, hit me!' Torrance groaned, clawing at the dirt.

Decker stared at the man's buttocks, his hand poised, knee back in position on the man's back. 'What? Say it louder!'

'Hit me! Fucking spank me!' the sprawled-out biker roared.

Decker grinned, then brought his hand smashing down onto the bare flesh. The shack rattled with the impact, the sound exploding in the men's ears. Torrance jarred into the ground, his butt cheeks rippling violently; never coming to a

40

complete stop, before Decker hit them again, and again, and again.

The big man burst into tears, Decker whacking his ass relentlessly, ruthlessly. Flesh fired crimson, fanned into flame by Decker's hand, filling Torrance with savage pain and pleasure, Decker with raw desire. He wanted to fuck that big ass, stick his hard, throbbing cock between those beaten buttocks and truly pound the man's butt, sear his insides like the outside.

'I'm going to fuck you, Torrance!' he gasped, between blows, sweat pouring off his face.

Torrance could only moan, embroiled in the conflagration consuming his ass and fire-storming through his body. His butt had gone just about numb under the brutal onslaught, each blow hitting him deep inside, striking at the core of who he was, his precarious sexuality. So when Decker's hand didn't bang into his cheeks any more, it was the worst kind of pain of all.

Decker straddled Torrance's legs, shoved his own pants down to his knees. His cock sprang out into the electrified air, hard as iron. He leaned forward and ripped the biker's doo-rag off, rubbed his hand around in the unwashed, matted hair; greasing his hand, then his cock.

'I'm going to stick my cock in your ass, Torrance – fuck you even harder than I beat you!' he husked, leaning over top of the fallen biker and prodding his shining, swollen hood in between the man's battered cheeks.

Torrance humped his ass upward, meeting Decker's cap with his pucker. Then he pounded the ground with his fists, when Decker pressed down hard. The pressure mounted, the tension soaring to explosive levels, Decker's cockhead squishing against Torrance's starfish. Then bursting through, bulbing ring and sinking into chute. Followed by shaft, inches and inches of bloated cock.

Decker ploughed his entire dick into the prone biker, going in slow and sure; not satisfied until his balls kissed up

41

against the man's blistered butt cheeks, then squashed against, his cock fully buried in Torrance's ass. He flattened his palms onto the ground on either side of the wide-body biker and pumped his hips, fucking Torrance's anus.

They both groaned, Decker pumping slow and languorous, bouncing lightly off Torrance's rump. Then torquing up the pace, driving harder and faster, pounding into the biker's gripping, sucking hole.

'You love it up the ass! You love me fucking you up the ass, don't you?' Decker raged, smashing his body against Torrance's butt.

'Yeah! Fuck, yeah!' the other man cried, pumping his own pulsating appendage into the dirt, in rhythm to the cock sawing his chute.

Decker pistoned faster and faster, now spanking Torrance's buttocks with his thighs almost as viciously as he had with his hand. His cock was a red-hot poker, sticking the biker's anus, going molten inside Torrance's velvet hot tunnel.

'I'm going to come in your ass! I'm going to blast your ass full of my come!'

'Do it!'

Decker pummelled Torrance, splitting the man in two with his battering-ram cock, reaming chute. Until he jerked, jolted by orgasm, his cock exploding, rupturing white-hot semen into Torrance's anus.

The biker felt the scalding spurts, and he grunted, shuddering with his own orgasm, his own cock going off and spraying into the ground.

The two men emptied out their balls, Decker filling Torrance's beaten-down ass, Torrance pouring out his pent-up lust into the dirt.

Decker spotted the kid slouched against the side of a building, barely visible on the edges of the halo of light shed by a sagging streetlamp. It was night, rain pouring down, the area the urban shithole. Decker's cock was hard and hungry in his pants as he slowly cruised by.

He went down an alley and came out onto the street opposite, drove back around. This time, he slowed to a stop at the crumbling curb, alongside the kid. He thumbed down the window and yelled, 'Hey, you need a ride or anything?'

The kid looked up from beneath his wide-brimmed cap. His face was young, pretty, dark as the night itself, eyes wide and showing white, lips plush and wet with a nervous lick from a neon-pink tongue. 'Huh?' He looked like a runaway.

Decker shifted the car into park, turned off the engine, got out. He'd liked the look of that empty alley for what he had in mind. The street shone slick with rain, some whores up at the corner, but no one else around. The kid was wearing a baggy basketball tanktop and shorts, sneakers. The smooth, ebony skin on his arms and legs gleamed with moisture.

'What's your name?' Decker asked, walking up.

'Fuck business is it of yours?'

Decker slapped the kid's cap off his head, revealing a burr of black hair. He looked 18, maybe 19. 'Don't mouth off to me, punk!'

'Anthony. My name's Anthony. So what?'

'So this,' Decker rasped, grabbing the kid by a bare arm and dragging him down the sidewalk to the mouth of the alley, shoving him in. His cock was a pulsing pole in his jeans, driving him on.

Anthony stared at Decker, his lean body shaking. He bathed his lips with that pink tongue again. Decker shoved him up against the greasy wall of the alley, mashed his mouth into the kid's mouth.

'Hey! What the fuck?' Anthony squealed, trying to wriggle away.

'Don't tell me you aren't selling it!' Decker hissed, pinning the kid's shoulders against the grimy wall. He kissed him again, hard, shoving his tongue inside the young man's mouth and tasting hot spit.

'OK! OK!' Anthony gasped, gulping humid air when Decker at last broke mouth contact. 'What you want, man?'

Decker grinned into the kid's frightened-looking face. 'I want it all. Only I'm not paying a cent for it.' He pressed down on Anthony's bony shoulders, pushing him down to the cobblestones. He pulled his erection out, smacked Anthony's face with it, stuffed it into Anthony's open mouth.

'Suck it, baby! Suck it!' he growled, the delicious heat and wetness enveloping his dong and suffusing his body. He gripped Anthony's ears and moved the kid's head back and forth, moving his own hips, fucking face.

Until he suddenly felt a sharp pain in his cock. His eyes burst open and he stared down, astonished. The kid was biting into his dick, shaft half in and half out of Anthony's mouth, sharp white teeth sunk right into the middle. 'Hey, what the ... Fuck!' Decker screamed, the kid biting his cock almost in two.

Anthony's lips curled up at the corners, into a grin, his teeth embedded in Decker's dong. Now he moved his head back and forth on his own, scraping his teeth along Decker's shaft.

Decker went rigid, unable to do anything for fear of getting his cock bitten right off, at the mercy of the young man.

Anthony pulled his head all the way back, finally releasing Decker's cock. But before the older man could regain control of the situation, Anthony grabbed onto his balls and roughly twisted them. He rose to his feet, bringing Decker up onto the toes of his feet. Then he spun the man around and shoved *him* up against the wall.

'I'm a cop, tough guy!' he hissed in Decker's ear. He pulled the man's arms back, slapped handcuffs onto his wrists before Decker could react. 'I should take you in, book you for soliciting, and assault!'

Decker froze against the wall.

Anthony grinned. 'Lucky for you, I'm a dirty cop. You like it rough, huh? Well, sucker, you're going to get it rough.'

Anthony popped Decker's jeans fully open, plunged them down the man's legs, exposing Decker's ass.

'Hey, no ... this isn't the way it's supposed to go down!' Decker whined.

'Not your way, man. My way.'

Decker heard a metallic click, then felt something cool probe in between his quivering butt cheeks. Anthony had snapped out his retractable baton, was pushing the tip of it into Decker's pale buttocks, pressing the tip up against the man's asshole.

Decker crumbled like a schoolyard bully. 'Stick it in! Fuck me!' he pleaded, his bluff called; but being on the receiving end just as ripe with possibilities as the other way around.

Anthony pushed the knob of the baton through Decker's pucker, into the man's ass. Decker cried out, the cold metal shocking his hot anus. Anthony pumped back and forth, fucking Decker's chute with the baton, not too deep, but deep enough.

'Stick it all the way in!' Decker begged.

Anthony pulled the baton out, slammed Decker up against the wall. 'I'm in charge here, asshole! And the only thing going to go all the way up your tight, white ass is my big, black dick! You want that, right?'

Decker nodded, his anus burning empty.

Anthony took a quick look around. The alley was empty, like the street beyond, the shadows deep. He pushed his basketball shorts down. His cock hung long, thick, engorged. He pulled a tube of lube out of a pocket and oiled the snake, letting Decker twist his head around to get a good look.

Anthony's cock stiffened up huge in his stroking hand. 'I'm going to stick every last inch into your ass, white boy. And you're going to like it.'

Decker whimpered, turning his face back to the wall. He'd been giving it out, now he was going to get it back, big-time. He jumped when he felt Anthony's slippery fingers slide up against his crack, groaned with pleasure when he felt two of those fingers plunge right into his ass.

'Better get you loosened up some, huh?' Anthony breathed in Decker's ear, pressing the pair of digits three knuckles deep into Decker's tight, pink anus. Then he pumped, finger-fucking the man.

Decker moaned into the brick, his body electrified. Anthony ploughed his fingers in and out of Decker's chute. He pumped him hard, ramming him up against the wall, ramming his ass.

Decker wallowed in it, rode it, his own cock as hard as the wall in front of him. He loved getting churned, his ass blazing with sensation.

Anthony yanked his fingers free and grabbed up his dong, slammed the mushroomed tip into Decker's pucker. His fingers had done the work; his shiny blue-black cap stretched Decker's starfish still more and then was immersed in anus. 'Here it comes, motherfucker!'

'Stick your cock up my ass!'

Anthony gritted his teeth and drove his prick into Decker's ass, gleaming liquorice stick gliding inside, more and more and more. Decker felt like his insides were being torn apart, all that cock filling his chute. Anthony felt the wicked gripping pressure, the resistance, but kept on pushing forward. Until all that showed on the end of Decker's white ass were Anthony's big black balls.

Anthony grated, 'Now you're getting what you deserve,' moving his hips back, pushing them forward, pile-driving Decker's ass.

Decker moaned and writhed, so wanting to grab onto his

own vibrating cock and stroke, but prohibited from doing so. His ass felt like it'd been pumped full to twice its normal size, wonderful sensations rippling up from his stuffed anus and flooding his body and brain.

Anthony gripped Decker's shoulders, shunted his massive cock in the man's chute. He bit his lip, moving faster, fucking harder, his face a glistening mask of sexual concentration.

The men grunted and groaned, Decker's buttocks shivering with the impact of Anthony's thighs striking against them, his body shivering with the impact of all that cock fucking his butt. He cried, spasmed, his own cock suddenly going off, hands-free, blistering-raw orgasm blazing through his body on the tip of that wildly thrusting dong.

Anthony grinned madly, slamming Decker's quivering ass, fucking in a frenzy. His flapping balls tingled, erupted. Pure, white-hot ecstasy shot out the end of his pumping cock, dousing him in erotic emotion, as he doused Decker's bowels.

Decker had learned to take it; take it and love it. Just so long as it was rough.

Pumping Ivan

I STARED AT IVAN "the Terrible" Teldov, the dumbbells in
my hands curling up and down on their own. The gym
owner-trainer was geared up for action in a pair of tight,
black shorts and a tight, blue muscle shirt, his chestnut-
brown, hard-rock body glistening with sweat. He was
looming over a guy sprawled out on a weight bench
desperately trying to wrestle a loaded barbell off his chest,
urging the groaning man on in his subtle, profanity-laden,
120-decibel way.

Ivan leaned in even closer, big hands on big, bunched
quads, square-jawed face inches away from the other man's
tear-streaked face. He screamed at the guy to push out that
final excruciating rep, spit spraying out of his snarling
mouth.

My cock was the hardest appendage on my
underdeveloped 180-pound, 18-year-old body as I watched,
bulging the mesh in my shorts. I was pumping iron, wishing
I was pumping buzzcut blond muscle-stud Ivan instead.

Just before closing time, it was my turn to get the Ivan the
Terrible training experience.

'Round 'em out at the top!' the big man barked, the gym
empty now. 'Like you're bear-huggin' someone!'

I clumped the dumbbells together over my head,
hurriedly banging out another set of chest flies, hopefully to
Ivan's satisfaction. The man's dimple-chinned face, bulging
bronze body, and Drill Sergeant intensity were more than a

48

little intimidating up-close, even after two weeks of getting yelled at.

'You wanna feel it right here,' he growled, reaching down and prodding my chest through my T-shirt. His warm, blunt fingertip ran along the swollen edge of one of my pecs, brushing over a nipple.

I shivered, the dumbbells jumping in my hands. I barely had the strength to bring them back together overhead to complete the set.

'What's next?' Ivan demanded.

I scrambled upright on the bench. 'Uh, like your plan says, I was, um, just going to do some sit-ups to finish off my workout.'

'Quittin' already?'

'I've been here two hours!'

He snorted, tousled my curly mop of brown hair. 'Crunch-time then, junior.'

The man of striated granite was actually only a few years older than me, but you'd never know it from the way he handled himself, and others. I lay back down on the bench and brought my feet up. He grabbed my knees, shoved my legs closer. 'Go!' he yelled.

I interlaced my fingers behind my head quicker than a perp on Cops, started crunching abs. Ivan grabbed the back of my head and pushed me higher, bumping my elbows into my knees.

'You wanna feel it right along here,' he snarled, letting go of my throbbing neck and yanking my tee up, poking my stomach.

I churned up and down like a madman, cock swelling along with my abs as Ivan traced my ribbed stomach with his fingertip. And when that thick finger trailed all the way down to my shorts, bulged the waistband and squirmed inside, I almost did a face-plant into my knees.

'You're gettin' a nice little six pack, kid,' he said, before snapping my shorts and turning and striding away.

I flew through 50 reps like nothing, then floated out of the gym, headed for the locker room, the warm memory of Ivan's soft fingertip still tickling my abs, teasing even lower, filling my pumped-up body, and groin. Until my dizzy brain suddenly registered the grunting and groaning of another type of workout going on, in the steam room.

I peeked into the sauna through a partially fogged-up window, and my cock flexed even harder. Two musclemen were putting in the most intimate of hot, hard male exercise sessions, one guy giving his buddy the iron bar from behind.

The black-haired dude was bent in half, clinging to an upper tier wooden bench, the blond hunk pounding cock into his ass, hard and fast, their built, bronze bodies gleaming under the muted lights, in the mist. I'd seen the pair around the gym before – Glen and Brendan – but never working out this passionately before. Glen's hips were flying, muscled buttocks clenching and unclenching, cock pistoning, hammering Brendan's sweet ass, rocking the moaning man almost loose from his perch.

I quickly grabbed onto my hardened dick through my satiny shorts and started rubbing, getting an eye and handful. Brendan was screaming, 'Fuck me! Fuck me!' Which was exactly what Glen was doing, head flung back and muscles surging, chiselled body splashing against rippling ass in the billowing steam.

I yanked my shorts down and cock out, getting skin-on-skin, fisting my raging member in rhythm to Glen's frantic thrusting. Until Brendan smacked the wooden bench with his hand, tapping out, and the guys hastily switched positions. Glen ended up hunched up on his back in the first row, anxiously pulling on his big, cut cock, Brendan clutching the guy's legs against his shredded body while he worked his own stiff prong up the guy's gaping asshole.

I went back to applauding the men's steamy exhibition with my hand on my cock, stroking even faster, as Brendan plugged into his hard-bodied lover. Glen groaned, tugging on his nipples, his cock, his blown-up, pec-plated chest heaving as Brendan hit bottom.

Brendan gripped his buddy's ankles and churned his hips, brutally cocking the blond, stretching out the man's chute with the hottest of warm-up exercises. 'Split me in two, fucker!' Glen hollered, pressing his balls down and heavy-stroking his prick.

I pumped my cock as Brendan pumped Glen, fantasizing even as I stared at the dripping muscle-studs that I was pumping Ivan. I had the hardcore trainer laid out on the end of the slippery steam bench, pounding reps into his hot, tight manhole, anally drilling him like he'd verbally drilled me so many times. My trim, toned body bounced off his smooth, mounded butt cheeks, cock ploughing his superheated vice of an ass. He screamed at me to tear him a new one, sausage fingers viciously twisting his fat nipples, ham fist urgently jacking his engorged cock.

And just when Brendan shouted out his ecstasy, thick muscles locking up and down his glistening body and tendons screaming, sprayed hot come into Glen's bowels, as Glen jerked ropes of the salty white stuff out of his own jumping cock; just when my own balls boiled up to the critical point and my dong went super-hard in prelude to unloading its joy, flooding my imaginary Ivan with my love; that's when the gym door suddenly whooshed open.

I stuffed my shorts full of cock and hustled my ass on into the locker room. I didn't want anyone spying on me, after all.

I stripped off my workout gear and jogged into the shower room, got the hot water going, building up some new steam, soaping my tight, blood-pumped body. I had the communal six-head shower facility all to myself, so I quickly got the dirty work out of the way – cleaning myself off. Then I got down and dirty, grabbing onto my quivering erection with my hand and the bar of soap and stroking again, dreaming again, the hot water washing over my stoked body in erotic waves.

The suds surged around my swollen prick, and I was engulfed by even more heat. I closed my eyes and took water in the face, urgently rubbing my cock, squeezing my nipples, fantasizing about Ivan's finger trailing down into my fur, moving slowly, lightly, exquisitely along the hard, pulsing length of my cock. I torqued up the pressure on my dick as Ivan the Terrible delicately swirled his finger around my bloated hood, brushing the super-sensitive underside where shaft met head.

'You're the last one here!' someone yelled.

My eyes snapped open and the bar of soap squirted out of my hand, went racing along the tile floor. Ivan was striding towards me, completely and utterly and breathtakingly naked, muscles-on-muscles body blazing a sun-kissed brown. His cock bobbed in between his thick, muscle-cut legs, heavy balls and the surrounding area as hairless as the rest of him. I crowded the wall, desperately trying to hide my excitement, and embarrassment.

He came right up next to me and twisted some taps around, spraying water over his ripped body-beautiful. 'Feels good after a tough workout, huh?' he said, tilting his head back, water splashing off his pec-cleaved chest.

'Yeah ... good,' I mumbled. My cockhead was kissing the slick, tiled wall, dick refusing to go down.

'You've made a lotta progress in only a coupla weeks,' he stated, glancing my way as I glanced away. 'You're even pumpin' in the shower now, huh?' He laughed.

I didn't know what to say or do. But Ivan knew what he was doing. He slapped my ass, hard, the sharp, wet contact echoing like a gunshot. My butt stung and my body surged.

The hardman put a heavy hand on my bare shoulder and gently turned me around, stared at my pointing, twitching cock, a warm, wonderful smile creasing his full, red lips. My balls went tighter than the guy's ass and a shiver ran through me.

'This muscle's sure well-developed,' Ivan said softly, reaching out and encircling my throbbing shaft with his fingers, making me jump. 'But it still needs regular exercise, right?'

'R–right,' I garbled, a wild tingling sensation shimmering all through my body as Ivan squeezed my cock. I gasped for air, got water, the man's warm, soft palm sliding up and down my shaft.

He stroked and stroked me, leisurely, wickedly, my head spinning like the water down the drain. Then he tilted my pole up and pressed it against my body, pressed his body against mine, his cock into my cock. He took me in his arms and kissed me. I gleefully threw my arms around the hunk, our hot, slippery bodies melting together, muscles fusing, his soft, wet lips pressing into my lips.

He kissed me harder and deeper, devouring me as I felt up his rugged back. He swam his tongue into my open mouth and bumped it into my tongue. He explored the inside of my mouth with his hungry, twisting tongue, choking me, painting my trembling lips. I tried to fight back with my tongue, but I was too weak in the face of his erotic onslaught, in his powerful grip, my body burning and my brain gone fuzzy. All I could do was feebly move my hips, grind my meat against his meat, secure in the iron man's iron grip.

Mouth still working over my mouth, Ivan drifted his huge hands down my back and onto my bum, gripping and squeezing my pale, trembling butt cheeks. I moaned into his mouth, and he lifted me right up off the water-washed floor, savagely kneading my buttocks, my cock sliding sensuously over his chiselled abs.

Finally, he broke away from my mouth, let me breathe again. I opened my eyes and stared at the man, his strong hands working my ass flesh to the point of pleasurable pain, our cocks squeezing together again. My eyes and mind suddenly cleared and my body brimmed with sexual energy. I grabbed onto the stud's chest, digging my fingers into the meat of his pecs, pinching his creamed-coffee nipples between my fingers. His eyelids fluttered and he groaned, and I gained even more strength from his loss of control.

I rubbed his streaming chest, rolled his swollen buds, his armoured body shuddering against me. I increased the pressure on his nipples, and he looked down at me, blue eyes gone misty. I stuck out my tongue and tickled a rigid jutter, and he jerked, fingernails biting into my bum. 'Yeah, suck my nipples!' he moaned.

I swirled my pink tongue around first one tan, pebbly areola and then the other, tasting the man, teasing the man, watching and feeling his rubbery nipples stiffen even further. I sealed my moist lips around a fully-blossomed bud and sucked on it, gazing up into Ivan's eyes. He bit his lip and plied my ass, overblown body trembling as I tugged at his nipple.

I bounced my head back and forth between his clenched pecs, licking and sucking his nipples. He grunted, 'Fuck!' when I sank my teeth into one of his buds.

Then he grabbed my head and pulled me up, mashing his mouth against mine again. I fought with his thrashing tongue this time, our slippery tongues entwining over and over, until he shoved me back and dropped to his knees, squatted in front of my dripping dong.

'You sure are built,' the behemoth marvelled at my feet, hot breath steaming against my cock. He gripped me at the base with one hand, cupped my balls with the other, nipping at my mushroomed hood with his ultra-white teeth. Then he took me in his mouth and sucked on my cockhead.

'Jesus!' I yelped.

Ivan pulled on my hood with his lips, fingering my tightened ball sac, pumping my pulsating shaft. He cushioned the underside of my dick with his tongue then wagged his tongue back and forth, and I went weak in the knees.

The big man pushed his head forward, my long, hard cock sliding easily in between his lips, down into the wet-hot depths of his cauldron of a mouth. I flung my head back and moaned, clutching at his buzzcut and shaking with delight. He sucked and sucked my cock, wet lips sliding up and down on my shaft, taking me down almost to the roots and then back up again, never letting up on the pressure in either direction, pumping me with his mouth like he taught the men in his gym to pump the iron.

I churned my hips, fucking the guy's mouth as he wet-vacced my cock. I thrust faster, he sucked harder, my balls tingling almost past the control point. He sensed it and jerked his head back, leaving me dangling.

'You're gonna pump my ass, big boy,' he declared, squeezing my cock, licking pre-come from my slit.

He stood up, and I got a good look at his prick. It was hard and high, but disproportionately small compared to the rest of his mammoth body. Then he turned his back on me and flattened his hands up against the wall, bending at the waist, showing me his bronzed, brick-hard ass. 'Fuck my ass!' he hissed over his shoulder, thrusting out his cheeks.

I quickly re-soaped my cock with a quivering hand, reaching out and caressing the man's heavy, round buttocks. Then I sudsed up his crack. He jerked when my fingers probed in between his water-pebbled mounds. Jerked again when I pulled out my fingers and plugged in my cap. I found his opening, gripped his hips, and pushed forward, plunging inside of him. He shoved backwards, his ass swallowing me whole.

'Jesus!' I groaned, the heated, velvet tightness unbelievable.

The temperature in that sexual sauna went nuclear as I started moving my hips, slipped, then got a good fucking rhythm going, churning Ivan's gripping chute. He clawed at the wall, head and back arched, thunder cheeks rippling as I smacked up against them, as I banged his ass.

I held onto his hips and on for the ride, blinking steam and perspiration out of my eyes, pistoning rock-hard cock up the guy's butt. I went faster and faster, oiling back and forth in that vice-like chute, stretching him out and pounding him down.

He desperately grabbed onto his flapping cock and fisted. I wildly slammed him over and over, the hot, wet smack of flesh against flesh filling my ears, the wicked pressure on my pumping cock filling my body with molten eroticism. My balls boiled out-of-control.

'Fuck, I'm comin'!' Ivan cried just ahead of me. He was on tip-toes now, his big, bad body dancing around on the end of my driving dick as he jacked streams of semen out of his ruptured cock.

My senses went into overload. I went into frenzy-mode, savagely spanking the guy's shivering bum with my thrusting body, plunging cock exploding deep in his beautiful ass. I was jolted by ecstasy, the one jumping around now, blasting sizzling jizz into my man's sexual core. I came for ever, with a terrible intensity that matched even Ivan's.

My big, tough muscleman works me hard in the gym, and I work him hard in the whirlpool, and the sauna, and the shower room, pumping iron and then pumping Ivan. I'm getting stronger every day.

Security Meltdown

I WHEELED UP TO the gate of the Plastech complex, waited. No one came out of the booth to challenge me. I exited the car, easily scaling the chain-link fence and dropping down on the other side. Not a sound, except the frogs croaking up a storm in the ditches. Not a security guard in sight.

The two-storey office building of the flexible packaging manufacturer was dead-ahead, the plant looming up in the darkness directly behind. I jogged towards the office, no one stepping out of the shadows to shine a flash on me, ask me what the hell I was doing.

I took the front steps two at a time, peered inside the glass double-doors. Dark, empty. I inserted a key in the lock and opened the door, slipped inside, pressed against a wall and listened. Nothing. Just the sound of the light buzzing over the door, the frogs raising a racket in the background. My blood went from simmer to boil.

I walked past the reception desk and into the hushed confines of the open-area cubicle farm on the first floor. No one around. No one slamming me up against the wall and frisking me. I cursed the darkness and the silence, the goddamn frogs.

Then I heard something. Coming from the second floor. A noise, low and long, like a wounded animal, or human. I charged up the stairs and down a hall, into another open-area cubicle farm. There was a light burning in a glass-fronted office overlooking the cubicles, at the end of the line, against the far wall. The noise came again, low and long, and louder.

I weaved my way through the maze to within ten feet of the lit office. Then I hit the brakes, hard.

I'd found my security guards – the guys hired to protect the Plastech plant from uninvited intruders like myself. They were inside the tiny office, Darren Schur standing, long legs planted wide apart, long arms gripping an upside-down Tony Valetti around the waist, the two men stark, raving naked except for their black boots, Darren sucking Tony's cock while Tony sucked Darren's. A hanging 69, for Christ's sake!

I froze in the dark, surveilling the situation. As Security Chief at Manguard I had a job to do – fire the two cocksuckers for dereliction of duty. But as a man who loved other men – a lot – I had a very personal reason for holding my position. I'm known at Manguard as being a short-fused hardcase with a raging Napoleon complex, but nothing makes this short, 40-something, shaven-head warrior harder, and happier, than the sight of two hot-looking studs doing sexual battle with one another.

I hadn't hired Darren and Tony, had never met them before, in fact; I'd been on mandatory three-week vacation when they'd come on-board. But I recognised their pretty mugs from the file photos, recognised the blue uniforms strewn all over the carpeted floor. And I was truly impressed with what I was seeing of the rest of them.

Darren was tall and blond and blue-eyed, hair shoulder-length and feathered, limbs long and lean, skin smooth and creamy-white. His cock pumping in and out of Tony's hanging mouth looked to be a whopping eight-incher, at least. Tony was medium height (from what I could judge), with a muscular build and model good looks, glossy black hair and sultry brown eyes, creamed-coffee skin. The guy's tan, veiny pole, that Darren was sliding his lips back and forth on, was an incredible nine inches or more, if I was any judge of cock size – and I was.

The two men entangled on the job in front of me were totally lost in each other, oblivious to my presence and probably any all-out assault on the plant. Darren was taking Tony's pipe about halfway down, head moving briskly, Tony's thunder-shaft glistening under the fluorescent lights. Tony's thighs were wrapped around Darren's neck, plump, round buttocks staring me and Darren in the face. He had his hands on Darren's hips, holding on, hair flying, pink, delicious meat gliding in between his lips.

Then Darren suddenly spat out Tony's monster cock and let out a long, low moan – the sound that had first attracted me to the sex scene – as Tony vigorously pumped the guy's dick with his mouth. Darren's blond-dusted body trembled, but he held on, held on to Tony. He opened his eyes and painted the inches and inches of Tony's jumping erection with his tongue. He mouthed the man's balls, licked the man's asshole.

I retreated a couple of steps, letting the darkness swallow me whole, but not compromising my wicked sightlines one iota. I unzipped my pants, one zipper tooth at a time. Then I eased a hand inside, drew my own baton out into the open, primed and yearning for action. Darren pulled Tony's butt cheeks apart and plunged his tongue home. I started fisting.

Despite my small vertical stature, my cock poles out at a rather impressive seven-and-one-half inches. And I covered every engorged, throbbing inch of it, swirling my hand up and down in conduct unbecoming a security officer. Tony's body vibrated, almost tumbling out of the blond's arms, Darren digging wet and insistent into his asshole.

Tony scissored his legs even tighter around Darren's neck, arching his head and crying, 'Yeah!' He bit into Darren's purple cocktop, hand-pumping the guy's shaft even faster than I was pumping. Darren fucked Tony's sexhole with his hardened sticker.

I slid a hand into my jacket, inside my shirt, onto a

swollen nipple. I gripped it and squeezed, biting my lip to keep from moaning like Darren, as my body flooded with heat. Hand flying on my prick, fingers pinching and twisting my nipples, I watched and waxed enthusiastic.

'Fuck, suck my cock!' Darren howled, his tongue out of his buddy's ass now, head flung back. He pistoned his hips, jamming his cock deep into Tony's hot, wet mouth.

Tears dripped from Tony's eyes down onto the carpet, as he took everything Darren gave him, throat bulging with cock, nose nuzzling blond fur. Darren quivered, inhaled the dangling man's dick almost to the three-quarter's mark. He kept Tony locked in his mouth like he was cock-locked in Tony's throat, fingers scrambling into Tony's glory hole and pumping.

Tony's body suddenly rippled, jerked, orgasm exploding inside of the man, flooding his lover's mouth with heated jism. I could tell by the white stuff leaking out of the corners of Darren's mouth. His throat worked overtime, desperate to take everything Tony had to offer. Then he, too, was jolted by orgasm, moaning around Tony's pulsing cock, legs shaking out-of-control. Tony jerked his head back, frantically tugging on Darren's glistening shaft, taking the come onslaught like a man – in the mouth, on his face, sperm spraying everywhere.

I watched it all, numb from the hood in, hand a blur on my rod, fingernails chewing my nipples. I wanted to come like Tony and Darren were coming, their gleaming bodies bucking with joy, but I was still a handful of swift strokes away. When my sweaty mitt slid out along the desk I'd been gripping and knocked a stapler flying into a metal trash can. The clatter echoed loud and clear.

The two cocky spurters in the office-turned-orgy room twisted their heads around, squinted into the darkness. I strangled my cock, hastily holstering and zipping up. Just as Darren dropped Tony, the guy rolling onto his back and up, and the two nude, dick-bobbing security officers charged out of the steamy room towards me.

They quickly collared me, grabbing my arms and pulling me into the light of the office. I stared at them, eyes bouncing back and forth between their handsome faces and hunky bodies like ping-pong balls. I tried to say something, but my throat was too dry to form words. I croaked like the frogs outside.

The big, built guards gave me the once-over, their eyes meeting at the suspicious bulge in my pants. I wasn't wearing my uniform (I was testing their work undercover), and they'd never met me before, but they didn't bother wasting any time demanding to know who I was, or what I was doing. Instead, Tony dropped to his knees and unzipped me, pulled the evidence of my excitement out of my pants and into his mouth, sucking on my bloated cap.

It was unprofessional as hell, on everyone's part, but what could I do? Darren had my arms pinned behind my back – loosely pinned, mind you – the long, tall blond running his wet tongue up and down my neck, in behind my ears. I could've escaped, sure, but I went limp as a noodle in Darren's strong arms instead, hard as a granite club in Tony's wet-hot mouth. I took it and loved it, Tony's plush lips sliding back and forth on my boiling shaft, Darren's thick tongue swirling around in my ear.

'I think we got the situation under control, huh, Tony?' Darren breathed, biting into my earlobe.

Tony popped my dripping dong out of his mouth and licked me up and down. 'Yeah, under control,' he murmured.

'Under ... control,' I mouthed, far from it myself. My head was spinning like a car-top gumball machine, body hot and heavy and seething with sexual electricity, cock a raging inferno on the end of Tony's slapping tongue. I'd tangled with plenty of guys in my time, but never been tag-teamed before. I was getting the third degree of my life.

Darren turned my face towards his and kissed me,

frenched me, traced the black line of my pencil moustache with the tip of his wandering tongue. Tony had me by the balls now, tea-bagging for all he was worth, my entire sac in his mouth, getting sucked. He juggled my balls around with his tongue and tugged on my pouch, Darren squirming his tongue into my mouth, almost right down my throat.

I couldn't breathe, I couldn't resist, I couldn't get enough. Darren pulled off my jacket, tore open my shirt, exposing my heaving, hairy chest, his tongue still doing tricks in my mouth. He cupped and squeezed my pecs, pinching and rolling my flared, needful nipples. A lightning bolt shot through me, dripping out the end of my quivering dick and onto Tony's upturned face.

The raven-haired stud kept on sucking my sack, pre-come oozing out of my slit and dropping onto his forehead. He bit into my balls, and I squealed in Darren's mouth. Darren twisted my nipples, mopping out the insides of my mouth with his tongue, my body and brain buzzing.

'Suck him! Suck his big cock!' Darren hissed at his buddy.

We both looked down at Tony, as the squatting muscleman slowly and wetly and sensually disgorged my bag. He looked up at us from under my towering, twitching cock, and grinned. Then he straightened his head and gripped my hips, staring me in the cap.

'Get ready, guy,' Darren warned, plucking my nipples almost right off my chest.

Tony squared himself away, brought his head forward, the shiny, mushroomed hood of my cock parting his lips, sliding into his mouth. He kept going, my shaft gliding inside him, oiling over his tongue, more and more and more of it.

I started to shake, violently. Darren held me tight by the nipples. More than half my meat was buried in Tony's heated mouth, but still he came on. Three inches, two inches, one inch of shaft showing – and then none. The man's nose dented my fur, my long, hard dong embedded to the balls inside his gripping mouth and throat.

I groaned, cock and body surging with a wicked tingling sensation that shook me down to my shoes. Darren and I gaped at Tony, at his bulging cheeks and throat, his soft lips pressing into my springy pubes, my entire inflamed manhood buried inside him. But the awesome deep-throater wasn't done yet, because, incredibly, I felt his tongue snake out of his mouth and lick at my balls.

'God in heaven!' I gasped, the erotic experience downright religious.

Darren was more practical. 'The guy can suck the nickel plate off a revolver,' he marvelled, biting into my neck, squeezing my aching nipples.

Hot, humid breath steamed out of Tony's nose and onto my groin, my pulsating member locked tight in the infernoic confines of the guy's throat. He looked up at me, brown eyes smiling. Before finally, slowly and deliberately, pulling back, letting my meat ooze out of his mouth raw and red and dripping.

I sighed in relief when at last my hood popped out from between his lips. Relief that I hadn't blown my load and brought a premature halt to the sizzling proceedings. I sensed that the boys-out-of-blue were just getting started working me over. And I couldn't have been more right, or grateful.

Tony sucked me some more, diving down to my pubes and back up again, the pressure on my shaft incredible. Darren bit into my tongue and pulled it out of my mouth, sucked on it like Tony was sucking on my cock, manhandling my chest all the while.

Then the two men abruptly ceased their erotic actions, synchronised like a well-trained, experienced team. Tony unbelted, unbuttoned, and jerked my pants down, then dropped to his ass and scooched backwards up against the wall.

'On all-fours!' Darren ordered, shoving me down.

I grabbed carpet, bare-assed and cock-hard, facing Tony's cut, upright prick on my hands and knees. The guy's recovery power was amazing. He stroked his tool, staring at me with an evil grin on his sensuous lips. Something whacked my ass. I twisted my head around – Darren, heavy, reinvigorated cock spanking my butt cheeks.

I was going to be the meat in a man-sandwich, and I couldn't have been hungrier. I grabbed Tony by the shaft and inhaled his hood, started sucking. The snake pulsed in my hand and mouth. He groaned, rubbing my bald head. 'Yeah, that's the way,' he muttered, thrusting his hips up off the floor, his cock deeper into my mouth.

I bit into his pipe. He gasped, shivered. Score one for the bad guy. I dropped my head lower, engulfing more of his dong. Hands riding my head, I bobbed up and down on the prime cut of meat.

I moved faster, sucking harder, Tony's cock feeling so very at home in my mouth. Until I felt something spray against my ass. I pulled gleaming dick out of my mouth and looked around. Darren was lubing up my butt and his latex-sheathed cock with a pocket-sized container, fingering my crack, a knowing smile on his pouty lips. 'You're going to take it up the ass, guy. Every inch of it,' he promised.

I sucked Tony back into my mouth, wet-vaccing again. Darren's cockhead pressed against my pucker, hot and insistent. He punched through, inside me. I choked halfway down Tony's shaft, Darren's cock sinking into my ass, filling me like I'd never been stuffed-full before.

The blond's body touched up against my trembling cheeks, his spike embedded to the hairline in my butt. I moaned around Tony's cock, the feeling exquisite, dizzying. The men moved their hips in unison, one cock ploughing my stretched-out chute, one cock pumping my stretched-out mouth. What a wild and wonderful sensation it was – getting anally and orally reamed at the same time. My body burned

64

bright as my face, my own dangling dick pulsing with energy.

Darren went faster, drove harder, rocking me back and forth. Tony thrust quicker, deeper, drilling the back of my throat. Darren's thighs slapped against my ass, cock sawing my electrified chute. Tony's balls slapped against my chin, powering into my raw throat. Darren groaned and Tony moaned. I gripped Tony's muscled thighs and tried to hang on.

Darren's fingernails bit into my waist, cock flying up my ass. Tony closed his eyes, body-beautiful clenching and unclenching, jamming me full of cock. I felt my balls tighten, my cock spasm, coming hands-free for the first time in my sexual life, the giant, churning cocks in my ass and mouth turning me into a live wire that just had to spew current.

'Fuck almighty!' Darren roared, pounding my hole.

'Fuck, yeah!' Tony bellowed, pumping my throat.

Warm spunk flooded my chute, hot, salty jizz filling my mouth, the two men bucking against me, pouring out their lust. I gulped and shuddered, clinging to consciousness by a whisker, my own cock spraying ecstasy, blistering orgasm sending me sailing.

When we'd finally dragged ourselves upright, dragged on our clothes, I fished around in my wallet for my Manguard identification. But the surprise was on me.

'We know who you are, Chief,' Darren admitted.

'Yeah,' Tony added, 'when you caught us going at it, we figured fucking you was the only way to maybe save our jobs.'

That was some sharp, on-your-feet thinking. I smiled at the grinning studs-in-uniform. These were my kind of men, all right.

Room Mate

I WAS READING THROUGH this old "dirty letters" digest I'd picked up at a garage sale along with some other books, when I came to a scene that shocked me – shocked my conception of what I was all about.

Two swinging couples were getting horny after a dinner out together and way too much wine later on in one of their homes. The men started fondling and fucking the wives – not their own – and the women were kissing and sucking and eating each other out. When suddenly one man's wife pulled the other husband's cock out of her mouth and offered it to her own husband to suck on. He hesitated, looking at the big, long, glistening pipe, at his wife. But urged on by her, the other man's hands in his hair, he took the guy's cock in his mouth and started sucking on it.

And my hard-on jumped from throbbing to raging. There was just something about the scene – so totally unexpected that in a heterosexual dirty digest a guy would suck off another guy, and enjoy doing it, like it was no big deal, the most natural thing in the world. So totally unexpected, and so totally erotic.

I was sitting on my bed, naked, back up against the headboard, erection in my right hand, digest in the left. I stroked harder, tighter, quicker, reading and re-reading that sizzling scene. I'd never felt so turned-on, even if with the couple of girlfriends I'd had in my short 19 years on this earth.

I shimmered all over with heat. My balls tightened, and

tingled. My cock went hard as rock in my sweeping hand, tall as it's ever been. I was just wickedly excited by the words and the mental picture of that man sucking the other guy's cock. To the point where the man bucked and came in the guy's mouth, filling it with cream, and he gulped it down.

I wildly fisted. Sperm bubbled in my balls, boiled up my shaft.

'Hey, Len, I'm home!' my roommate called.

I jerked, coming, arching up off the bed, riding the surging joy in my cock, spurting high into the air. Over and over and over.

'You there, Len?'

I bounced up and down on the bed, throttling my spouting dick.

'Yeah, I'm in my bedroom, Tim!' I finally gasped.

Tim was my new roommate. I suddenly pictured *his* cock in my mind, me sucking on it like the man in the digest, as I squeezed the last drops of sheer pleasure out of my prick.

I was really confused now. I was sure I wasn't gay, but ... I couldn't stop thinking about men's cocks – long, smooth, bulbous-headed cocks. What would they feel like, pulsing in my hand? What would they taste like, filling my mouth? Why had I chosen Tim as my roommate?

The guy was small and soft-spoken, with glossy brown hair and mild brown eyes, a lithe body and smooth, golden-brown skin. He was quiet, had a good part-time job with which to pay the rent while he attended college; I'd thought those were the reasons I'd chosen him, when he'd shown up in answer to my ad in the student newspaper.

But maybe there'd been a deeper, subconscious reason. Girls called him cute, and he was. He was almost feminine in some of his mannerisms, kept himself silkily groomed. But he'd had a significant bulge in his white briefs, the one time I'd seen him in his underwear on the way to the bathroom.

We'd only been living together for a month, and now I watched him more closely. Maybe too close for comfort – his and mine.

Two mornings after I'd been jolted by the story in the digest, I was passing Tim's bedroom, when I saw him stretched out on his bed through the cracked-open door. I stopped in the hall, looked into his room.

He was lying on his back, his head turned to one side on his pillow, just a single white sheet drawn up to his waist. The skin on his stomach and chest shone supple in the soft morning light, his nipples tan and taut-looking. He looked so soft and sensuous. I felt my cock harden, rise up in my jeans.

I gulped. I was getting turned-on by my roommate – my *male* roommate. I couldn't stop it ... didn't want to stop it. What I yearned to do was pull that thin, white sheet down even further, so I could see Tim's cock. I just knew it was as lean and smooth and luscious as the rest of the guy. I wanted to hold it. I wanted to stroke it. Jesus, I wanted to suck it!

Tim rolled over onto his side, and the spell was temporarily broken. I stumbled away, my head spinning.

That night, Tim rushed out of his bedroom and into the kitchen, where I was making dinner for the both of us. He was wearing only a pair of tight, white briefs.

'Aw, sorry, Len,' he said, placing a hand on my shoulder and jumping up onto his tip-toes to look at what I had frying in the pan. 'I should have told you – I'm going out for dinner tonight.'

His hand was warm on my tingling shoulder. I could smell the sweet freshness of his body so close, feel the heat. 'H–hey,' I gulped, 'no problem! Just more for me, then, right?'

Why was I yelling? Because my cock had been zapped

with electricity at Tim's touch, and I had to cover it up. Didn't I?

Tim sunk his chin down onto my shoulder and sighed. 'Looks good, too,' he breathed. His warm, humid breath bathed my reddened ear, his groin pressing up against my shimmering butt.

The fork shook in my hand. I moved closer to the stove, to hide the pounding bulge in my jeans.

'Oh, well,' Tim said, finally breaking away from me. 'I'll just have a snack. It could be a long night.'

He laughed and padded over to the refrigerator. He pulled it open, bent down and peered inside. I turned my head and looked at the guy's bum filling out his briefs. His cheeks were taut and rounded, his smooth, brown legs pouring out from beneath the rising hemline of the underwear. I could see the skin where the swells of his buttocks began.

The meat spluttered and burned in the pan, my own meat surging in my pants. I wanted to drop the fork and fill my hands with Tim's cheeks, grip and grope and squeeze the cute little pair.

Fuck, now men's asses were turning me on!

But they really weren't much different from girls' asses. Except that there was a long, hard cock around the other side. Grease jumped up and bit my hand, unnoticed.

'An apple will do, I guess,' Tim said, straightening up and shutting the fridge. He walked by me, adding, 'Toodle-loo, handsome!'

I jerked off two minutes after he left. Only this time, I didn't need any digest to stimulate my imagination. I just thought of Tim, in the morning with the sheet up around his waist, so mellow and ripe, in the early evening in his underwear, so close and so warm.

I was watching a late-night talk show when he returned, and flopped down on the couch with his head in my lap.

69

I was so surprised I dropped the remote, the man hitting me where it hurts so good. 'Ever have one of those dates where *everything* goes wrong?' Tim said, seemingly completely unaware of the effect he was having on me.

I stared down into his fine-featured, almost feminine face, his limpid brown eyes. His little head was directly over top my groin, his soft, brown hair cushioning me in warmth. 'S–sure!' I stammered. 'Sometimes nothing goes right – right?'

He looked up at me, and his plush lips broke into a glossy smile, his eyes shining. 'That's right.'

My cock was rapidly inflating under his head, no stopping it. I reached down and touched his hair, stroked it, desperate to distract him in some way.

He murmured and rolled onto his cheek – in my lap – on top of my groin. His hot, golden skin was against my cock. I swelled up like I'd been stung.

There was no way he couldn't notice, my erection lifting his head. I flooded with heat and desire. I was going to bend down and place my lips on Tim's cheek, turn his face to me and press my mouth against his mouth.

Fuck, I wanted to kiss a man!

But Tim was no ordinary man. He was so soft and warm and succulent. He was right in my lap, on top of my throbbing cock. I bent my head down ...

'Oh, well, no use crying over spilt milk,' he said. Then lifted his head and pushed off the couch.

I gasped for air, my chest heaving and face burning. As I heard the door to his bedroom close.

It was Sunday afternoon, when things finally came to a head. A soul-shattering, mind-blowing head.

I'd just come back from the grocery store, and yelled at Tim that I'd picked up his yoghurt. Getting no response, I put the bags down in the kitchen and walked down the hall, looked into Tim's bedroom. No Tim.

I walked further down the hall, past my bedroom, headed for the bathroom which housed our washer and dryer. Sunday was laundry day. And then I froze in my tracks, slowly backed up, looked into my room.

Tim was sitting up on my bed, back to the headboard, legs stretched out – completely and utterly naked! He held my dirty digest in his left hand, his right hand riding up and down his long, tall erection!

'Hi, Len,' he said brightly, looking right at me ... and stroking.

He gestured with the digest. 'Interesting reading. Especially this one dog-eared story about the two men and their wives. I think I like it almost as much as you do.'

I walked, stiff-legged, into my room, my eyes full of Tim's nude, golden body, that large, jutting cock in his little, shifting hand. I stopped and stared at the man and his beautiful erection.

He set the digest down on the bed, slowly swirling his hand along the smooth-skinned length of his cock. Then he took his hand away and patted the comforter next to him. 'Come over here, Len, and sit down. Please?'

His cock towered up from his loins. I gulped, got my feet moving again, coming closer. I looked down into his warm, shining eyes, at his lithe, lovely body topped by that glorious cock. Then I collapsed down next to him on the bed, and he took my right hand and placed it around his penis.

We both groaned, a shiver running through our bodies.

I was holding a man's cock, stroking a man's cock! It beat fiercely in my hand, foreskin shifting deliciously under my palm. I pumped Tim's cock.

He moaned and closed his eyes and leaned his head back, his body trembling. I leaned my head closer, and kissed the man on the lips.

He kissed me back, his mouth soft and wet and lush as any woman's. But this was no woman; this was a man, his hard-on filling my hand, straining in my hand as I stroked him.

He kept his arms at his sides, letting me kiss his mouth, his chin, his neck. His skin was hot and velvety. I dropped my mouth down to his chest, swirled my tongue around a hard, rubbery nipple. Pumping and pumping his tremendous erection.

'Oh, God, yes, Len!' Tim breathed, tremors rippling through his body. As I licked one of his nipples, sucked it right into my mouth and tugged gently with my lips.

It was immensely erotic. My head spun and my body flushed red-hot. I was making love to a man, jacking his cock.

I bit lightly into Tim's nipple, making him whimper. I fisted his cock, shaven balls to mushroomed cap, and he moaned.

I lifted my head and he opened his eyes and we stared at another, ablaze with undeniable passion. 'Suck my cock, Len! Please, suck me!'

I licked my lips, swallowed. I shifted slightly over and lowered my head, looking at Tim's cap, his slit. Then I gripped his dick tight at the base and stuck out my tongue and licked Tim's hood.

'Yes!' he cried, jerking with pleasure.

I shot my tongue all the way out and swirled the thick, red, wet appendage all around and around his handsome cockhead, bathing it in my saliva, painting it with my tongue. I tasted the spongy, intimate flesh, the salty drop of pre-come that welled up from Tim's slit. I swallowed another man's come!

There was no holding back now, no need to. I slid my lips right over Tim's hood, capturing the swollen tip of his dick in my mouth. He shuddered. I dropped my mouth down his shaft, consuming his cock, just as much as I could.

It was everything I'd imagined and more. Holding a man's cock in the steaming cauldron of my mouth, feeling it beat, tasting its engorged hardness ... sucking it longer and thicker still.

'Yes, Len! Suck my cock!' Tim cried.

As I bobbed my head up and down, pulling on the man's erection with my mouth. I'd never done it before, but I was a natural – sucking tight and deep and rhythmically. *It was natural* – one man sucking another man's cock.

Tim bucked his hips up off the bed, unable to control himself, pumping into my sucking mouth. The man's hood plugged the back of my throat, his shaft bloating my cheeks. I tongued up and down the underside of his cock, pulling hard with my lips, moving my head faster and faster and faster.

'No! Oh, God, Len, I want you to fuck me! Will you fuck me?'

I instantly became uncertain all over again. I'd kissed a man, stroked his cock, sucked his cock, but sticking my cock in his ass and ...

Tim showed me the way, patiently and gently and oh-so-sensually. I was quickly as naked as he was, me sitting on the bed with my back to the headboard now. Tim sprayed lube onto my cock, rubbed it in. I jumped and groaned at his touch, then revelled in his supple stroke.

He let go of me and straddled my cock, rubbed his butt with lube. Then he gripped my slickened dick and brought the head back to his ass, staring me straight in the eyes.

His cock jutted out over my stomach. My cap jammed up against his pucker. He bit his lip and pressed me in harder, pushing back with his ass. My hood exploded through his ring, and he sat down on my cock, swallowing me whole with his anus.

It was a stunning rush of emotions, my prick spearing into the man's hot, tight chute. I grasped Tim's bent knees. And he leaned back and gripped my quivering thighs, his cock arching up in front of me, my cock embedded, throbbing, in his ass.

I was on fire with feeling, trembling out of control. Tim bounced up and down, fucking himself on my cock.

We gasped, groaned. I pumped my hips, driving back and forth in his chute. He bounced faster, higher, impaling himself on my raging hard-on over and over, his cock flapping with joy.

It was overwhelming to a man-virgin like me; to Tim, too. He tore a hand off my leg and grabbed onto his cock and fisted, wildly riding my cock.

I yelled, 'Fuck!' at the top of my lungs, and spasmed, orgasm detonating like a bomb inside me. Sperm blasted out of my cock and into Tim's butt.

He wailed and quivered, hot semen leaping out of his prick and splashing down on my chest and stomach, striping me with his orgasm. We came and came, me pouring out my lust into the gorgeous man's ass, Tim blazing his all over me.

Tim confessed he'd agreed to be my roommate for the same reason I'd taken him on – mutual attraction. He'd been trying to seduce me, apparently, ever since he'd moved in. Who knew? Not me. But my poorly hidden dirty digest had provided the final piece to the seduction puzzle; the answer to the riddle of my own sexual identity.

I don't secretly, shamefully fantasize about men any more. I openly love one – named Tim.

Foot Bridge

I'M THE BOSS OF a road repair crew for a private construction outfit. We do a lot of work for the State of South Dakota, watering and oiling down dirt roads, spreading asphalt and pouring concrete on highways, and shoring up vehicle and pedestrian overpasses as required. The work's hard and usually hot, but the pay's good and the fringe benefits are often more than even I bargained for.

Come early summer we get the greenhorns fresh out of high school or on-break from college to spell off the regular guys on vacation. It's my job to break these new guys in; in some cases, make 'em or break 'em. Like Rafael, from this summer just past.

'What would you like me to do, Mr Hunter?' he asked, once we'd spilled out of the crew cab and into a blazing dawn out on Highway 14.

'First off, I'd like you to call me Dave,' I said.

The guy looked like he was built more for office work than highway work. He was maybe five-eight, slim, with skinny arms and legs that were wrapped up in a plaid cotton work shirt and green nylon work pants, despite the 90-plus heat. His black hair was cut short, eyes brown and intelligent, and he had an almost delicately-featured face.

'You'll be shovelling and spreading asphalt. It's gonna be hot and it's gonna stink,' I told him, pulling no punches. It was the worst job available, but that's where I start all the new men, and women.

He nodded downright eagerly, and we started unloading

the truck. Then we sat around on our asses, scarfing down the coffee and doughnuts we'd bought in Montgomery, waiting for the machine operators to show up. When they finally did, we got down to the serious work of resurfacing an overpass that carried vehicle and foot traffic over the highway.

Twelve sweat-soaked, lung-burning hours later, we broke for the day. We piled back into the truck and headed for town. Rafael and the other four guys in my crew zonked out as soon as they hit the bench seats, stayed that way for the 20-mile drive in. I was plenty tired myself, but I wasn't going to let the guys see it. I may be pushing way past 50, my crewcut as grey as it's out-of-style, but I can still lay down a hard week's work on the road with the best of them. As Nana used to say, 'That one, he built like a brick shit house, and just as dependable.'

When we eventually rolled into the Come N' Stay Motel, the woman tenting the muumuu behind the counter informed us that we were all sharing rooms instead of getting singles. The new girl back at the office had screwed up our normal sleeping arrangements. I quickly claimed Rafael as my bunk mate. He'd been the lightest snorer on the ride back to town.

I tossed my gear onto one of the queen-sized beds, said, 'Gonna grab a quick shower. Then we can go and get some chow.'

'Sure,' Rafael responded, setting down his own bag.

I turned the jets on full-blast, relaxing under the hot spray, letting the water soak into my sore muscles. After ten minutes or so, I reluctantly stepped out of the tub and towelled off, padded back into the room to throw on a clean shirt and a clean pair of pants. And that's when I got a couple of surprises.

One, Rafael hadn't cranked on the air-conditioning, and the room was stiflingly hot, humid with steam. And two, the young guy was stretched out on his bed in just his underwear, watching TV, his bronze legs gleaming smooth and taut, his golden-brown feet crossed and wickedly arched.

I had to stop and catch my breath. What does it for me, what's done it for me ever since I was a Boy Scout in hot pants, is a well-turned pair of legs with a pair of shapely peds attached. I've been worshipping male lower limbs and feet for 50 years and counting, got the footprints on my dick to prove it.

'All done in the bathroom, Mr – Dave?' Rafael asked.

'Huh?' My eyes were running up and down the guy's toned, caramel-coated legs, following the curved contours of his feet, bouncing over his slender, wriggling toes.

'Can I use the bathroom now?' he said, his eyes leaving my face, shifting lower.

And that's when I noticed that my cock, which had been dangling between my legs with the nonchalance of casual roommate nudity, had suddenly stiffened up, as it took closer note of things. 'Huh? Oh, yeah, sure,' I mumbled.

He slid off the bed. I followed his flashing legs past me and into the bathroom, watching the muscles ripple sensuously on the shiny limbs. He popped his head out the door, looked me directly in the cock, and said, 'We'll get something ... to eat after I'm done, right, Dave?'

'Riiight,' I breathed. The door closed again. My cock was a hardened slab of meat, rising up and sniffing the steamy air. I met it with a warm, accommodating palm. The sound of running water and young man laughter filled my reddened ears, as I vigorously fisted.

I inhaled soup, salad, steak, and baked potato.

'Jeez, you're sure hungry tonight, boss,' Fat Manny commented, mopping up the remains of his own 32 ouncer.

'Yeah, hungry,' I mouthed, staring at Rafael across the table.

'We're gonna try out that new bar on the corner. You

comin'?'

'Nah, I don't think so. I'm gonna take a dip in the pool, hit the sack early. How 'bout you, Rafael?'

'A swim sounds great,' he responded, poking at his inch-thick wedge of semi-raw beef.

Manny snorted, said, 'You kids behave yourself,' as he pushed the table away from his gut and heaved to his feet. He and the other guys trundled off down the empty street towards the neon oasis, while Rafael and I legged it back to the motel.

The Come N' Stay had a scenic view of the Interstate on one side, the bald prairie on the back side. But it did boast an inground swimming pool and Jacuzzi tucked away in a corner of the three separate buildings that made up the place. And when I watched Rafael stroll out of the bathroom in his bathing suit – a red Speedo that bulged in all the right places – his legs stretching out long and lean, his small, tender feet tiptoeing through the carpet, I vowed to heat up that pool and soak tub way past their normal temperatures.

Rafael's body was smooth as a sheet of copper, slender but wiry, his nipples dark like his eyes. I trailed after his bouncing bottom, his swishing legs, as they and him made their way out of the motel and into the green water of the medium-sized swimming pool.

It was just before ten, the temperature still hovering in the low 90s, but we had the pool all to ourselves (after I'd shooed away a couple of kids who should've been in bed by then). We swam four or five laps, me right on Rafael's tail, following in the wake of his kicking, pale-padded feet, his churning, glistening legs. Then we paused to catch our breath in the deep end, and I splashed water in Rafael's face.

'Hey!' he yelped. He grabbed onto the silver ladder at the edge of the pool and lay out on his back, kicked water in my face.

My mouth was hanging so far open, watching those playful peds kick out at me, those golden legs flex on the surface of the froth, that I almost drowned. I spat chlorinated water and grabbed hold of one of his mischievous feet, the other. He thrashed his legs around, but no way I was letting go.

His feet were warm and wet, incredibly smooth and soft, exquisitely curved. They were almost dainty in their elegance, and I gripped and squeezed them, thumbed their bottoms, my cock and resolve hardening. Rafael stopped struggling and stared at me with his liquid-brown eyes, floating on the surface of the suddenly stilled water. The "deep-end" was less than six feet deep, so I was standing, the water just up to my shoulders, which made it easy for me to lift the guy's left foot and sole-lick him from rounded heel to outstretched toes.

'Jesus,' he breathed.

He didn't try to pull away though. I hard-licked the hourglass bottom of his other foot, my big, calloused hands now gently cradling his slender, tendon-cleaved ankles, putting his feet up on a pedestal where they belonged, where they could be righteously worshipped by a fetisher like myself. I dragged my velvet-sandpaper tongue over the contoured sole of his left foot again, and his legs started trembling, his foot-bottoms crinkling, telling me I was getting through to the guy, bridging the generation gap one glorious foot at a time.

'D–don't stop,' he whimpered, confirming my thoughts.

I shoved my thick tongue in between his big toe and the first piggy in line, slithered it around. I went down the plump-topped row on his left foot, tonguing in between his toes. His legs really started shaking then, the water rippling with my erotic footwork.

'Jesus, that feels good!' he gasped.

'Tastes good too,' I muttered, popping his cute little pinky toe into my mouth and sucking on it.

I went back up the row, sucking on his toes this time, one by wiggling one. His foot-digits were neat and trim, oh-

79

so-succulent, and when I took his big toe into my mouth and tugged on it, he moaned with pleasure. And almost as breathtaking as the sight of the guy's sensuously moulded feet and legs, was the sight of his swelling cock. The snake in his soaked-through Speedo was shifting around on the water's surface, expanding dangerously with desire.

I consumed Rafael's right foot, lapping at his sensitive foot-bottom, writhing my tongue in among his delicate toes, sucking and nibbling on them. His cock strained the thin material of his skimpy swimsuit, his entire body trembling now as I fed on his feet.

I couldn't get enough of the guy's pretty peds, my hunger for man-feet and legs a thing that could never be fully satisfied. I lapped at the curved tops of his feet, pressing his peds together, my own cock tenting the loose, wet fabric of my trunks.

I opened his legs up again, and this time I nipped at his ankles, bit into the bunched muscles of his calves. Then I shoved his left leg up higher into the air, dunking him in the water. I swabbed the soft, vulnerable back of his knee with my tongue, my hands shaking now with excitement. He tasted wonderful, his legs and feet a goddamn delicacy. He had to conk me on the head with his leg to get himself upright and breathing again.

I attacked his other leg, but he was ready for my oral assault this time, urgently rubbing his cock as I sank my teeth into his calf. The sight of what I'd done to him and his cock drove me crazy, and I waded in between his legs, my big mouth open and hungry for meat. I shouldered his thighs and grabbed onto his waist and captured his balls in my mouth.

'Jesus!' he yelled again.

I was like the shark in Jaws, swallowing the guy whole as the boat went down, tugging on Rafael's sac through the damp material of his bathing suit, juggling his balls around with my tongue. His head went under the water, popped up again. He anxiously scanned the horizon, the motel windows, for curious onlookers. But I didn't give a damn. I was a relentless man-eating machine. The whole town could've come out and watched the spectacle, for all I cared.

I sucked on Rafael's pouch, my throat working. He closed his eyes and moaned, abandoning himself to my loving mouth. A different kind of warmth not air or water-related was washing over him now. I pulled him down a bit, unmouthed his balls and dragged my tongue up the rigid outline of his cock.

He bit his lip and clung to the metal ladder, as I licked his shaft over and over. I soon got sick of the taste of spandex, however. I yanked his Speedo down, let his dick pop out and catch some air, some direct tongue. His cock was clean-cut and golden brown, veined and throbbing. I teased its tensed surface with the tip of my tongue, and Rafael groaned, did a pelvic thrust into my face, slamming his hard cock against my soft lips. I tongued his naked shaft, slow and sure, from fur-matted balls to mushroomed head.

'Yes! Yes!' he urged, knuckles white on the railing, eyes wild.

God, but it felt good! Inhaling the musky scent of that young man, his muscled thighs resting hot and light on my big shoulders, his tightened sac and swollen cock within easy reach of my mouth, the warm air and water swirling all around us. It was enough to make a guy poetic, if he was so inclined. Me, I bluntly lapped at his shaft, then swallowed his hood.

'Fuck!' he wailed.

My lips sealed around his cap, I wagged my tongue back and forth, scouring the sensitive spot where shaft meets head. Then I took in more of his cock, bending it back like a lucky guy pulling the lever on a slot machine. Rafael arched his slick body to meet my demanding mouth, and I quickly swallowed his meat down to the balls.

I kept him there at that impossible angle, staring at him,

his cock filling my mouth and throat, choking me, my face half-submerged in the water. He shook like he meant it – like he was close to blowing his load. Or maybe his muscles were just wearing thin. Either way, I pulled back a bit, let some of his shaft glide out from between my lips. I stopped its progress with my teeth, biting into his cock halfway down. I started sucking him off, bobbing my head up and down on his dick, polishing his hardness with my lips and tongue.

'I'm–I'm going to come, Dave!' he warned.

Come to the poppa! was all I thought. I kept right on sucking, blowing that guy with a technique perfected over five decades, vacuuming him down to the furline and then suctioning back up his shaft again, over and over.

His body bowed rigid as his dick, and then he shuddered, groaned. His cock jerked in my mouth, and I was flooded with warm, salty spunk. I kept my lips locked on his spasming cock, milking him, his thighs squeezing my neck like a vice. The young man spurted his joy repeatedly, forcing me to swallow fast and often. I drank in his essence without wasting a drop, proudly watching as he thrashed around in the water, blown away by my cocksucking.

He lost his deathgrip on the ladder and almost went under for good when he'd finally finished emptying his balls in my throat. I dragged him to the surface. I wasn't done with him yet.

'I wanna foot-fuck you,' I whispered in his ear.

He nodded vaguely, gasping for air.

I helped him out of the pool, admiring how stiff his bobbing cock still remained. Then I eased him into the hot, swirling waters of the Jacuzzi. I stripped off my own trunks, let my own cock catch some air. It was hard as a divining rod, twitching like it smelled water – and feet.

I dropped into the tub and stood up to my waist in the bubbling chop facing my slumped lover. I fisted my submerged member, getting it good and fully jacked for action, my grizzled chest heaving with excitement and anticipation.

'You–you don't want to fuck me in the ass?' Rafael gulped, sitting up higher.

'Sure I do,' I replied, grinning and fisting, fisting and grinning. 'Later. Right now I want those pretty feet of yours.'

He nodded wearily and extended his legs underwater. I grabbed his ankles, clapped his soles on either side of my raging cock. He went under, came up spluttering, clinging to the sides of the Jacuzzi. He was very, very flexible, like I'd thought he'd be, and his foot-bottoms gripped my cock in the best bowlegged fashion.

I started pumping my hips, fucking the guy's feet. My dick glided easily back and forth between his soft soles, the smooth, heated sensation sending a shiver up my spine, a lightning bolt through my groin. I pumped faster and faster, stirring up the agitated water even more with the brute force of my foot-lust.

Rafael stared at me, struggling to remain top-side, as I ruthlessly fucked his peds, his legs shuddering with the impact of my thrusting body. I gripped his toes and pistoned my cock in between his soles, the tension, the tingling in my balls, building and building with every furious cock-stroke.

Then I abruptly pulled him up out of the water, spilling him back onto the indoor-outdoor carpeting. I scrambled up onto the shelf where he'd been sitting, fucked away again. My cock went numb, flying in between his feet, my muscles locking up to the snapping point. I tilted my head back and churned like a madman, bellowing, 'Fuck, yeah!' at the moon and the stars, consumed by the dizzying sensation of total release.

I blasted white-hot come onto Rafael's chest and stomach and cock, pumping out rope after rope of sticky, sizzling sperm, the wicked foot-friction sending me sailing. 'Til I was drained as an end-of-season swimming pool.

The next day I put Rafael on a new job – sitting in a chair under an umbrella holding up a "Slow" sign. I wanted the young guy off his gorgeous feet during the day, 'cause I was going to be on them every night.

Dropping a Load

I CAUGHT FAT ETHEL'S eye behind the counter, pointed at my empty coffee cup. She snorted and ambled on over with the jug, poured me some more of the good ol' dark stuff. I had a long haul in front of me, and just like my rig needs gas, I need caffeine to keep going. Trucking was no easy business in the spring of '38, and I needed to stay on top of the game.

That didn't mean, though, I didn't always keep my eyes open for a little roadside diversion. I swung around on my stool, mug of mud in hand, and surveyed the crowded truck stop. My red-veined orbs quickly focused on one individual in particular – the blond-headed kid peering in through the screen door of the joint, licking his lips and staring at the steaming food on the white crockery, nostrils working hard to suck in the heady smell. He was hungry, no doubt about it. Just my kind of Joe.

'Lookin' for work?' I asked him, after I'd settled up with fat Ethel and banged on out of the eatery.

He glanced up at me, all nervous and shy, sky-blue eyes blinking. 'I'm looking for anything, mister. I haven't eaten in three days.' He twisted his cap around in his small, sunbrowned hands.

He was wearing dusty blue overalls and a white shirt, worn boots, his face and bare arms golden-brown, his lips plush and red and wet.

'Well, today's your lucky day, kid. I'm pickin' up a load of oranges 'bout 30 miles down the road, at the Hoskins spread. Could use some help loadin' it aboard and haulin' it to the San Fran fruit market. You know how to drive a rig, strong enough to lift crates of oranges?'

A bright, white smile broke over his pretty face. 'Sure, mister!' he gulped. 'My father was in the trucking business back east – before the accident. He taught me all about it.'

I nodded. I was old enough to be his father. But the lessons I'd be handing out were going to be of the off-road variety. 'OK, hop aboard.' I walked over to my beaten-up truck.

'Uh, mister!' the kid yelled. 'Can I just go to the bathroom first?'

'Sure. I don't wanna haul any more weight than I have to.' I grinned, watching those tight, appetising buns in the thin overalls run into the diner.

We made good time. The kid's name was Dennis; he'd come out to California just a few weeks earlier, looking to get into the fruit and vegetable hauling business, hearing the land was lush and the opportunities endless.

He was right about the land, dead-wrong about the business. Trucking was a cutthroat racket, competition for loads fierce. I wasn't above sawing some throats myself, which is exactly what my intentions were with Hoskins. I'd gotten a hot, juicy tip that he had over a hundred crates of oranges that were a week away from rotting, so he needed to unload them fast. I'd have the guy over a barrel, and I planned to pluck his fruit cheap.

'I'll do all the talkin',' I told Dennis, as I pulled the rig off the highway and onto the dirt road that led up to Hoskins' farm. 'You just take notes this time, OK?'

He smiled that sweet, shy smile of his, and something blossomed in between my legs.

Hoskins was a tall, stringy guy with a nasty disposition. 'Buck-twenty-five a box? You crazy? Oranges are going for six bucks a crate, maybe more, down on the Embarcadero, and don't you try and tell me different!'

'Maybe, maybe not,' I replied laconically, winking at

the kid. 'But you got to get 'em there, 'fore you can sell 'em.'

Hoskins hawked a wad of tobacco down at my shoe. 'You can take your–'

'OK! Let's go, Dennis. This guy obviously doesn't wanna do business. I hope he's got the machinery for making orange juice, 'cause that's all that fruit is gonna be good for in a couple of days.'

We started walking back up the road to my rig.

'Hold on,' Hoskins grumbled.

We kept walking.

'I said, hold on!'

'You're going to make a big profit, aren't you, Mr Jameson? Buying those oranges for a dollar a box and selling them for six?'

We were back in the truck, on the road, hauling oranges now. The kid had moved fast once I'd nailed down the deal, stripping off his shirt in the heat of the sun as he loaded the crates onboard.

I looked at his bare chest, the succulent puffy brown nipples that capped his smooth pecs, just above the line of his overalls. 'Maybe even six-fifty a box. There's a bad strain of the flu going around 'Frisco right now, don't forget.'

We hit a bump, the truck and load jostling. I had to keep my eyes on the road.

Dennis cocked his head, listening. 'I think maybe some crates have come loose, Mr Jameson.'

'Bill,' I reminded him. I might be more than twice his age, but I was no old-timer. I turned the rig onto the shoulder of the road. And now was a good time to prove it.

We climbed down out of the cab, me right on Dennis' swishing little tail. He never made it to the back of the truck, because I grabbed his arm, spun him around, pinned him up against the side of the rig.

His young, lean body burned hot as the sun against my

87

rugged, needful physique. He looked up at me with clear, questioning eyes. And then his eyes lost their questions, got a little misty, as I gave him the answers by grinding my cock into his groin, up against his cock. 'Mr Jameson,' he breathed.

I slammed my mouth against his, planting my lips on his soft, lush lips. I poured on the loving, boiling inside and out, clasping the young man in my arms and devouring his mouth. His arms tentatively encircled my torso, then hugged tight, when I swarmed my tongue into his mouth and thrashed it around.

We melded together, our cocks connecting and squeezing, his surging up hard as mine. I explored his dripping, crimson mouth with my tongue, then rimmed his plush lips, licked up and down the smooth, tender skin of his neck. He moaned, rolling his blond head against the canvas side of the truck.

I grabbed up his arms and plastered them over his head, exposing his damp, tangy armpits. I thrust my tongue in, licking up and down the flesh and hair of one pit, the other, lapping up his sweat and heat. He was as fresh as they come, and I revelled in the taste, smell and feel of the guy, tonguing his armpits.

I unhooked his overalls. He moved forward a bit, away from the side of the truck, and the straps dropped down along with the overalls, fully exposing his golden chest. I instantly clutched a pec in each hand and kneaded the warm, ripe, brown mounds, giving Dennis my outstretched tongue to suck on. He captured it between his lips and really pulled, just as excited as I was now.

I let him tug on my tongue, as I felt up his boyish chest. Then I broke loose and brought my mouth lower, down to his nipples. I swirled my tongue all around one dark bud, the other, teasing them higher and harder, tasting their rubbery textures and pebbly areolae. Dennis gasped, shivering in my grasping hands, on the end of my spinning tongue.

Hunger welled up inside me to new heights, and I captured a rigid nipple in my mouth and sucked on it. I tugged, pulled, bit, almost tearing the lovely jutter right off the guy's chest and swallowing it down my throat. I bobbed my head over to his other glistening bud, sucked on that stiffened protuberance. Until Dennis and I just couldn't take any more.

He squirmed against the side of the truck, then squirmed right out of my hands and mouth, dropping down to his knees on the gravel shoulder. 'I want to suck you!' he gasped. 'Please, Mr – Bill, I want to suck your cock!'

The kid needed meat, like all growing boys. I batted his scrambling hands aside and cracked open my belt and fly, shoved my jeans and drawers down. My veiny root plant sprung out in front of him, bulbous cap brushing his lips. I shivered when he gripped my swollen shaft with his hot, little hand, shuddered when he tugged on it.

'That's the way!' I groaned, feeling his warm, earnest strokes all through me.

He stretched me further out with every jack of his hand, my dick throbbing under his soft, moist palm, bloated hood straining only an inch or so away from his pretty lips. His hot breath flowed over my groin, my obscenely swelled-up manhood looking huge and hugely erotic in his small hand, in front of his young face. He opened his mouth up wide and slipped his lips over my knob, and I buckled like I'd been socked in the gut.

'Jesus, fuck, yes!' I rasped, the kid swallowing my hood, sucking in shaft.

His mouth was a wet-hot cauldron, consuming my monster erection. I grabbed onto his fine, blond hair and jerked him even farther down my dong, bringing his pouty lips to within a couple of inches of my tightened balls. He gagged, unable to swallow any more, but what he had inhaled was more than enough to turn me molten by the side of the road.

He looked up at me with his watery eyes, his reddened cheeks bulging with my cock locked down in his mouth and part of his throat. I quivered, the pressure intense, skyrocketing. My cock beat wildly inside him, like my heart in my chest.

Until, at last, he pulled his head back, and my dong exploded out of the crucible of his mouth in a burst of hot air and spit. He was right back all over it in an instant, sucking me into his mouth, pulling back, dragging his lips and tongue along my shaft, hoovering my dick with a raw, honest enthusiasm that left me weak in the knees and the head, breathless.

The pure, sweet cocksucking went on for a glorious minute or two, the kid gripping my pulsating rod and blowing me from clenched hand on up, over and over. There was no traffic on the highway, just the sun beating down on the two of us, birds singing, leaves rustling.

But for the next part of our road initiation I required a little more privacy.

So, when Dennis pulled me right to the boiling brink with his wet sucking mouth, I scooped him up off the roadside and led him out into a field, behind a covering of trees. My bobbing cock shone in the sunshine, like Dennis' nude body, when I helped him shove his overalls all the way down.

His dick wasn't quite as large as mine, but it would be a nice, luscious mouthful nonetheless, once we hit 'Frisco and got a room. Now, I just gave it a couple of affectionate strokes, stirring the semen in Dennis' balls. Before I pushed the kid down into the doggy-mounting position, and the big dog got in behind.

His ass was as round and ripe as any pair of cantaloupes. I slapped the bronze cheeks, making them ripple, him moan. Then I greased my cannon with spit, shoved a pair of dripping digits in between his ass-melons and scrubbed his smooth crack.

He jumped against my fingers. I probed his pucker, sticking the tip of a finger inside, popping his ring. He wiggled his bum around on the end of my digit in delight, and I went two knuckles deep into his searing sexual core, loosening him up just a bit for the massive, meaty onslaught to come.

I pulled my hand away and gripped my dong, spreading his cheeks with my other mitt. His pink pucker winked at me. I licked my lips, sweating profusely. Then I steered my mammoth cap up against his tiny starfish, and we both shuddered with the heated impact. I pushed forward, gritting my teeth, the kid's cheeks and body shivering.

'Fuck!' I growled, driving hood through his resisting ring, delving shaft deep into his gripping anus. I didn't stop until my balls kissed up against his bum, my huge spike impaling his swollen bottom.

He undulated his ass. I rutted around, getting all I could of the wicked feeling of his hot, tight chute hugging every inch of my cock. It was as fine a feeling as I've ever felt in my life, just me and the pretty boy under the sun, my cock embedded in his ass.

I gripped both of his hips, pumped mine, fucking his bum. He groaned and banged his fists into the field. I went slow and sensuous, stroking long, pulling out to the cap and then ploughing all the way back in again, over and over. His ass sucked on my cock just as much as I plugged it.

'Fuck me harder, Bill! Faster! Really fuck my ass!'

He couldn't wait. And neither could I.

I dug my fingernails into his flesh and flung my hips back and forth, ramming his butt, reaming his chute. His cheeks rippled with the heavy impact of my thighs banging against them, his body rocking to my frenetic rhythm, my axe splitting him in two.

I hammered his peachy bottom, pistoning his chute. The blazing friction was incredible, my thrusting cock going numb-hard in his swallowing anus. He took it and loved it as much as I did, grabbing onto his own flapping cock and fisting.

It was too much. My balls boiled, my cock surging with imminent explosion. I wanted the kid to taste the fruits of his labour. So I ripped my dick out of his gaped ass and spun him around, speared into his open mouth.

'Fuck, yes!' I howled, going off in the kid's mouth, blasting fiery come right down his throat.

He gripped my balls and sucked on my cock, squeezing, draining every last spurt of semen out of my body and gulping it down. As he jacked hot jizz out of his own prick, spraying up into the air again and again.

He brought me to my knees, into his arms.

Which is when I heard my truck start up, glimpsed it rumbling off down the road. I scrambled to my feet and raced after it, cursing myself for leaving the keys in the ignition, for getting so completely diverted in the first place. They didn't call it "thieves' highway" for nothing.

Then I got another kick in the crotch, when I looked back and saw a dusty car pull up, Dennis jump inside. They roared past me, the kid sticking a hand out the side of the fast-moving vehicle and waving and yelling, 'Thanks for the load, Mr Jameson!'

Campus Rumpus

JEREMY AND IAN WERE in Jeremy's dorm room, sitting at his desk pushed up against the wall, Jeremy frustratingly trying to drill the fundamentals of chemistry into Ian's head. It was no easy task.

'See,' Jeremy said, 'when a base and an acid–'

'Hey, why don't we take a break?' Ian interrupted. 'My head is spinning.' He slapped Jeremy good-naturedly on the shoulder, almost knocking the studious young man's glasses right off his face.

Jeremy was small and slender, with dark, velvety skin and a delicate, fine-featured face, intelligent brown eyes. The exact opposite of Ian, in other words, who was a blond-haired behemoth with a boulder of a head and a jutting granite jaw, grey eyes, freckled skin, a muscular body built for the defensive line of the college football team, where he really excelled. The mismatched pair had come together thanks to the university-mandated tutoring requirements it bestowed (or belaboured) on its more brainy students, to help out those less academically but more athletically gifted.

Jeremy sighed and set down his textbook and scientific calculator. 'You've got an exam coming up in a week, you know,' he reminded the buzzcut giant.

'I also got a football game coming up on the weekend,' Ian countered, scooping a pigskin up off the floor of the dorm room. 'What say we chuck the old ball around, huh? Loosen up the muscles – brain and body.'

'The human brain doesn't have any muscles. It's–'

'Come on!' Ian's whack on the back sent Jeremy sprawling across the table.

Out on the grassy field in behind the old dorm building, Ian heaved the football to Jeremy, a tight, perfect spiral despite the big guy's ham-fisted approach to the game. The ball passed through Jeremy's tentatively extended arms and punched him square in the chest, knocking him backwards onto his butt. Had his eyes been open he might've had a better chance of catching the ball, perhaps.

As it was, the football rebounded off the tumbling young man at a right angle and bounded all the way down the bank of the river that ran alongside the university.

Ian lumbered over and grabbed one of Jeremy's small hands in one of his huge mitts, heaved him to his feet, just about wrenching the science major's shoulder out of its socket. 'You almost caught that one,' Ian said. 'Next time, use your hands.' He grinned solid white rows of teeth and jogged over to the riverbank, down.

Jeremy stood in the early-evening sun rubbing his chest, the grass stains out of the back of his pants. He looked at the watch on his thin wrist, wondering what was taking Ian so long. The guy seemed to be moving even slower than his comprehension of elemental chemistry.

It was a warm night, perfect studying weather. Jeremy had an exam of his own to ace in physics in two days. So, finally, after at least one minute had passed, he threw up his hands and trotted over to the riverbank, looked down.

Ian was stretched out on the grassy flat at the water's edge, flat on his back.

Jeremy snorted and scrambled down the bank, stood over the sunbathing giant. 'Playtime is over, Ian. We have to get back to work.'

One of Ian's eyes popped open. He squinted up at Jeremy. Then one of his thick arms reached up, hand gripping Jeremy's wrist, pulling the man down onto the grass next to him. 'Hey, lie down a sec and enjoy nature,' he

94

rumbled. 'That's biology, right?'

Jeremy was thrown onto his back on the soft, warm bed of grass. 'We aren't studying biology, Ian,' he grumbled, scrambling to get back to his feet and into his textbooks.

Ian rolled over on top of him, pinning him to the ground. He grinned in Jeremy's face, eyes twinkling, huge, heavy body enveloping Jeremy's small, thin frame. 'Anytime you want to get up, just go ahead and try,' he teased.

Jeremy squirmed, twisted, wriggled, but it was no-go. The solid mass on top of him was unmovable, the muscled arms locking his arms up over his head unbendable. Sweat bathed his face, and he blinked it out of his eyes, looking up at Ian looming large above him.

And then both young men felt what all of Jeremy's struggling against Ian's hot, hard body had really wrought – a raging erection in Jeremy's pants, pressing up against Ian's groin.

Jeremy went limp everywhere else, staring worriedly up into the footballer's eyes. Try as he might, he couldn't control the reckless flow of blood into his cock; it went harder, bigger, thicker, pumping up against Ian. Both men felt it, no way around it.

Ian scowled down at Jeremy.

Jeremy bit his lip.

Ian's lush mouth broke into a wide grin.

Jeremy's pretty face registered fearful surprise.

'Looks like you *are* interested in football, after all, huh?' Ian breathed into Jeremy's face. He pumped his hips, driving his cock into Jeremy's erection.

Jeremy could feel the other man's swelling excitement, rubbing against his full-blown enthusiasm. He closed his eyes and moaned softly, the wonderfully warm sensation of one man's cock stroking against another man's cock filling his body. He shimmered with swelling pleasure from head to toe. Then he started, when he felt Ian's soft, wet lips press down into his.

Ian kissed Jeremy's plush lips, lightly. Then harder, more heatedly, mashing his big mouth against Jeremy's pert mouth, consuming the undulating young man. He thrust his tongue into Jeremy's mouth and thrashed it around.

Jeremy was overwhelmed by the power of Ian's passion, the relentless thumping of the man's hard cock into his hard cock. He feebly tried to fight Ian's tongue with his own, but his sticker was pushed aside, so he just lay there and revelled in the onslaught of Ian's tongue swirling around and around in his mouth.

Ian pulled back, up, lifting his suffocating body off of Jeremy. He crawled down to Jeremy's crotch. 'Let's see what you got going on down here,' he growled.

Jeremy whimpered, as the big man tore his belt open and ripped his fly down, skinned his pants and underwear down his legs, Ian lifting Jeremy right off the ground with the strength of his movements. Jeremy's cock flopped out into the open, onto his stomach, stretching out long and black as liquorice.

'Wow, for a little guy, you're really packin',' Ian marvelled, staring at the night-shaded tool.

Jeremy gulped, his cock quivering like the rest of his body, anxiously anticipating the impact of Ian's hand or mouth on his most sensitive organ. There was no escaping it now. He was going to be ravished by the big man, any which way the big man wanted. Which was just what Jeremy wanted. He jumped a couple of inches off the grass when Ian gripped his throbbing shaft with his huge, hot hand.

Ian stroked, shifting his paw up and down the pulsating dong, squeezing it tight, pumping it hard, admiring the size and texture and coal-black colour. Then he dropped it, shoved Jeremy's legs apart, bent down in between and licked the young man's pube-pebbled balls.

'Ooooh!' Jeremy moaned, the slap of Ian's wet tongue

on his scrotum jolting him with feeling. He rolled his head around in the grass, the man vigorously licking his nuts, tightening his sac with sensation to the point he thought it and he would burst.

Ian devoured Jeremy's pouch, tugged on it.

Jeremy's eyes popped open. He stared down the length of his heaving torso and twitching prick, watching Ian suck on his nut sac. The heated tug, the big man's agile tongue probing and juggling his balls, made Jeremy surge with pleasure. His cock arched up into the air, pre-come oozing from the gaping slit.

Ian pulled his lips slowly off Jeremy's balls, leaving the man's sac glistening under the sun. He went lower, gripping Jeremy's thighs and diving his tongue deep in between the man's legs, licking at his perineum, stroking the thin, sensitive bridge between penis and anus, curving his long tongue up to lap at Jeremy's crack.

Jeremy's entire body arched along with his cock, wilfully urging Ian to tongue his erogenous zones, quivering all over with excitement. Ian's rough searching mouth-organ found Jeremy's pucker, squirmed against it, the man blowing hot air out of his nostrils and against Jeremy's balls.

'Oh, God!' Jeremy gasped, shaking.

Ian dragged his tongue back along Jeremy's crack and perineum, up over his balls and along his shaft. He spread his thick, red lips over Jeremy's blue-black hood and pulled it inside, upwards.

Jeremy gripped the turf on either side of his body, tearing at the grass, as Ian brought his cock up and swallowed it down, the man's head dropping, mouth consuming. The pulsing length of Jeremy's ebony tool was disappearing from view, devoured by Ian. Until there was nothing left to the naked eye but Jeremy's squished balls, his dong locked inside the wet-hot cauldron of Ian's mouth and throat.

Jeremy moaned, pounding the ground with his little

fists. His body beat to the frenzied beat of his cock in the other man's mouth, out of control. The damp, searing pressure was incredible, unbearable.

Ian lifted his head, dragging his lips along Jeremy's thundering shaft, right up to the bloated knob. He held the man's cock up there for a moment, the shaft gleaming, then he dropped his mouth downward, sucking up Jeremy's cock again. He did it over and over, blowing Jeremy deep and devastating, blowing apart what little sexual self-control the young man possessed.

'Ooooh, Ian, I'm coming!' Jeremy managed to bleat in the nick of time.

Not that it mattered. Because Ian only grinned from around the length of dark meat, inhaling it whole again, asking to be blasted. Jeremy bucked, exploding in the other man's molten mouth. He jetted with absolute joy, jumping up off the grass on the geyser of his ecstasy, spraying Ian's throat and mouth full.

Ian swallowed almost it all, taking the heated spurts deep. He gripped Jeremy's balls and squeezed and sucked everything out of the radically trembling man that he could, leaving himself with a mouthful of sperm. Then he flipped Jeremy over, spat some of the slippery semen onto the man's butt, then onto his own hard cock, which he pulled out of his jeans.

Jeremy hugged the ground, quivering with the aftershocks of all-out orgasm. He barely heard Ian growl, 'I'm going to fuck you now!' But he felt it, knifing into his cloud of bliss, as Ian pushed his come-smeared cockhead in between Jeremy's taut cheeks and up against the man's asshole.

Ian gritted his teeth, gripping his huge, swollen-angry pink pole at the base, shoving the mushroomed purple tip against Jeremy's pucker. Jeremy's dark cheeks cushioned Ian's cock, his ring holding tight. Ian pushed harder, applying enormous, unstoppable pressure. Until Jeremy's rim widened, Ian's hood plunging through, inside Jeremy's anus. Hard-driven shaft followed immediately, sinking inside scorching hot chute.

Jeremy chewed grass, wallowing in the wicked sensations of another man's cock filling, stretching his ass. The feeling was intense. His bung swelled to the bursting point. Until, finally, Ian's blond-dusted balls kissed up against Jeremy's trembling butt cheeks, the immense dong buried full-length.

Ian didn't waste any time. He planted his hands on either side of his gasping fellow student and pumped his hips, thrusting his cock back and forth in Jeremy's anus, fucking the man like a dog fucks its bitch. Right out there in the open under the sun by the edge of the river.

Sweat poured off Ian's face and down onto Jeremy's neck, the sharp, wet crack of Ian's thighs against Jeremy's cheeks rending the sultry evening air. The big man pounded his cock into the prone man's ass, reaming Jeremy's chute, relentlessly, powerfully. Jeremy's ass cheeks were shocked over and over by the crash of Ian's body against them, his own body shivering wickedly with the savage, burning sluice of cock in bung.

'Fuck, yeah!' Ian roared, pumping harder, faster. He pile-drove Jeremy's ass, plundering the young man's anus for all he was worth.

It went on and on. To the point where Jeremy just about passed out from the punishment. He gasped for air, suffocating, his head spinning, body ablaze. He'd never been fucked like this before. His whole butt had gone numb; he was just a sucking hole, for a man to piston until he blew out his balls, poured liquid fire inside.

'Fuck, I'm coming!' Ian cried, pumping in a frenzy.

He frantically sawed Jeremy's chute. Then jerked, jolted by the white-hot orgasm that welled up from his flapping balls and blasted out the tip of his churning cock. He shot burst after burst of sizzling jizz into Jeremy's bung, shaking uncontrollably up above the man's laid-out body.

Jeremy felt the heated splashes against his bowels, his body flooding with a new kind of bliss. His own cock spasmed, leaking semen into the grass.

Ian pulled up, his cock sliding out of Jeremy's devastated ass. Sperm oozed up along with the drained dong, and Ian went back down on his hands and knees and licked his own come out of Jeremy's crack, sucking it out of the man's rendered asshole. Then he flipped Jeremy over on his back again and went full-length over top of the guy, like it had all begun.

Ian kissed Jeremy's gaping mouth, opening up his own mouth so that the come flooded inside. They swirled the semen and their tongues together, cocks pressing tight.

'Back to the books now I guess, huh?' Ian said, grinning, licking a string of jizz off Jeremy's lips and swallowing it down.

'Yeah,' Jeremy groaned, staring up into Ian's eyes, basking in the salty taste and musky smell and rugged feel of the big guy. 'But we'll need to take plenty of breaks. You've taught me that.'

Penal System

THEY BROUGHT THE NEW "fish" in that morning. Me and the guys were milling about in the yard, batting around the idea of shanking Jenkins the stoolie, when we saw the van pull up to the gate, watched them unload the new prisoners from behind the chain-link, razor-wired fence that runs all around the yard.

There were ten of them all together. Six of them I already knew, returning guests of the province. I'd been in the jug a long time, you see.

Three of the strangers were nothing to write home about, two fat, middle-aged guys who had "biker gang" tattooed all over them, obviously transferred in from another province for someone's protection, or to keep them separated from their extended family; while the third unknown was an elderly gent, a crown of white hair atop his bony skull, probably a first-time embezzler who'd been shafted on his retirement gift and dipped his hand into the company till after 30 years of dedicated service.

But the fourth guy was something special. He was about 25 years old, small, slender, with glossy, chestnut-brown hair and a pretty, delicately-featured face dimpled at the chin, big brown eyes. He looked nervous as the rest of them, but I liked the look of the bulge in his prison pants, visible to this naked, discerning eye even from 50 feet away. When you've been in the can for as long as I have, you judge a man by his crotch. I was mightily impressed with this latest recruit to the penal system.

And when they shoved the young man into my cell to become my mate, I vowed to go the system one better – and make him my bitch.

I didn't get a chance to chat him up right away, because the chow bell sounded, and we went marching on our stomachs down to the food hall. Then later, I was behind the plate catching a game of slo-pitch out on the dusty yard. I like catching, and pitching. And with a ruggedly handsome mug and a relatively hard body – if I do say so myself – I get my fair share of both. Being cooped up with 600 other guys helps.

His name was Brad Tatum, and we finally got to know each other a little better in the confined space of our cell before bedtime.

'What're you in for?' I asked, stretching out on the bottom bunk and looking up at the guy.

He was leaning uneasily against the back wall, next to the toilet. 'Uh, this and that. You know.'

I sure as hell didn't, not from that evasive answer.

The bell sounded for lights out, and Brad proved just as evasive to pin down physically. I grabbed onto his pants leg as he attempted to climb by me and up onto the top bunk.

'Why don't you join me down here for a while?' I said, all soft and silky. 'It can get pretty lonely the first night.'

He shook off my hand, swung his legs up onto the bunk. 'No thanks.' Later, 'What are you in for anyway, Louie?'

Communication is the first step in any relationship. 'I'm a safecracker, one of the best boxmen in the business – or used to be.'

'Oh yeah?'

I heard Brad roll over onto his back, and within a few minutes I was sound asleep.

And I was right in the middle of a three-man shower room train, dreaming contentedly, when I suddenly awoke with a start. That warm hand swirling up and down my cock in the steaming mist of the shower room dissolved into a warm body snuggling in next to me on my bunk. I turned my head, stared into Brad's soft, gleaming eyes. 'Hi, Louie,' he said, kissing me on the lips.

I was already hard as a ten-year stretch, and that lengthened it pleasurably. I put my arm around Brad, drawing him in even closer. He was as naked as I was, his hot body melding into mine, one of his slender legs draping over my thighs, one of his slender hands sliding up onto my chest.

'I figure since we're going to be bunkmates for a long time, we might as well be close,' he purred.

I grinned from ear-to-shining-ear. Then I pulled his head close and planted my mouth on his, drawing inspiration from his warm, wet kisser, the humid air flooding from him to me. His fingers glided onto one of my nipples and pinched it, rolled it, as we deep-kissed one another.

It was quiet up on the third tier, just the two of us in our small, warm cell, in each other's arms, and mouths, beating together. I pushed my tongue up against his tongue, and we entwined our slippery stickers, the pair of us frenching like we were Quebecois.

Brad's hand moved lower, down my heaving chest and stomach, onto the pulsing stretch of my cock. 'Yeah!' I groaned into the guy's mouth, his fingers lacing my shaft, pumping.

I surged in his hand, in his arms. He slipped his head down and batted his wet tongue against one of my stiffened nipples, buzzing me full of even more feeling. He rotated his talented mouth-organ around first one nipple and then the other, still pumping my cock with his hand. This guy could walk and chew gum at the same time; he was nowhere near as inexperienced as he'd first looked.

'I've done some adult movies,' he confessed all over my chest. 'Quite a few, actually.'

A porn star! In my bunk! This was worth eight years of

waiting.

Brad showed off some more of his skills, pushing the blanket right off the both of us and trailing his tongue down the path his hand had already taken. My skin burned wherever he licked, and my cock blazed, when his tongue met up with my cap.

He bent almost double down on me, stroking my shaft, twirling my hood with his tongue. The sensations were to die for. Two years – less, with good behaviour – looked damn doable now, an absolute joy.

Brad popped my knob into his mouth and sucked on it.

'Fuck, yeah!' I moaned, thrusting some of my throbbing shaft into his sucker.

He craned his neck lower, taking almost all I had to offer, gripping my dick at the balls. I thrust back and forth on the bunk, creaking those springs like they'd never been built to creak, plunging my cock in and out of Brad's moist, molten maw.

He went all the way, deep-throating my dong. Turning right around on the bed so that his knees straddled my head, his ass up above me, his cock hanging down into my face. The guy was built for pro fucking, all right, his dick boning out eight inches straight down, bumping my lips.

I swallowed hard, wallowing in the rich, wonderful sensations of Brad blowing my meat. Then I opened up wide and tapped his ass, and he lowered his dangling sword down inside me. He drove right for the hilt, his smooth pulsing cock filling my mouth and beyond. I'm a seasoned vet, been cocksucking for decades, but that much prick left even me gagging somewhat with the sheer volume of it all.

But I gulped to, with delight. They never feed you enough in the joint. I sunk my fingers into Brad's taut little cheeks and sucked on his wicked prong, moving my head up and down, inhaling pipe like a crackhead.

He reciprocated full-throttle, mouthing, throating my slammer in rhythm to the sucking I was giving him. We were a well-oiled sexual suction machine, blowing each other stiff as the provincial flag out on the high tower.

We escaped the bars, our shackles, finding freedom in one another's mouths. Until we reached paradise, our balls boiling simultaneously.

I sucked faster, harder. I tasted salty pre-come, gave it back. A burst of hot jizz coated the lining of my throat. I bucked up into Brad's mouth, blasting back. He spurted for an eternity, making my Adam's apple do hard, enjoyable labour, swallowing all of his spunk. It tasted delicious, especially with my cock erupting into his velvety kisser, spunking him just as excitedly and voluminously.

He snuggled back into my arms afterwards, and I held him tight. He kissed my sperm-slick lips, licked them clean. This was one sweet bitch I'd been blessed with by the authorities.

But I should've known better. Nothing or no one comes free in the joint.

By the second day, Brad had lost all of his innocence and tentativeness, like it had been an act all along. He asserted his new-found confidence, as I was gripping the bars of our cell before bedtime. I felt his hands grip my shoulders, his hard cock drive up against my backside.

'We're going to bust out of this tomb,' he rasped in my ear. 'And we're going to need a good boxman – on the outside. See, I got a three-year sentence for heisting a jewellery store, but I don't intend to serve it. But I do intend to hit that store's safe again – successfully this time.'

I heard him loud and clear, feeling his rod grind into my butt cleavage. A guard passed by, said, 'Lights out, Louie.' In more ways than one, I thought. I'd be a lifer with one more strike against me.

Brad encircled my waist with his arms and popped my pants open, pulled them and my underwear down. The guy had the moves, no doubt about it. And he had the cock to back it up; it wedged between my cheeks, naked as my ass and plenty harder.

'Like it, huh, Louie?' he said, pumping, frotting my crack. 'We'll have all the time in the world to do it – on the outside.'

He jammed me up against the bars with his thrusting, my cock jabbing right through. My butt burned, crack buzzing. I could've taken it that way all night long, myself. But the guy wanted to do things his way, on his schedule.

He pulled his dong out of my crack, and I heard him spit four or five times. Then I heard his hand stroke up and down his foreskin. And then I felt – man, I felt – his meaty hood bust in between my cheeks and bash up against my butthole.

I bent forward, pushing back, gripping the bars with one hand, my own steel with the other. Brad grunted and shoved, banging on my backdoor. He ploughed in, he ploughed deep.

'Christ!' I groaned, the guy sticking me whole-hog.

Thank God I'd had a lifetime of eating cocks and contraband with my ass, otherwise I might not have been able to handle every inch that he handed me. As it was, I went dizzy with all that dick wedged in my chute.

He started pumping, churning my anus with his thunderstick. I did my best to stifle my moans, getting rocked, getting cocked. My ass was ablaze, stuffed and chuffed like never before. My cock was a numb slab of meat in my hand, sticking though the bars and boiling at the balls.

'You're going to make us rich, old man!' Brad snarled, driving my ass.

His thin thighs spanked my trembling cheeks, his fat prick penetrating me, plundering me to the core. He thrust faster, riding my backside, blowing my insides and mind.

I wildly stroked, getting wildly fucked. Brad upped the tempo to frenzy level, battering my behind, reaming my rectum. I gulped, and jumped, getting ready to fire off my cannon.

But then Brad suddenly decelerated; still stroking, sure, still stoking, only now slow and long and excruciatingly hard. 'You're going to do as you're told, old man, aren't you? I'm not going to have any trouble with you, am I?'

He pumped a little faster, showing me exactly what I'd be blowing if I didn't answer the right way. I answered the guy, eagerly pushing back, swallowing his cock up with my anus, sucking on it with my chute-walls.

He grunted his satisfaction as boss, and resumed his fearsome rump-thumping. The interlude had left me hanging on the edge. And now I went sailing over, gasping, jetting, my cock exploding in my flying fist.

I vibrated like the tiers with the men tramping down, shooting sheer ecstasy out of the tip of my prick, Brad banging away at my rear. He growled – giggled! – in total control of the situation and his sperm, a true pro. I felt the hot splashes douse my bowels, as I doused the outside walkway with my hot splashes.

We slept apart that night. Brad preferred it that way.

'He's got a tool in his trousers,' I informed the warden.

Smithers looked up at me suspiciously. 'What kind of tool, Louie?' The man knew my proclivities after eight years daily living together.

I grinned sheepishly and looked down at the floor of his office. Brad wasn't the only one who could act. 'Some sort of digging tool,' I replied. 'For busting out.'

They strip-searched Brad. I wish I could've been there, to at least see that incredible dong one last time. But they quickly found the sharpened spoon I'd carefully taped to the underside of his lengthy prick while he lay sleeping that morning, shipped him into solitary for a 30-day stretch.

See, my parole was coming up in three weeks, and I wasn't going to let any punk kid – no matter how porn and streetwise – blow it for me. Plus, when I crack a safe, I share the contents with no one.

Dirty Dick

'IT'S MY WIFE. I–I think she's cheating on me.'

The guy glanced nervously around the sparsely-populated diner, back at me, his fingers drumming up a jitterbug on the Formica tabletop.

I casually shook a coffin nail out of the deck on the table, stuck it in my maw and set fire. 'What makes you think that?' I blew smoke.

He was a good-looking tike, blue eyes and blond-streaked hair, a cute face and slim, small, cuddly body. He was the kind of joe you want to wrap up in your arms and protect against all comers. Until he bit you in the balls and turned tail for some other hunky specimen. He looked like he was just that petulant enough below the surface to do something like that. I could tell. I make it my business to know people, inside and out.

He gazed into my hooded brown orbs with his electric blue. 'Oh, it's just a suspicion. But she's been acting strangely lately, going out places without telling me where. You know, stuff like that.'

I took another pull on the cancer stick, deep into my lungs and out at him. 'Uh-huh. So you came to me.'

His eyes beamed, face shining, a perfect white smile splitting his kitty puss. 'Yes. I've, um, heard you have quite a reputation in this, er, field.' His little pink hand shot across the table and briefly gripped my rugged mitt.

'They don't call me "Dirty" Dick Stenner for nothing,' I confirmed.

'More mud, Dick?' Bernice barked, wallowing over to our table on a cloud of rancid grease.

'Nah. My bowels are good, thanks. What about you, Toby?'

Toby James jerked his pretty little head back and forth, a tad ticked I'd used his real name in public. Not knowing what I knew – that you could trust Bernice like a man trusts his basset hound to bring him his slippers after a hard day. The Corner Diner was practically my office, and Bernice and her equally lazy husband got a rake-off in fees because of it.

She grunted, slowly shifted her load back around like a barge turning in a channel, steamed back in behind the cash register way down at the other end. Toby and I were in the far booth, nice and private-like.

I stood up and pulled a notebook out of my front pocket, along with a pencil, intent on making some scribblings. My cock was bulging the front of my tan summer slacks, long and hard, and I gave it a little inside stroke as I pulled pad.

Toby's eyes lit up like the jukebox in the corner, staring at all that thinly-disguised dong. He seemed surprised, as well as delighted. But he shouldn't have been, if he knew my reputation like he claimed.

Most dicks make it a habit not to get involved with their clients. I'm just the opposite, in (Sam) spades. This job can get pretty boring, pretty routine, if you don't use your pretty clients for more than just meal tickets.

I sat back down and put pencil to paper, said, 'Where does she work? What does she drive?'

Toby vaguely recited the details in a hushed, reverential voice, all the time working his shoes off beneath the table. By the time we got to his wife's hobbies and habits, one of his pert little stockinged feet had landed in my lap, on top of my cock.

'She, uh, goes swimming every Thursday night at the Millennium Pool on Rochester,' he breathed, rubbing his tender tootsie up and down my inflated length and fluttering his long, dark, curly lashes at me.

His sliding foot was warm and a little moist. I surged harder, bigger, tighter in my trousers. The guy had a talented ped; he was tapping my dick to its full potential.

'I'll need a picture,' I growled, spreading my gams wider apart.

Toby's other foot rose up and found a home on my groin. He needed both feet, to handle the snake swelled up there. He gripped me with his socked toes on either shaft-side, pumped up and down, real nice and smooth.

'A picture?' I repeated.

He was almost under the table, stretching his little legs as far as they'd go, his feet keeping their toe-holds on my cock.

Then he was under the table. Just like that. One minute his blond head and blue eyes and lush, red mouth were peeking up over the edge, the next minute they were gone.

Bernice didn't notice a thing, too busy chewing her cud and her way through another romance novel. When would the dame learn; love was all around her.

Toby's hands were all over my dick now, taking up where his peds had left off. He wrestled my zipper down over my massive boner with a two-handed tug, and pulled me out into the open down below, covetously clasping my rod and pumping.

I jotted some notes down on my pad, to control the tremor in my body and brain, the surge in my red-hot blood. The guy's bare hands were even better than his stockinged feet, stroking up and down my bared cock, tugging me with both his soft, hot mitts.

I jerked when he cupped and squeezed my nut sac, jumped when he popped my hood right into his heated wet head-hole. Bernice glanced over, but her eyes were as myopic and jaundiced as her outlook on life, and she soon went back to her reading.

Toby gripped my balls and gripped my shaft at the base, tugging on my hood with his lips. His mouth was a wet-velvet place any man's cock would feel welcome in. I clenched my fists and rode the wonderful rush, his mouth pulling on my cap. Then I bucked like a dollar bill, when my under-the-table client opened up wider than even I'd expected and hummered three-quarters of my hammer into his mouth.

'Yeah!' I grunted, agreeing with the sensuous point he was making in his own defence.

He enveloped me in superheated moistness, my rod pulsing hot in his face holster. He started bobbing back and forth, hoovering my pole like he meant to get to the bottom of my balls. I dove my hands under the table and my fingers into his silky hair, holding for the rollercoaster ride. The little big-mouthed man blew me with a ferocious intensity.

He was so good, too good. My balls were on full-boil after only a minute of his pressurised sucking, my shaft beaming come-hard in his pussy-like mouth. I shoved his head back. 'You gotta come clean with me, Toby,' I rasped, 'if you want me to come hard down your throat.'

He scuttled back over to his side of the table, popped up into view. 'What–what do you mean?' he gulped, wiping his gumby mouth, his rubber lips stretching back into shape.

I knew he was hungry, starving. So I fed him my best line. 'We're going to conclude this meeting in the back room,' I said, jerking a thumb at the hall that led to the men's room. 'Provided ...'

His eyes leapt to high-beams, his tongue shooting out. He squirmed on the vinyl benchseat like he had ants in his ass.

'Provided you tell me the real story.'

He bobbed his head again, just as eagerly as before. And sure enough, he was as good at spilling as he was at sucking. 'The truth is, I think my wife is checking up on "me". I found a Continental Investigations card in her purse when I

111

was going through it the other day. And I just thought you could, you know, use your contacts in the private investigator field to find out for sure for me.' He grinned like a puppy dog expecting a belly rub.

'Why didn't you just say so?'

'Well, I thought you PIs had some sort of code of ethics – about not divulging or delving into other colleagues' cases or something. But if I hired you to follow my wife around, you'd have to tell me about every man she met with – including any dicks.' He shrugged, cutely.

'Ethics!' I hacked. The guy'd just been sucking my dick, and he was talking about PI ethics. He'd seen too many old TV shows. 'OK, you've told me the truth. Now let me show you how it's going to be.'

I got up, crotch bulging harder and heavier than ever, only with a damp stain outlining my manhood in my pants now. Toby shot out of his seat and into the hallway, rocketed through the men's room door.

I trailed after him, hung the "Out of Order" sign onto the knob. Bernice and her husband appreciated the fact that sometimes a man just needed a private place to think, to work out the tough kinks on a case.

Toby was waiting for me by the sink, his pants down around his ankles. He sure as hell knew what a rear office was all about. His butt sported a twin pair of tautly mounded cheeks, propped atop smooth and shapely stems.

I got in behind the guy, got a real good grip on his case. He moaned and shivered, as I sunk my big paws into his little seat cushions. They filled my broad palms with rich, pliable flesh, and I squeezed, kneaded, groping for answers that were all too obvious. This guy swung both ways, hard, judging from the size 7 erection steeling out from his loins.

I crowded up closer to him, tore a hand off a cheek and reached around, grasped his dick. He moaned, thrusting his body back against me. He was hot as a pistol, piss-stick beating in my hand. I tugged on it, shifting foreskin, shunting man with my own cock to his ass.

'Fuck me! Please, Dick, fuck me!' he pleaded.

It sounded like an idea. I let go of him and unbelted, skinned down my slacks. My cock burst free, and I grabbed onto it, jammed it in between Toby's cheeks; making the both of us mouth off, jump like we had the heebie-jeebies.

My iron rod was enveloped in cheeky heat. I wrapped my arms around the little cocksucker, shoving my hands up into his shirt and onto his bare nipples, as I pumped his crack, frotted his dry, hot, satiny-smooth butt cleavage. His nipples stood to attention between my pinching and rolling fingers, his body quivering under my cocky interrogation.

I bent my bean down and bit into his neck. His butt cheeks clasped my cock in a loving embrace. His skin was like shimmering silk. I tongued all over his neck, in behind his shell-shaped ears, inside his ears, churning his cleavage, pulling on his nipples.

It was too much for even me to take. It was time to really live up to my Dirty Dick nickname, cross the boundary between client and comehole. I pulled back, grabbed up a tube of lube out of my ankled pants, and greased my gun, stroking long and hard for Toby to see.

He craned his neck like the Exorcist kid, gripping porcelain sink up front, sticking his bum way out back. I grinned at him, swirling my fingers all over my bloated tool. Then sticking a pair in between his buttocks, blasting them with lube.

He was super-sensitive down there, like most men, just a lot looser. I scrubbed his crack with a real erotic flair, then shot two fingertips into his hole, punching past pucker and into bung proper. I sunk those pair of pokers, slow and sensual, into his ass. His legs trembled out of control, his anus swallowing my digits whole.

'Oh, God, Dick, that feels so good!' he whimpered.

It felt pretty good from my end, too, nice and hot and slick and sexy. I pumped my prodders, plunging the little blond's ass, stoking his chute. He was all gripping velvet, butt muscles contracting to suck on my plugging digits.

'I'm on the case now, baby!' I gritted in his ear, fast finger-fucking him. 'I'm on the case!'

I reached around with my free hand and grabbed onto his flapping cock, fisted him in rhythm to my flying fingers. Toby shot up onto his tip-toes, his body arching like a bow, cheeks shimmying, cock jumping. I could've brought him off with just my two mitts, right then and there. But my name wasn't Dirty Hans Stenner.

So I yanked my fingers free, flung my hand off his cock. He was wide open and wound up for the meat of the matter now. I gripped his hip, my slickened dick, speared gleaming cap into his cheeks.

'Yes! Fuck me!' he cried, my hood hitting home.

I gritted my teeth and ground forward. My cockhead bulbed ring, popped through, my python-shaft snaking into his rectum, inch by over-engorged inch. I filled his ass to bursting with my cock, only stopping when there was no full-hose left to dole out, my heavy, hairy balls kissing up against his pretty, perfect behind.

It was a tight, searing fit. I revelled in it, rutting around inside the man's anus. He almost tore the sink right out of the wall, on fire with the filthy feel of so much dong bloating his ass.

I could've lifted him right off the floor and into my arms on the strength of my cock alone. Instead, I gripped his narrow waist with both hands, started moving my hips, fucking his ass.

It was slow, tough, terrific work at first, I had him packed so full. I pulled back right to the cap, watching his stretched ass lips suck on my hood, then slowly, slowly drilled back in again, submerging my bone to the balls in that wanton butt tunnel.

Perspiration dewed Toby's quivering body-beautiful, sweat prickling my concentrated mug, as I fed him pipe up the rump in measured, manly strokes. Until it got easier and easier to move, my prick gliding in and almost out. Which is when I turned on the full rubber hose treatment, fucking the rear-humped man harder and faster, faster and harder.

The hot, wet crack of hardened thighs against softened bottom filled the one-seater can. Along with the ragged grunts and groans and gasps of men getting it on, one man getting pummelled with pole up the back end. I smacked into Toby so hard I almost sent him smashing right through the mirror, tattooing his butt, reaming his chute.

He stared into that mirror with wide-open eyes as glazed as Easter ham. His mouth hung open and his chest billowed for air, his body and rectum getting jolted beyond repair by a madman thundering prick into his ass from behind.

I threw back my head and roared, slamming away with a cock gone molten.

'In my mouth! Come in my mouth!' someone screamed.

I just had sense enough left to rip my dong out of Toby's ass and stuff it into his mouth, as he spun around and hit tile with his knees. 'Fuck!' I howled, letting loose, just as the man's lips and mouth and throat closed on my cock.

Sperm blazed out of my pipe and straight down his pipe, again and again and again. I jerked like a puppet on his last strings, Toby gulping like a drain. I emptied a full tank of boiling ball-batter into the pretty boy, and he swallowed up every last spurt.

I didn't bother informing the guy that I already knew for a fact that his wife had hired a dick to check up on him. See, I was that dick, doing some freelance work on behalf of Continental Investigations.

Was it a conflict of interest to work for two competing clients at the same time? Was it unethical of me to fuck Toby up the ass, after I'd just banged his wife that morning, mouth and tits and pussy?

Hell, they don't call me Dirty Dick for nothing.

Scuba-Doo

I WAS LYING IN bed half asleep, wet-dreaming about Leeza the huge-titted scuba diving instructor, when Ethan came into the room. I was naked, the sheet covering my lower half, but doing a poor job of covering up my obvious arousal.

I pretended to be fully asleep, squinting through slitted eyes at my buddy. He was wearing his blue Speedo and nothing else, his lean, bronze body glowing in the muted light of the room, obviously just come back from a morning dip in the hotel pool. He was now staring at the dip in the bed, at my painfully obvious erection.

He padded closer, smiling. 'Oooh, Jaaake!' he murmured, doing a not-so-bad imitation of breast-blessed Leeza. 'I want you sooo bad.'

He stifled a laugh. I groaned and shifted around, keeping up the charade of being asleep, trying to shift my dick into a less up-thrust position, and failing.

'Can you teach me the breast-stroke, Jake?' Ethan went on in his Leeza voice.

I snorted and licked my lips, sealing my lids shut.

That was a mistake. Because it didn't prepare me for Ethan suddenly diving right on top of me. The guy landed with an oomph, scaring the hell and squeezing the air out of me.

'Oooh, Jake,' he breathed in my face from two inches away now. His big brown eyes stared into mine, his lithe, golden-brown body burning against my body, his cock

116

pressing down on my erection. 'I can feel how much you want me,' he purred, undulating his hips, grinding his cock into mine.

The guy had a bad knack for taking a joke too far.

'OK, OK,' I groaned, more than a little uncomfortable – with the positioning, and the fact that my dick was actually swelling harder with the hot, manly pressure applied. 'You caught me.'

Ethan went on rubbing his loins against mine, wetting his plush, red lips and flashing a bright, white smile. 'It's not Ethan, Jake,' he stated femininely. 'It's Leeza. Leeza with the big, succulent tits and round, ripe ass and wet, juicy pussy.'

He ground his groin into mine, pumping. And damned if I didn't feel *his* cock hardening, lengthening up against my throbbing hard-on. My head spun and my vision blurred. Things were going too far, our bare bodies burning together, joined inferno-like at the barely clothed cocks.

'Uh, OK, Ethan, that's–'

He kissed me. Right on the lips.

'I can't hide my feelings for you any more,' he breathed, his eyes half-closed and mouth half-open. 'From the first time I saw you by the pool, I knew we'd become lovers.'

He kissed me again, his lips soft and warm and slightly moist. I shivered beneath the guy, despite the suffocating heat. And when he gently planted his mouth on mine a third time, I grabbed onto his taut, mounded butt cheeks and kissed him right back.

He moaned into my mouth, his fully-erect cock pulsing against my pulsating organ. He slid his kitten-pink tongue between my lips, and I thrust my hips up, pumping his cock with my cock. We were on vacation, in Hawaii, what the hell!

I swirled my own tongue around his wet, probing tongue. He gripped my head, his long, slender fingers sliding into my dark hair and rubbing my scalp, his hips moving against mine. He smelt of sun and fun and chlorine, just like lovely Leeza. I jammed my mitts into the sides of his Speedo and really gripped and groped his bare ass, fucking his cock.

He moaned, pumping back in rhythm. Our pricks squeezed together, slid together, the heated friction driving me wild. The whole thing was crazy, insane, but there was no stopping it now – we were too turned-on to turn off.

Ethan arched up and skinned his swimsuit down, then my sheet. Then he flopped back down on top of me again, driving his naked cock into my naked cock. The dick-to-dick sensation was incredible. I wrapped my arms around the guy and flat-out sucked on his outstretched tongue like I was sucking his cock. I could feel his heart pounding away, in his chest and his prick.

He pulled his tongue out of my mouth and rimmed my lips with it, then sealed his mouth over mine. We moved faster, thrusting harder against one another, our cocks getting rubbed to the point of explosion.

Ethan moaned into my mouth and shuddered in my arms. I felt his heated sperm shoot against my belly and cock, the guy's butt cheeks jumping in my hands with every burst.

I frantically pumped, then bucked, spraying Ethan's belly and cock with my semen. We jerked against one another, tight together, our hot seed mixing in blazing spurts.

We lay in each other's arms for about a minute afterwards, groins glued at the cock. I kept my eyes closed again, feeling a whole lot weirder now than when the thing had first started.

Then Ethan rolled off me and onto his back, next to me on the bed. 'That was nice,' he said, like there was nothing strange about two buddies getting off on each other. He slid his hand onto stomach, down my stomach, onto my cock.

I spasmed with surprise and delight, his slim, brown fingers wrapping around the shaft of my semi. He started stroking, our sperm lubing his erotic movements. And damned if my dick didn't stiffen again, swelling up pulsing in his pulling hand.

'Feels good, huh?'

I'm not sure if he was talking to me or himself, but it sure did feel good – the guy tugging on my cock soft and sensuous. He could feel my response in his hand, so I didn't say a word, just lying there and taking his handjob, tingling from head to toes.

His hand swirled up and down the length of my re-erected dick, gliding over shaft and up and around hood. He was a man, so he knew exactly how to handle a cock. And he knew how to handle a man, too, as I found out when he said, 'How 'bout doin' me? Lending me a hand?'

I turned my head on the pillow and looked at him. His soulful eyes looked back into mine, a warm smile on his full lips, his hand bobbing up and down on my prick. When in Hawaii ...

I slipped my arm under his and reached down and grasped his cock. He moaned and closed his eyes, his dick jumping up in my hand, swelling. It was weird touching another man's cock, but we had just fucked each other cock-to-cock earlier, so it didn't totally freak me out.

He stroked my prick and I stroked his, the pair of us looking at each other as openly and honestly as I've ever looked at anyone before in my life. His cock surged full-length in my hand, the power I had over the guy, the feeling of his hand on my cock, filling me with shimmering heat. We were shoulder-to-shoulder, and I leaned in and kissed him, on the lips.

He murmured his approval, his mouth breaking partway open as I pressed my lips home. He kissed me back, and we smacked one another repeatedly, languid, sultry kisses, pumping each other's cocks. Then we were kissing harder, more passionately, devouring one another's mouths. His tongue bumped into my tongue, and we spun our tongues together, jacking each other just a little bit harder and faster.

It was so warm and sweet and luscious. Just lying there in bed, kissing and frenching, fisting, no one else and no other sound in the world. It was too good to last too long. I felt my balls tighten and tingle, my cock stiffen to come-shooting strength in Ethan's caressing hand.

He felt it too and released my prick. I kept on pumping his, staring questioningly into his eyes.

'You know what's better than a handjob, don't you?' he said. Then: 'A blowjob,' he answered for me, playfully licking the tip of my nose.

'Uh, Ethan, I'm not sure ...' Making out like we were man and Leeza, mutually masturbating each other, were two things, but actually getting blown by another guy? That was a whole other kettle of tropical fish. 'I'm not sure I want you ... sucking my cock, Ethan.'

He laughed. 'Well, don't worry, you're going to suck my cock too.'

He rolled back on top of me and kissed me before I could say anything else, pressing his come-smeared groin into my come-smeared groin. Then he slid lower, down to my chest, cupping my pecs, lashing his tongue across one of my stiff, pink nipples, the other one.

'Mmmm!' I moaned, my chest ablaze with the guy's loving.

He didn't let up, twirling his neon-pink sticker all around my jutting nipples, washing them in his hot spit. Then sealing his lips around one and sucking on it, tugging on it.

I arched my chest up into his mouth, my nipples tingling wildly. He swallowed my other bud, pulled on it. Then he nipped at my nips, biting into them, pulling back, stretching them out so far my mind almost snapped along with the rubbery protuberances.

His tongue trailed down my chest and onto my stomach, the guy's downy brown head dipping lower. I clutched at his fine, soft hair, as he shot his tongue into my bellybutton and swished it around.

I knew where he and his hot, wet tongue and mouth were headed, and was powerless to stop it; had no intention of stopping it now, if I ever had had. So when his tongue slithered down over my lower abdomen and into my pubic hair, I just groaned and quivered; and when he nudged the tip of my prick with the bottom of his tongue, I full-out cried, 'Fuck! Suck me!'

He touched his tongue down on the base of my outstretched cock and licked upwards, dragging pure delight the entire length of my wildly beating manhood. I arched off the bed, jamming my shaft against his lips. He lapped my prong like it was a melting popsicle on a hot, humid Hawaiian day.

I trembled with the wicked sensation of getting my dick licked. Ethan lapped over and over, almost tonguing my foreskin right off, making my slit tear with pre-come – which he promptly snapped up with a flick of his talented tongue.

When I could hardly take any more, he suddenly cupped my balls, shooting my erection up off my stomach and up to his waiting mouth. His lips flowered open and flowed over my bloated knob, consuming me in warmth and wetness.

I clawed at his scalp, watching him envelope my cockhead, then tug on it, his cheeks sucking in and out. The pressure was intense, the pulling sensation immense. And it only got better, as Ethan curved his head down and swallowed up more of my cock, his lips and mouth sliding down my shaft almost right to the balls.

'Fuck, yeah!' I bleated, the guy's head bobbing in my hands, the guy sucking on my cock.

He gripped my hips and blew me apart, tugging tight and hard and quick, wet-vaccing my prong like no man, or woman, had ever done before. Until he abruptly pulled his head up and my dick fell out of his lusty mouth. 'It's better together,' he said.

I just lay there, panting, as Ethan scrambled around on the bed so that his knees were straddling my head, his cock hanging over my face. We were quickly in the 69 position, man-sized. I reached up and grabbed onto the guy's taut butt cheeks, squeezed them, craning my neck and opening my mouth and snagging his smooth, tan, bulbous cap with my lips.

He groaned. His meaty hood filled my mouth, salted with our semen, and I wanted more, and more. I slid my lips up along his arrow-straight shaft and he shifted his hips down, gliding cock into my mouth and just about right down my throat.

I gagged only a little. It tasted so good, so right, another man's cock in my mouth. I was so enthralled that I hardly felt Ethan tilt my prick up and take me into his mouth. But I *did* feel it, and it felt great.

I bobbed my head back and forth, sucking on his throbbing cock, nudging his hanging balls with my nose. He sucked me right back, plunging his mouth down to my sac and pulling back up again, blowing me wild. I gave as good as I got, gobbling cock like a pro.

I slid my hands across Ethan's ass and probed at his manhole with my fingers. His cock jumped in my mouth, as I ploughed a prying digit right inside the guy, plugging anus for the very first time. He gripped my clenched thighs and sucked fiercely on my dong, his head flying up and down.

I'd tasted his seed, our seed, but I wanted more – I wanted him flooding my mouth with his hot, sticky lust, like I was about to cream his mouth. So I sucked harder, faster, squirming another finger into his anus and wiggling both around. He moaned, the rapturous sound vibrating up through my cock in his mouth and all through my burning body.

It was too much. My balls boiled over, out of control. I bit into Ethan's shaft, three-quarters up, and bucked, blasted, shooting into his sucking mouth. Just as hot, rubbery semen shot against the back of my throat, flooding my mouth; the pair of us going off simultaneously.

I sucked, swallowed, spurted; pouring out my joy, drinking in Ethan's. He filled me to overflowing with his cock and come, my throat working frantically to keep up, as I jetted my own sheer white-hot ecstasy into his gulping mouth.

When we'd finally emptied ourselves totally into each other, Ethan swung off my head and slipped back into my arms. We swirled our tongues together, tasting our come all over again, our cocks pressing back into the position that had started all the lovely mayhem in the first place.

Ethan gently ground his groin into mine, and I ground back, our cocks squeezing out their last drops of man-juice. Then the guy rolled off me and said, 'Ready for another scuba lesson, stud? I'll meet you down by the pool. Leeza awaits.'

Mob Scene

I WAS GRINDING A taco down to size when he alighted on the stool across from me.

'You a dick?' he purred.

'I've been called worse.'

'They call you "Stiff" Pecker, don't they – private eye?'

'Pee-car,' I pronounced it right for him. 'Stiff Pekar.'

He grinned, coolly, batted his lashes. 'Why the Stiff?'

I grinned back, took the rest of the taco wide-mouthed, chewed nice and slow, gulped with gusto. 'Maybe because of the kills I rack up in my racket. Maybe for other, less violent, reasons.' I batted my own lashes.

He said his name was Logan Morgan, he was looking for someone, didn't know the town that was swinging San Fran in the earlier 70s, so he needed a local's help. He had short, black hair and baby-blue eyes, to go with his baby-face and toddler body. He looked good enough to cuddle. But so did a chipmunk, before it sunk its choppers and claws into you, busted your nut.

'Logan Morgan, huh?' The name just didn't rhyme with the Brooklynese accent he was doing his best to cover up, jive with his obvious olive complexion. 'Just who are you searching for in our fair city?' I could've said "fairy", the way things were changing, the way the guy looked at me, and to me. But I let it ride, for the time being.

'His name is Dix Handler. He's big into photography, filmmaking, that sort of thing. A close relative of his is sick, wants to see Dix before he croaks, er, dies. I'm a friend of

124

the family. I said I'd try to look him up, since I live in LA. Dix left home a while back, sent some letters along the way postmarked 'Frisco.'

'That certainly narrows it down. 'Dix Handler' you say, Logan Morgan?'

The guy wetted his pouty lips, pursed and proffered a moist smile. 'That's right. I have a picture of him.'

He stood up to his full five-foot-three, pulled a wallet out of the back pocket of his black pants nice and slow so I could see the leather curve over the contours of his right buttock. I envied that leather some. Then he pulled a pic out of the wallet and handed it to me, sat back down, I think. He was that small.

It was a single frame from a film, clipped off from the main thread. I had to hold it up to the cloudy sky, got a pretty good gander at a man's face close-up. He didn't look anything special – young, with lots of hair, hippie-type.

'This all you giving me to go on?' I asked, setting the frame down on the plastic table.

'And some incentive,' Logan pitched, drawing three $100 bills out of his wallet, tossing them onto the pic.

'Anything else?'

He grinned that warm-cold knowing smile of his, and we adjourned our tête-à-tête to the deserted back lot of the taco storefront.

He gripped my crotch, looking up into my eyes. I felt the heat of his soft little hand, my cock's interest in his case growing by leaps and bounds. I took his head in my hands, bent my gourd down, planted my lips on his kisser.

His mouth was just as wet and willing and supple as it looked. He kissed me back. We chewed on each other's lips, Logan gathering my rapidly inflating shaft in his hand and stroking, tugging me through my slacks. I gave back as good as I got, diving my mitt down in between his legs, clutching the rod he was packing.

The wind rustled our hair, the sun making a rare

appearance and beaming down upon us, seagulls cheering us on. I tasted tongue – hot and slippery and urgent – and I spoke back in its language of lust, swirling my own sticker around his twirling mouth-organ. Our hands working each other's members like we welcomed home sailors down at the docks for a living.

'Pull out your cock! I want to stroke it barehanded, jerk you off!' Logan breathed in my maw.

I was thinking of another kind of bare – that went with "back" – but a dick's got to take what he's offered. So I pulled my paw off his crotch, unzipped, unloaded. He did the same, and our naked cocks met in a love embrace, 'Frisco-style.

I shook with delight when our slits kissed. Moaned with pure pleasure when Logan laced his fingers around my hard, beating shaft and stroked skin-on-skin. His cock jogged upwards, not too big, not too small, olive in colour with a swelled purple crown. I took it in hand, intimately welcoming it to the City by the Bay. We shook dicks, sealing our deal.

We kissed some more, frenched some more, Logan pumping me, me pumping Logan. Our hands moved faster and faster, our cocks stretching harder, bodies burning hotter, tongues flailing ferociously. A bum stumbled by and caught an eyeful, muttered a disparaging comment about lax city ordinances, went back on the prowl for a bottle.

'Oh, Stiff!' Logan mewled in my mouth. 'I think I'm going to ... I'm going to ...'

He did; jerking and jetting. His cock surged in my shunting hand, shooting ecstasy out the tip – hot, sticky, rubbery strings of ecstasy.

I felt his hand tighten on my cock, yank. And I spasmed, blew jism. We shook, rattled, and howled in each other's hands, popping off and pouring out, burst after starburst.

I promised to be 'in touch', and he took it just like I meant it.

126

"Shutterbug" Murphy owned a camera shop on Polk Street. He sold cameras, film and equipment out of the front of his store, pornography out of the back. The city was becoming a hotbed (pardon the pun) for the stuff, an X-rated Hollywood of the north, with the emphasis on "wood".

Bug was trying to cajole a kid into upgrading to a Nikon telescopic lenses on his grandpa's Speed Graphic, when I barged into the store.

'Stiff! How's it hanging?' he bellowed, blowing smoke not just from the cigar crowding his mouthflaps.

'Long as my kneecap, why?' I responded, giving the Bug a lascivious wink.

He grimaced. The kid packed up his relic and amscrayed, leaving Bug with no sale.

I gave him an opportunity to make back his money, though, dropping the clip of Dix Handler down onto the glass counter. 'Recognise this photog?'

Bug lip-walked his cigar from one side of his mush to the other, picked up the frame with a pair of portly digits and screwed a magnifier into a jaundiced orb. Holding the clip up to the light, he studied it. Then horked out a laugh, lowered the pic. 'Yeah, I recognise everything,' he chortled mysteriously.

I wasn't fond of the company, so I got the dickering started, tossing a fin onto the glass.

More chortling, wet and phlegmy as the man's stogie.

I added a sawbuck to the mix.

'I can wrap this case up for you lickety-split, Stiff,' he stated (and try saying that three times). 'That's gotta be worth something to you.'

The pile grew to 50 bucks, my bile along with it.

'That's Dix Handler,' Bug informed me.

'For crying out loud and lusty!' I wailed. 'I know what the guy's phony handle is!'

'Do you know where to find him?' Bug hastily added,

clump of a hand closing anxiously over the growth of cabbage. 'Did you know there's a prick in the picture? That the clip is from 16 millimetre stock, blue movie shoot?'

I admitted I didn't. 'What prick?'

Bug showed me, tucked away down in the right hand corner of the frame, past Dix's face – an erection. A Dix in the foreground, a dick in the background. 'He's a pornographer?'

'He ain't Yuosuf Karsh.'

'What's his real name?'

'Don't know that. But I know he hangs out at the Humping Camel – that's where all the up and comers in the jizz biz go to scout out fresh meat for the grindhouse.'

I pocketed the pic, said, 'What and where's the Humping Camel?'

'Never heard of it?' Bug eyed the geetus in his grip.

I shook my head.

He shrugged, chewing his stub. 'It's a swinger's club on Ashbury. 725, I think. It's the place to get down, and go down, if you know what I mean.'

His rheumy wink would've given a blind man a soft-on.

725 Ashbury was a big, old, tall-storeyed, gabled-galore Victorian house painted a fire-engine red. There were fires burning indoors too, judging by the endless stream of beautiful people who were eagerly marching through the front door. Blackout curtains adorned every window, music throbbed out into the street. I joined the throng making for the inside, intent on sniffing out my man.

There were two bouncers stationed just inside the door. I didn't have a membership card, wasn't on any list, so I punched my own ticket.

The guy on my right went down like a sack of codfish when I clipped his jaw with an Alcatraz-hard fist. The guy on my left threw his hand at my face, but I parried, swung low, bringing a punch up from the fault line below. It caught him in the beanbag. He went cross-eyed like Jerry Lewis, sat down like Gandhi.

I strolled down the hall, opened the door at the end. And was assailed by sex with a capital XXX.

There were naked men and women everywhere, in every conceivable position, exploring every inhabitable orifice. The cloying smell of sex funked the giant room, and groans and grunts and moans and the creaking and swooshing of furniture and cushions, the frenzied tattoo of flesh striking flesh, filled the hot, humid air.

There were sofas, divans, loveseats, settees, sectionals and flat-out mattresses, the designer's nightmare load-bearing couples and threesomes and foursomes and moresomes of every colour, creed, and chromosomal make-up. Two black men were stretching the eagerly greased sexholes of one redheaded woman just off to my left. While to my right, four women were linking up in a midget's daisy chain, lapping cunts like pussycats lap tuna juice straight from the can. And dead-ahead was the rest of the roiling sea of fucking flesh, along with a number of men and women just standing along the walls and watching, in some cases jerking and jilling.

I put my own back to a free spot on a wall, scanning the frothy mass for my man. I didn't find him, but three other men found me – found me out.

A svelte blond gripped my hand and pulled me off the wallpaper, into his arms for a passionate kiss. As another man, an equally slender-bodied brunette, began peeling my slacks open, button and zipper. The blond kindly arched away to give the brunette easier access to my over-engorged cock, and he pulled it out, popped it into his mouth.

'Jesus!' I gushed, getting hit with a wet velvet hammer between the legs.

'No, silly,' the blond cooed, squeezing my neck. 'He's Tristan, and I'm Percy. And he's Tyrell.'

I jerked my head around, following Percy's green eyes.

There was a huge bodybuilder standing behind me, his teeth gleaming white in a smile, skin gleaming black on his swollen nude limbs, snake between his legs gleaming with intent at my backside.

I opened my mouth to protest what looked like impossible penetration. But Percy drew my pan back around, plopped his petal lips back on my kisser. As Tristan down below gobbled up just as much of my pulsating rod as he could, then sucked on it – hard, quick, tight pulls than almost took off my foreskin.

I felt thick fingers dig into the back of my slacks, yank them down to my knees. I felt heavy hands grasp my bare butt cheeks, squeeze, knead the trembling pair. I braced myself for what was going to happen next, using Percy's mouth on mine and Tristan's mouth on my cock as a buffer.

And then it hit me – sweet Tyrell's tongue in my ass.

He'd squatted down and parted my rump right in the middle, stuck his warm, wet, neon-pink tongue where the sun don't normally shine. His slick mouth-member plugged into my asshole, and I vibrated like I was drawing 10,000 volts. The guy was an ass-eater, and he was ravenous.

Percy captured my own tongue between his pearly white teeth, sucked on it, in rhythm to Tristan wet-vaccing my dick. In time to Tyrell plunging his hardened blade of a sticker in and out of my anus. It was a dick's life, and I was loving it.

Percy moved lower, splitting my shirt open in a shower of buttons. He kissed one rigid pink nipple, the other, making my chest swell and my head spin. Then he slapped at my jutters with his tongue, licking them, lapping them, sucking them into his mouth and tugging on them. It was an awesome accompaniment to what was going on below, the trio of men playing me like a sexual instrument.

Tyrell had stopped fucking my butthole with his tongue, had spread me even wider, squished his tongue deep inside. He had a good three inches of face-snake buried in my ass, squirming around inside my chute. My bum blazed with the passion of it.

Tristan was cupping my balls, giving the bubbling sac a playful squeeze now and then, as he hoovered my meat from base to cap, over and over. He stopped only long enough to bite into my hood, Percy biting into my buds, before he went back to cocksucking like the skinflute virtuoso he was.

It was too much for me, too wild, too wicked. I've seen my share of astonishing things in my years of gumshoeing, experienced a lifetime of lowdown living, but I'd never felt anything like those three men were dishing out and serving up. 'Christ, I'm going to come!' I bleated.

Tyrell rammed my ass with his tongue. Percy groped my pecs, plucked my nipples almost right off my chest with his teeth. Tristan sucked me right over the edge.

I jerked, jolted by mind-blowing orgasm. The men scrambled around down in front of me, and Tristan hosed them all and himself with my spurts of sweet joy. He spray-painted one man's outstretched tongue, the other's, directed a couple of soul-shattering gouts into his own gaping and gulping mouth. I flopped around like a puppet on live wire strings, gushing sperm and sensation.

It took me a few minutes to regain my senses, my reason for being ... there. I was on the trail of Dix Handler, and the trail was hot.

I walked across the room, past the acrobatic exhibitions of all-out sex, followed the red velvet road up a staircase to the second floor. There were individual rooms up above, each and every one of them put to good use.

I poked my head in, got an eyeful, sometimes a splatter, pulled my head back out. And it was at door number six, at the end of the hall, that I finally hit paydirt of the non-procreating kind. Dix Handler, manning a camera, shooting through a two-way mirror.

The room was little more than a broom closet. Dix was so engrossed in his work, in the scene on the other side of the one-way looking glass, that he didn't even hear the slight snick of the door slipping open. I could see his reflection in the glass, recognised the broad forehead and long nose and plush lips and bushy brown beard and moustache from his freeze-frame photograph. I also recognised the mayor of Oakland on the other side of the mirror. His honour was polling two constituents of the buxom variety.

I said, 'Psst!'

Dix jumped like Tyrell had popped him one in the pucker, almost knocking his tripod and 16 millimetre into the next room.

'Stiff Pekar,' I introduced myself. 'I was hired to find you. A relative of yours is–'

Someone grabbed my arm, yanked me backwards, filled the doorway in my stead. 'Thanks for showing the way, hawkshaw. I'll take it from here,' he gritted.

It was Logan Morgan, sounding a whole lot more Lower East Side. He had a gun in his mitt, pointed at Dix, getting ready to squeeze.

I pulled my own rod, blasted.

The bullet banged into Logan's gun, turning it red-hot. It flew out of his fist, his convulsion helping it on its way.

He turned on me with a petulant snarl. Just in time to catch a size-12 in the sperm bank. I set him straight, and flat, with an uppercut that went from toe to head – his.

'OK, Dix, let's take it from the top. What's this all about? Why's this torpedo – Logan Morgan – gunning for you? Using me as a birddog?'

We were in Dix's flop, a one-room deep in the Castro district; low-rent, like the guy. He was hugging the end of his sofa, me pulled up in front on the back of a chair, interrogation-style.

'I don't know! How do I know!' he squealed for the tenth time.

I'd had enough. The racket on the other side of the

wafer-thin wall – a man and a woman road-testing the heavy-duty springs of a mattress – was giving me a headache, and a hard-on. 'OK, I'll just leave you to your own misery. Logan'll find you again, if he has to hire someone else to do it. And this time I won't be there to stop him.'

I got up, spun the chair back around, looked down at the trembling man. 'I figure him for mob muscle, out to collect on a contract.'

Dix whipped his head up and stared at me with saucered brown eyes. I made for the door. He made with the plea bargain.

'OK! OK! You gotta promise to help me if I tell you!'

I mumbled something vague, might've sounded like a promise.

'I filmed a guy – a few years back – with another guy. You know, some man-on-man action.'

'Just doing your job, right?'

'Sure. Right. This one cat wanted me to film it, for his sake. But he's dead now, and – and ... and the other guy's an up-and-coming gangster, in Chicago. He was, you know, just out to 'Frisco on a lark back then.'

'Let me guess, you kept a copy of your "work", for yourself?'

Dix nodded, something like professional pride in his eyes.

'And then you started blackmailing the guy in Chi? Tried to cash in even more?'

The eyes became sheepish. But the head bob was the same.

'Let's see it,' I said. 'Maybe I can figure out a way to get you off the hook.'

Dix sprang off the sofa and snapped a screen up to its full height on its stand against one wall, then jimmied three floorboards loose, extracted a silver can of film from the cubbyhole. He sprocketed a machine and got me to switch

133

off the light. And we sat side by side on the sofa, as the screen lit up with the scene of two men getting it on in the way the Good Lord originally intended.

I recognised the mobster in the picture – his mug had made the west coast papers about six months earlier. That was probably how Dix had figured out he had dynamite, as well as jack-off material, on his hands. The other man in the skin flick I didn't recognise, but I did admire the way he worked a dong in and out of a man's asshole.

Dix admired it too. So much so that he leaned over and unzipped me, extracted a measure of my appreciation for his auteurship out of my pants. He poured his soft, juicy lips over my cap, bore down on my shaft with his wet-hot mouth.

'Yeah!' I groaned, digging my fingers into the man's wild hair; staring at the Technicolor image of the one man drilling the mobster in the ass. If only crime was so sexy.

Dix hit my balls with his lips, taking my pipe right down his drain. I bucked, singing the guy's praises. He pulled back up, plunged back down, deep-throating me like a male Linda Lovelace.

I spun around on the sofa, stretched out, Dix never losing his lip-lock and mouth-clamp on my cock. But I got him to swing around, too, so that we were in the sweet 69 position, Dix over top of me, his cock, when I freed it from his bell-bottoms, dangling down hard and longing to my open mouth.

I sucked him inside. He shuddered, moaned. His voice vibrated through my prick in his mouth. I bobbed my head up and down, pulling on the man's smooth, slim, bulbous-headed appendage; as he ploughed his mouth up and down, throating me to the full length of my cock and endurance.

I only managed to get a few more hard tugs in on his dick, before I felt my balls boil ominously. I pushed the guy up, barked, 'Take off your jeans! Get on the table!'

If I was going to save his ass, I was going to have his

ass.

He understood, explicitly, stripping off his jeans and stretching out flat on his back on top of the wobbly table he ate off of and was going to get fucked off of. He lifted his legs, clutched his thighs. His pucker winked at me, pink and inviting, crack hairy as his head. I shuffled forward, hefted my schlong, hit his hole with the hood.

'Yeah, man, drill me!' he moaned in the lingo of the day.

I gripped one of his thighs with one of my hands and pushed dong into his ass with the other. The men on-screen moaned their approval, as I made cockheadway, surging through his squinting browneye and into the tunnel beyond. I went deep and delicious, long as I had available to me.

When my sword was fully impaled, I grabbed hold of Dix's other thigh, started rocking him back and forth on the table. He squeaked like the furniture, grabbing up his own cock and stroking to my stroke.

It was as hot as LA in the summertime, flamingly gay as 'Frisco in season; me fucking Dix in the ass while the projected men did the same. Our grunting and groaning, the splash of my thighs against Dix's butt cheeks, spliced into the erotic soundtrack.

My balls had never fully settled down, and now they went from simmer to boil again. I just couldn't last in the vice-tight, oven-hot pressure of the man's ass. I just wasn't that much of a stud, despite my wooden appearance. So I turned on the burners, searing Dix's chute with my sawing dong, rocking and cocking like a madman.

The men in the film howled out their ecstasy, no acting involved. I bellowed, and blew, doing a jig, spurting a free-for-all into Dix's ass. Still having sense enough, however, to smack his hand off his cock and jerk him myself. He erupted like a geyser, pulsing out spume, as I pumped his butt full of protein.

***

I mailed the blue movie to a high-level mobster in Chi-town, let those good Catholics clean up the mess in their midst, fit filmed man with a pair of cement testicles if they so desired. That cost Dix any more blackmail money, but it also took the baby-faced heat off him – no more mobster, no more need to protect his position with the help of a hitman.

One thing I didn't tell Dix, though, or the boys in the black suits and white ties back east: I got Bug to make me a copy of that well-shot, scorchingly hot mano-a-mano film. For personal reasons only, of course.

The dick business isn't always so engaging, after all.

Beau for a 'Bo

I WAS SNOOZING ALONGSIDE the tracks on a sweet bed of grass in a ditch, when I felt something tugging at me. At first, I thought it was the handsome cop in my dream, tugging me gently by the sleeve and off the train and into his arms, preparatory to taking me home and stuffing me full of food and cock.

But then the sad reality of 1933 came back upon me, as I woke up. I squeezed a red-rimmed orb open and spotted a young, brown-haired kid tugging at the bindle my feet were draped over, preparatory to taking it away from me and emptying me of all of my meagre belongings. 'Get your greasy mitts off that, punk!' I growled.

The kid jumped like I'd jabbed him with a cattle prod. He stared at me from his crouched-down position, eyes wide and baby-blue. I relaxed a bit, loosened my grip on the rock I always slept beside so I could brain such an interloper.

But the kid didn't take off like a rabbit, like I expected. He kept right on thieving like a fox, tugging my battered grip out from under my battered feet and trying to make off with it.

He jumped to his feet, clutching the old leather bag (my last surviving remnant from the Jazz Age), and turned tail. I shot up like a spring and grabbed his tail, my bag.

A brief tug-of-war ensued. And then the grip busted apart like a train uncoupling, spilling my belongings onto the grass. A whistle blew, a freight rumbling out of the yard half-a-mile down the line.

I let go of the kid's jacket, more concerned now about gathering up my clothes and books and razor and hopping that train coming down the tracks, than punishing the young robber like he deserved. We hoboes have our priorities, and the first one is riding the rails.

But once again the kid didn't bolt. Instead, he scooped up my cardigan, and then ran off with it. I gave my chase, hot on his bony heels.

For a lean, lithe strip of an 18-year-old youngster, he was surprisingly easy to catch, even for a 35-year-old, grizzled veteran of the hobo army like me. I grabbed onto his jacket after 50 yards, was pulling my cardigan out of his hand, when that whistle blew again, the tracks vibrating now as the freight picked up speed. Night was fast-approaching, and I preferred spending it in the relative comfort of a closed boxcar than an open field.

The cardigan decided the issue. It ripped apart at the well-worn seams. 'You can have half!' I yelled at the kid, turning and racing back to my ruptured bindle.

I just had time to shovel most of my stuff into the broken bag when the train thundered alongside, headed for highball. I raced to keep pace, tossed my bag into an open boxcar where it exploded again on impact, swung myself aboard. My hands slipped on the metal railing, slick with sweat from the tussle, but I didn't go under the wheels.

I saw the kid still standing by the side of the tracks, watching me with, I swear, a wistful expression on his face.

I got red-lighted 50 miles down the line, a bull catching me sleeping in the car as we approached a watering station. He sent me sailing with a blow from his club. We were slowing down, so I didn't hit the ground *too* hard.

I spent the night in an open field.

Morning came, afternoon. My crust of bread and can of beans were consumed. I found some twine in the ditch and did a serviceable job of tying my grip together. Good for another thousand miles on the Southern Pacific.

I tramped to the next station down the line – a one-horse farming town known for being hard on beggars – tramped on past. I lay low, until I finally heard that plaintive whistle and felt the ground a-rumble. Then I rose up and raced alongside the freight, tossing my grip inside a half-closed boxcar and following up with my body.

My luck was still holding – all bad.

There were four other 'bos already on board. Three of them were looming over the fourth stretched out on the floorboards in a corner. One of the three had his pants down around his ankles, his ass showing pale as the face of the moon.

I'd jumped into the middle of something I wanted nothing to do with. One thing you learn fast on the road is to mind your own business. Only, now these fellow travellers were wanting to make me their business.

'What you got in the bag, 'bo?' one of the three rasped, a short, thickset guy with a face as unshaven as a bear's butt.

The other two turned to look at me. One was wearing a slouch hat and a leather jacket that had lost its sheen a century earlier, his torn pants tied at the waist with part of a clothesline. He was tall and thin, with a pockmarked face. While the man next to him had a wide, pie-like face, a wide body to match, his cock bobbing hard and stubby in between his stubby bare legs.

I snatched my bag up off the shuddering floor and started backing away. They should've let me go, let me leap back from whence I'd come. But they were greedy bastards; they wanted my booty like they wanted to stick it up that prone 'bo's booty.

The short guy charged me, tucking his chin into his chest and driving headlong for my gut. I dodged to the side, grabbed onto his dirty collar and turned his trajectory slightly, sending him flying over the open side of the rattling boxcar and out into the wild blue yonder.

139

The tall 'bo hauled a chain out of a jacket pocket, started swinging it. I dodged in and swung my bindle up into his face, catching him under the chin. My bag burst and the bum went skyward, lifted clean off his dirty feet by the force of the blow. He landed with a jarring thud on his back, rolled the wrong way to avoid me – right out the other side of the boxcar. We could all hear his forlorn wail as he hit the grading at 30 per.

'Tough guy, huh?' the wide-body 'bo with the dangling dick glowered. He carefully tucked his rod back into his roadworn trousers, eying me menacingly.

I was hoping that stretched-out 'bo would rise up and ride the guy's back like the guy had been about to ride the 'bo's ass before I'd intervened. But he just lay there in the darkened corner of the boxcar, not doing a damn thing to help.

Cock secured, moon-face pulled a jackknife out of his pants pocket, flicked it open. The blade glinted in the sunlight cutting in through the half-open doors. I sneered like I'd find it a pleasure to pick my teeth with the pig-sticker, after I'd beaten the pig holding it senseless. And that guy moved forward, then sideways, stepping off the moving train and out into the early-evening air.

I could hardly believe it.

The fourth 'bo hardly could, either. He slapped my face, whined, 'Why'd you drive them all away?'

It was the kid who'd gotten away with half of my cardigan!

I smacked him back across the face, my blood still boiling and body still shaking from the recent dust-up, and from the sheer ingratitude of the little ingrate.

His head snapped to the right, brown hair flying. He snapped his head back, a warm grin spreading across his face, a strange sheen taking hold in his big blue eyes. I looked down and noticed that his jeans were crumpled up around his bony knees, his cock jutting out from between his thin legs, long and hard and beautifully sculpted. 'Slap me again!' he hissed. 'Rough me up! Please!'

There were all kinds on the road. This kid was one of the strangest, and one of the prettiest. He had a delicate, oval-shaped face and plush, red lips, slender hands and fingers, smooth skin tanned a tawny brown. My cock hardened in my pants looking at him and his wiener like my appetite whetted looking at a load of red-hots at a ballpark.

He shoved me in the chest, making his cock jack up and down. I grabbed his girlish shoulders and shoved him down to his knees. His fingers were light and agile, pulling my hard-on out of my pants before I could even stop him, had I wanted to.

His hot hand on my pulsing rod was like a sweet, jarring slap to the mush. His hot, wet mouth engulfing my bloated hood and half of my swollen length was like a warm wave of sunshine washing through my shimmering body. I grabbed onto his ears and jerked his face into my groin, driving my dong right down his throat.

He gagged, blowing snot out of his gasping nostrils. But he clutched my buttocks in a death-grip, not even letting me take a step back. I pumped my hips, fucking his face.

It was searing heat and bathing dampness and velvety tightness, plunging back and forth in the kid's mouth and throat. My cock bent, dove, the kid sealing tight with his lips. Sucking.

I flat-out slammed his face, my fingernails biting into his ears, his biting into my ass. My balls slapped against his pert little chin. He blew steam over my groin, the glistening length of cock that actually squeezed out from between his lips, before gliding back in again. My body temperature rocketed, pouring molten cock into that young man's coke furnace of a mouth and throat.

I couldn't hold it, the pressure too intense. I was going to blow.

The kid sensed it. For all his young years, he knew men,

well.

He jerked his head back, and my prong popped out of his mouth on a tidal wave of hot spit and air. 'Fuck me! Fuck my ass!' he moaned. He caught my bobbing cap between his teeth and bit into the shining knob.

I yelped and shoved him backwards. He went sprawling prone onto the floorboards. He instantly shot his legs up into the air and skinned his pants right off. Then he gripped his bare butt cheeks and spread them, offering up his pink hole to my hungry eyes and cock.

The train shunted, throwing me forward. I went down on my knees, before the kid's upraised ass. I gripped his cheeks, plied them, revelling in the smoothness, the sweet suppleness. And then I bent my head in and licked his cute asshole, tonguing his pucker.

His bum shivered in my hands, his legs shaking up above. I lapped at his crack, from tailbone to fuzz-dusted balls. His butt cleavage was as tawny and tasty as the rest of him. My cock raged between my legs, anxious to plunder that delicious pink hole.

I rose upright on my knees and gripped my dong with one hand, his right leg with the other. I poked at his hole with my spit-slickened cap.

'Drive it home! Drive it deep!' he howled, knuckles white on his ass, tearing his cheeks apart.

He gaped wide and pink before me, and I plugged my hood into his butt, ploughing through his rim and into his anus. That's when he let go of his cheeks, so that his ring closed in on my cap, gripping me tight.

I shuddered, grabbed onto his ankles, thrust my hips forward, leaning into the young man. My cock speared into his chute, full-length. We both cried out, as my balls squished up against his butt cheeks, my cock embedded in the kid's luscious anus.

I rutted around in his ass, wallowing in the wonderful sensations. He spat in my face, begging to be fucked and fucked hard. I licked his hot saliva off my lips and spat it back at him. He stuck out his long, pink tongue, and I flogged it with my tongue. Then I churned my hips, pumping him like he and I wanted him to be pumped.

He was red-hot and vice-tight. I rocked him to and fro, plundering his anus with my erection, reaming his impudent butt. He gripped my hands on his ankles and rolled up almost in two, taking and loving every pistoning inch that I slammed inside him.

The train humped along the tracks at a good rate of speed, as I humped that kid with a savageness and sensuality borne of too many lonely nights on the road. I smacked my thighs into his cheeks over and over, my iron-hard cock swelling his bottom, sawing his chute. It was wild, wicked. I had the strength to go on and on, fuck the kid so raw that his anus wept with delight. But my balls didn't have the willpower.

The searing, sucking pressure on my shunting dick made my nuts boil, then burst. 'Fuck, kid, I'm coming!' I grunted, pumping at a panic pace.

'Come in my ass! Fill my ass with your hot seed! Please, mister!'

He didn't ask much. Just what I had to give him.

I thrust hard and long and deep a couple more times, then jumped, jolted by earthquake orgasm. My cock exploded in the kid's ass, semen spouting out the tip in head-spinning spurts, flooding his tunnel.

Through the tears of sheer joy in my eyes, I saw that he was jacking his own cock, semen leaping out and into his twisted face, onto his extended tongue. I blasted his ass to overflowing, riding it and my own sperm with my thrusting cock.

143

The kid works for me now, stealing stuff from other 'bos, mainly. Only problem is, he keeps getting caught. Like he wants to get the beating and bitch-fucking that follows. But we always meet up again, making life on the road a helluva lot more *hard* for the both of us.

Heavenly Body

MY GIRLFRIEND, SARA, GAVE me a telescope for my birthday. I'd expressed some tepid interest in astronomy during the long course of one of our evenings together when we weren't having sex and should've been, and she'd run out and bought the stargazer for me. She was always trying to encourage me to use my mind, rather than my hands (all over her hot little body).

To please the woman, I set the instrument up on the balcony of my tenth floor apartment and promised to faithfully study the night sky every chance I got, when we weren't out for dinner and a movie and an unsatisfying petting session in my car. I planned, of course, to pitch the nerd-tool over the railing or misplace it some other way the first chance I got (like the first time I broke up with Sara).

But one Sunday night, shortly after my girlfriend had left me all alone and longing again, I actually did plug my orb into the viewfinder, took a quick gaze at the sky. And couldn't find one damn star or moon. Apparently, the thing didn't work real well when it was overcast.

So, I trained the tube downward, onto the apartment building across the way, hoping to maybe pick out at least one earthbound heavenly body in a state of undress or coitus. But as I scanned across and up and down, I located nothing more exciting than a geriatric broad in a sports bra sweating to the oldies. I soon gave that up, before I strained the telescope and my neck with all the flopping and floundering around.

But then I locked onto the apartment next door, and found some actual nudity, though not quite the kind I was searching for. It was a guy – a long, lean, sun-bronzed guy – slouched on his big white sofa with his long, hard cock in the upright and locked position, jacking himself off while he watched something dirty, no doubt, on the big-screen TV in front of him.

The magnifying powers of the mini-Hubble brought everything up close, right into my face. I could clearly see every smooth contour of the man's pretty face, every straw-blond follicle on his head, the jutting tenseness of his tan nipples and the tightened intensity of his six-packed stomach, the mushroomed meat of his hood, the smooth and impressive length of his shaft – as he swirled his slender brown hand up and down the towering erection.

I stared at him through the lenses, transfixed. And as I watched him tug on his boner, I felt something boning out in my shorts. I was actually getting hard, spying on another man jerking off!

I pulled my head up, looked around, frightened, excited. There were no other people out on the balconies bordering mine. I reached down and rubbed my cock through my thin shorts. Yup, I was erect all right, pitching a tent that was only supposed to be pitched by woman-watching and wrestling.

But maybe it was all because of my recent frustration in dealing with and being dealt out of Sara. Or maybe it was due to the fact that just a couple of night ago I'd stumbled onto some gay porno in my wanderings on the internet – two young, buff, tanned studs stroking, then sucking each other off – and been mildly turned-on by the mellow eroticism of it all. But whatever the cause, I was pulling a stiffy like nobody's business, peeping in on that luscious lad across the way minding his own dirty business.

I applied my eye back to the viewfinder and gripped my dick, stroked. Jacking off through my shorts like that pretty boy was bare-handing himself.

He ran his left hand up his stomach and onto his chest, pinched and rolled a rigid nipple between his fingers. As his other hand picked up speed on his cock, pumping faster, harder, with the smooth, practised ease of a man who was used to handling pricks. More than his own, I quickly found out.

Because right then, another guy appeared, naked as the man on the couch. He walked in behind my voyeuee, looking at the TV, at the glorious sight of his friend stretched out in front of the television with his big dick in his shifting hand. This guy had black hair, was just as tanned, sported a more muscular body. He hefted his own cock and touched it down on the blond's shoulder, startling him.

The guy stretched his long neck back on the couch and looked up at his friend. Then grinned, as the standing man slapped his hardening cock right down onto the sitting man's face.

'Let the gaiety begin,' I marvelled, rubbing my straining member with a new passion, focusing in hard and tight on the pair of fellows.

Blondie arched back even further and opened his mouth, and the brunette fed his cock inside. He tottered closer, smooth-shaven balls squishing against the guy's nose, vein-ribboned shaft delving deep into his friend's mouth, almost right up to those balls.

Blondie took every inch of that lovely dong into his mouth. His cheeks and throat bulged with the meat. I scrambled my shorts down, grasped and fisted my own cock skin-on-skin, never breaking eye-contact with that sizzling homoerotic scene across the way.

The dark-haired dude pumped his hips, fucking Blondie's mouth. He reached down and played with the sucking guy's nipples, reached lower, grabbed onto his pal's massive erection and picked up the stroking where the man

147

had left off.

It was wild, so totally different from what I'd so long considered sexy, been conditioned to think is sexy. Here was a muscle-hunk getting sucked off by his pretty love-buddy, while he pulled on that man's penis, and I was as aroused as I'd ever been, tugging tube steak as excitedly as that sucked-off man in the apartment building opposite.

There was no time to analyse my feelings. Because my balls were already tingling, tightening, my cock surging come-hard in my flying hand. Blondie bucked, and blasted, his lover pulling rope after rope of hot, white jizz out of the man's jumping cock. Then the brunette shuddered, the muscles all over his blazingly nude body clenching, as he shot sperm into the blond man's mouth, pumping with his hips, and his hand.

I bit my lip and whimpered, my own cock exploding in my fist. Semen spurted up into the air and rained down on the green-carpeted floor of the balcony. I was jolted over and over, like the beautiful boys across the way, shimmering with blissful heat as I jetted my joy.

It was about a week later that I got a knock on my door as I was searching the apartment opposite for sexual life. I was dressed only in my bathrobe, with nothing underneath, having come out to the balcony and the telescope prepared to come. But I answered the door all the same, and came face-to-face with the blond guy I'd been studying so closely the past seven days.

'Hi, my name's Darcy,' he said with a friendly smile. 'May I come in? There's something I'd like to discuss with you.'

My mouth gaped open and closed like a fish, as I floundered for a response. The man was even better-looking, more breathtaking, to the naked eyes.

He walked by me and into my apartment. And he couldn't help but notice the open sliding doors, the telescope mounted out on the balcony, pointed not up but across. He turned back to me, grinning. And then he unfastened the trenchcoat I just then noticed he was wearing, shrugged it off his shoulders, and let it drop.

I gasped for air like that flounder out of water. The guy was totally naked, stunningly nude as I'd seen him so many times before – only this time he was in the same room with me, and I wasn't hidden behind the glassed-in safety off a long-range optic device. His bronze body gleamed under the muted lights, smooth and hard, nipples erect, cock dangling long and large.

'I've noticed you watching from across the way,' he purred seductively. 'Why haven't you just come over and introduced yourself? Troy and I don't have an exclusive relationship, you know.'

'But – but I'm not gay!' I gulped.

It sounded ridiculous, especially with the way my wide blue eyes were travelling all over Darcy's body, focusing in on his cock; the way my own cock was protruding from between the terrycloth folds of my bathrobe, risen up all on its own with the sight of the luscious dude so near. And yet, it was also true. I'd never been romantically involved with a man before, never had sex with any man before.

All that was about to change, for the better.

'Gay or straight, I like what I see,' Darcy murmured, coming up close to me, slipping his slender fingers into my brown hair and teasing my tingling scalp. 'And I think you've liked what you've seen, haven't you?'

I had to nod at that undeniable fact. And Darcy pressed his warm body into mine, his warm lips making contact with my lips, first softly, then harder, more urgently. I grabbed onto the guy and mashed my mouth into his. I just couldn't help myself.

We kissed excitedly, passionately, holding each other tight, our cocks melding together in the heat. His body spray was sweet and subtle and it filled my dizzy head, as his supple tongue slipped in between my lips and filled my mouth.

My own tongue sprang to life, wrestled with his, the warmth and wetness absolutely wonderful. He pushed my bathrobe down off my shoulders and pulled it open as we frenched, and the garment slid off my body and to the floor. Leaving both of us naked.

I clutched his hot body to mine, groaning in his mouth as our bare cocks came together foreskin-on-foreskin. He pulled his head back and stared at me, his limpid brown eyes hooded. 'Getting gayer?' he asked.

I was a raving, flaming homosexual for the man. He was that desirable. I kissed my way down his long neck, licking, biting into the smooth brown flesh, onto his chest. I clutched his clenched pecs and wagged my tongue back and forth over one of his rubbery nipples, the other stiffened bud. He moaned his approval.

I captured a nipple in my mouth and sucked on it, revelling in the taste and texture. His chest and tits were as hairless as any woman's, his pebbled areolae a delight to my swirling tongue. I bit into his other nipple and tugged at it, making him arch his back and whimper for more.

I dropped lower, gripping his slim, smooth sides and dragging my tongue down his stomach, his lower abdomen, his cock rising up to meet my mouth. I was on my knees on the carpet, the man's erection right in front of me, twitching before me.

'Suck it!' Darcy urged. 'Suck my cock!'

My hands sweated against his skin, my throat gone bone-dry. I stared at that swollen, bobbing hood. And then I slid my lips right over it, consuming the man's cap. It felt right, delicious.

'Yes!' Darcy gasped, shivering. He grasped my head, urging me to inhale more of his beautiful cock.

I did, pouring my wet-hot mouth over his shaft, swallowing up three-quarters of his tremendous erection.

His knees buckled, my head spun. I had a man's cock in my mouth, throbbing in my mouth, filling my mouth.

Then I was sucking on it, moving my head back and forth, wet-vaccing Darcy's meat. I slid my hands down onto his taut, trembling butt cheeks for a better grip, and he arched his back, his cock thrusting into the back of my throat.

He was loving the loving I was giving his dick, and I was loving it too. It came naturally, sucking quick and tight, slow and sensual, downing just about his entire prong and then drawing it back out of my mouth dripping and shining. I sucked him like I liked to be sucked, like any man would want it.

I moved my hands over his butt mounds so that my fingers met at his cleavage, dug into his crack. He pumped his hips, fucking my mouth, diving cock down my throat. I looked up at him, on fire with lust, wanting him to douse me – come in my mouth, flood me with his hot seed so that I could joyfully swallow it down.

But he had other ideas. He knew I thought his body a work of art, and he wanted me to appraise it in the most intimate manner a man can – by fucking him up the ass.

We stumbled over to the couch. Darcy sat in my lap, my straining prick spearing up along his shaven nut sac and poling against his cock. He was light, tight. I kissed his chest, tongued a nipple, lapped one of his tangy armpits.

He pulled some lube out of a pocket of his discarded trenchcoat and sprayed a blast on my cock. I jerked at the feel of the cool mist on my raging prong. Jerked again when Darcy gripped and greased me, rubbing up and down the length of my cock, jacking me to new heights and hardness.

'Fuck me in the ass!' he hissed, lifting himself up, poking my hood in between his butt cheeks.

I grabbed onto my cock. He spread his cheeks, lying back on my heaving torso. I ploughed my cap up against his pucker, stood stymied there for a breathless second, then plunged through. He shifted his body downwards, his anus swallowing up my erection.

It was hotter and tighter than any girl's pussy. I was buried balls-deep in another man, squeezed sensationally by his ass walls. I could feel my cock beating inside him. I fucked him, thrusting back and forth in his chute. We both moaned.

Darcy shifted on top of me, meeting my thrust with his movement, the pair of us oiling together in perfect rhythm, my cock plunging his ass.

I was bathed in sweat, ablaze with the blowtorch heat of Darcy's body, the searing shunting of cock in anus. I gripped the guy's hips and pumped mine, fucking him harder, faster. He gripped his flapping cock, stroking the rock-hard appendage to keep pace with my reaming.

'Oooh ... fuck!' I groaned, overcome by it all. I thrust in a frenzy, then bucked, shooting white-hot sperm into Darcy's ass, again and again and again.

He yelped, his jerking cock going off in his hand, spraying his chest and my face. The guy came like a fountain, all over the place because of my ass-buffeting, with just about the same mammoth intensity as me.

I still play it "straight" with my girlfriend, Sara. She's never been happier, because now she doesn't have to fend off my animal advances any more; I get all the loving I need from Darcy now. Who knew astronomy could be so satisfying, satiating even?

Office Poly-dicks

I'M NOT ONE TO normally mix business and pleasure, but as I watched Barron strutting around my office when we were working late one night, his big, muscular buttocks clenching and unclenching beneath the thin material of his tight suit pants, his gleaming, powerful, coal-black arms flowing majestically out of his short-sleeved shirt, his thick nipples wickedly indenting the light-weight fabric, my hardened cock told me that, for at least one night, I had to do all I could to make pleasure my business. And who am I to argue with a hard cock?

Barron had been with the firm for about six months, ever since he'd graduated from college with his mechanical engineering degree, but even in that short time, he'd already impressed the partners and the rest of the staff with his intelligence and work ethic. His clean good looks, warm, brown eyes, and heavily-muscled physique had also impressed more than a few of the partners, including myself, and many of the ladies in the typing pool. He'd worked on a couple of small projects for me, and I'd quickly become the studly overachiever's biggest fan.

'You want to take a break, Barron?' I asked, as the youthful up-and-comer spread a set of blueprints out on a table next to my desk and bent over them, his round, heavy ass filling my eyes, and cock.

'Huh?' He turned his head in my direction. 'Sure, whatever you want, boss,' he said, his sensual lips breaking open to reveal blindingly-white teeth.

I would have to hold him to that statement, I thought to myself, then glanced at my watch. 'Let's take a ten-minute break and then we'll polish off the rest of the proposal. We'll call it a night no later than 11 o'clock. OK?'

'Sounds good,' he replied. 'I'm going to grab a soda. You want anything?'

I only smiled and shook my head, watched him leave the room, thinking how much, for a big man, he moved like a cat – smoothly, sinuously, silently. I spun around in my chair and gazed out the window, at the twinkling, night-shrouded city spread out below, and I ran a few Barron seduction scenarios through my lust-addled mind – strategies for getting the ebony hard-body to bury his liquorice stick up my itchy ass, to pound my petoot with the same intensity he brought to his work, to grab onto my waist for dear life and hammer my rippling bum 'til he exploded in a blaze of come inside me. Then it'd be my turn.

I didn't even know if the gorgeous go-getter was queer, but I did know that he didn't have a girlfriend, and that he'd already given the cold shoulder to a few of the firm's secretaries who'd chased after him with their tongues hanging out. And I knew something else just then; I knew that in thinking about Barron and the heated erotic possibilities that accompanied the young man, I had almost unconsciously unzipped my pants and pulled out my cock, was stroking myself in a practised manner like I was home in my recliner with a gay porn magazine spread out on my knees.

I shot a quick glance around the back of my chair, saw no one, and kept right on stroking, never one to leave a job unfinished. I thought some more of Barron's rock-hard, noir body, naked and glistening with sweat as he pumped my stretched-out chute full of sperm. I pulled a Kleenex out of my pocket, a second one on second thought, and kept them handy, my balls tightening ominously as I vigorously fisted and fantasized. I stared blindly out the window and swirled my hand up and down my straining cock, earnestly polishing my meat to certain orgasm, visions of Barron dancing through my head.

'Need a hand with that?' someone asked from behind me. 'Or a mouth?'

My hand froze on my pole. I slowly turned my head, my neck cracking, and looked up at Barron standing directly in front of my desk, a big grin on his beautiful face. I struggled to gather up my shattered wits, and asked lamely, 'W–what do you mean, Barron?'

'I can see your reflection in the window, Leonard,' he replied matter-of-factly.

I whipped my head back around and looked at my own reflection – the reflection of my hand-wrapped cock. I'd been caught red-fisted, but my embarrassment quickly faded away when Barron stealthily moved around the desk until he was in front of me, openly admiring my clenched cock.

'That's quite the marvel of engineering you've got there,' he quipped, his warm eyes re-establishing what little erection I'd lost when he had surprised me. 'Mind if I take a closer look?'

I was speechless, but any words I might've mumbled would have been lost, anyway, when I swallowed my Adam's apple when Barron dropped to his knees and pulled my cock out of my hand and into his. His huge, hot hand engulfed my swollen dong, and I ran a wooden tongue over cracked lips and groaned; groaned again when he started pumping me.

'Yes,' I breathed, my body flooding with heat as he stroked my dick and stared into my eyes.

He leaned closer and kissed me – a soft, lingering kiss full of greeting and promise. I gripped his shaved head and mashed my lips against his, and we kissed as two men should kiss – long and hard and deeply. We devoured each other with our mouths, my exposed passion bursting into full-flower as I hungrily chewed on the lips of that night-

155

shaded giant.

He returned my fire, pulling on my pulsating cock continuously while we kissed, his hand moving faster and faster. He slid his tongue in between my lips and scoured the damp interior of my mouth, until I met his slashing tongue with my tongue. We excitedly frenched each other, slapping our slippery, pink pleasure tools together over and over as the buff beauty urgently tugged on my steel-hard shaft.

'Let me get a little more comfortable,' he breathed into my face, before breaking away from my mouth and cock and rising to his full six and a half feet.

He unravelled his tie and unbuttoned his shirt, tossed them aside, and I gaped in astonishment at his magnificent upper body. The guy was an absolute monster, his hairless arms and chest thick and hard, striated with muscle, ripped, his abs chiselled out of polished, black granite, his dark nipples large and protruding. My mouth watered like a Pavlovian dog as I stared at the built-for-manhandling hunk, at his rippling muscles, but he wasn't done disrobing just yet, thank God. He kicked off his shoes and unbelted and unzipped his pants, pulled them down and off in one fluid motion and stood there, three feet in front of me, clad only in a pair of tight, white briefs and blue socks. His cock bulged out the stretchy material of his underwear, obscenely, like a coiled snake that I knew would grow incredibly large and long when fully aroused.

'Want to take it down the rest of the way, Leonard?' he asked quietly, moving closer, his cock twitching in his underwear, growing, striving to break free of the constraining garment.

I gulped, slid forward in my chair, and gripped the sides of his briefs with shaking hands and pulled down. His cock sprung out into my face, brushing my nose and lips, and the ebony dong quickly swelled in size as I watched in hot-blooded amazement, kept on swelling until it stood a good nine inches out from his pubes, huge and heavy-looking, arrow-straight and jerking slightly as I breathed on it. I anxiously grabbed it, my fingers barely fitting around, and marvelled at its size and heat and pulsing power.

'Yeah,' Barron grunted. 'Stroke it, Leonard. Stroke my cock!'

I was only too willing to oblige the young stud. I pumped his tremendous, blue-black cock with my hand, the sweat on my palm providing just the right amount of lubrication. My body temperature rose to fever level as I lovingly tugged on Barron's big cock, regarded it hungrily, my lips mere inches away from its mushroomed head. I stuck out my tongue and tentatively licked at his slit, his cock jumping in my hand as I did so. Then he did the unthinkable – pulled his dick away from me.

'I'm working for you, remember?' he commented, before dropping to his knees again, in between my legs. He took hold of my prick with one hand while he pushed me back in the chair with the other.

I looked on, enraptured, as the eager-to-please engineer gripped my cock at its base and flicked his wet tongue across my hood. I groaned, held on tight to the arms of my chair, and then thrust my hips up and urged Barron to paint the shaft of my raging cock with his ultra-pink tongue. He swirled his tongue all over my bloated cockhead, bathing the hood in his hot saliva, and then he dragged his velvet-sandpaper tongue all the way up from the bottom of my throbbing dick to the tip, in one slow, superheated tongue-stroke. I trembled with excitement and let the warm waves of sexual pleasure wash over me, as Barron lapped at my cock, his flattened-out tongue repeatedly licking the underside of my dong.

'God, that feels wonderful,' I moaned, overwhelmed by the awesome sensation of his slimy tastebuds on my cock-flesh.

'It gets better,' he said, momentarily halting his tongue-lashing to blow on my quivering dick. He ran his tongue the length of my prick one final time, then opened wide and swallowed my hood.

'Jesus!' I gasped, squirming around in my chair as he popped my swollen cocktop in and out of his warm, wet mouth.

He closed his lips over the top of my hood and sucked, his tongue pressed firmly against the super-sensitive spot where shaft became head. Then he took a lungful of air in through his flared nostrils and lowered his head, began going down on my cock. My muscles tensed to the tearing point and my brain came close to snapping as his lips inched their way down my dong, slowly, sensuously, surely, until he had three-quarters of my meat lodged in his mouth. And, God bless him, he didn't stop there.

I impetuously shoved my hips upward, and his nose burrowed into my pubes. The talented oralist had the entire length of my cock buried in his mouth, and throat, and I was overcome with the incredible feeling of heat and tightness. Then the wicked man-eater turned the sexual tension up another few notches by pushing out his tongue and lapping at my balls.

'God almighty!' I bellowed, getting all religious in praise of Barron's righteous sword-swallowing. I twisted my head from side to side, revelling in the wanton glory of his ferocious deep-throating, the pressure rapidly building to the boiling-over point in my tongue-teased balls.

He looked up into my eyes, my size-large cock locked between his lips, wedged in his craw, and I lost it. My dick exploded and I cried out in ecstasy, blasted white-hot semen straight down that snake-charmer's throat. I frantically pumped my hips, Barron's head bobbing up and down and his throat working as he consumed load after load of my spurting come. I came for what seemed like a blissful, sexual eternity.

And when my ruptured cock had at last sprayed jizz for the final time, I slumped back down in my chair, exhausted and exhilarated, and felt the last tremors of all-out orgasm slowly fade from my body. Barron kept my spent cock imprisoned in his throat for a good while longer, milking me of come, until he finally lifted his head and my dripping dong tumbled out of his mouth.

He smacked his lips with satisfaction, then leaned forward and frenched me, giving me a taste of my own sticky medicine. 'Mind if I fuck you up the ass, Leonard?' he asked politely.

'Would you?' I quipped, sliding out of my chair like I was minus a backbone, when Barron got to his feet.

I stood up and wandered past him, shut the open office door, and then slowly and shakily stripped off my tie and shirt, shoes and pants, until I stood there buck-naked save for my boxers and business socks. He strode over to me, his muscles moving like they were sheathed in oil, shining huge and powerful under the bright, fluorescent light, and I let him slide down my shorts, before stepping out of them and into his arms. We held each other and kissed, his lips and tongue rekindling my smouldering fire, our cocks pressing hotly against one another. Eventually, I broke his embrace and took a step back, and admired his monster cock as it pointed accusingly at me, imagining what it would feel like to have that python buried to the hilt in my ass.

Well, there was only one way to find out for sure. I swallowed hard and collapsed to my knees, then down onto all fours. 'Fuck me, Barron!' I said, sounding a hell of a lot more casual than I felt.

He nodded his head, appraising my naked brown body with his eyes. I may be 45 years old, with more than a few grey hairs on my head and chest, but I've always taken good care of myself. I'm nowhere near as muscular as young-gun Barron, but I'm lean and hard and have a tight, round ass that has garnered more than its fair share of compliments, and cocks. So, I dropped onto my elbows and shoved that big, mocha man-catcher into the air, urging my young lover to stick it with his cock, to hard-ride the two of us to blistering orgasm.

'Here I come, Leonard,' he warned, spitting into his hand and onto his cock, onto my ass. He rubbed his enormous dong with the hot spit, getting it good and greasy, oiled for action. Then he rubbed saliva into my asshole, probed a finger up my butt.

'Yes!' I grunted, burying my face in my arms, the feeling of his finger wiggling around in my chute turning my cock from semi-hard to fully-erect.

He slid a second finger into my bum, pumped them in and out and slapped my quivering cheeks with his gargantuan butt-plug, before pulling his digits out and easing his cockhead in. I groaned when his puffy hood pushed hard up against my starfish, then penetrated my pucker and slid inside me. I desperately reached back and spread my ass cheeks, my face pasted to the carpet, inviting Barron to fill me to over-full with his giant cock.

He gripped his dick and pressed forward, and his tremendous organ sank into my tremulous ass like a spike into the warm, wet earth. He grabbed hold of my waist and thrust his hips forward, just as I thrust my ass backwards, and his over-sized man-tamer dove deep into my chute, 'til his bone was buried to the balls in my stretched-out glory hole.

'That feel OK, Leonard?' he asked, attentive subordinate that he was.

'Feels great!' I hissed, lifting my head. 'Now fuck me! Fuck me!'

His fingers dug into my flesh and he began pumping his powerful hips, slowly at first, his cock barely moving in my packed-tight ass, and then faster and faster. Soon, he was banging my butt with reckless abandon, his immense balls loudly smacking my cheeks as he pummelled my bum. I gripped my cock and frantically tried to fist it as I was jolted again and again by his bludgeoning cock-thrusts.

'Yes! Fuck me harder, Barron!' I had the nerve to yell, sweat pouring off my face and pattering onto the carpet, my hand flying up and down my jerking cock.

He savagely hammered my ass, his fire-hardened steel pistoning relentlessly back and forth in my chute, sending shockwaves of pure, unadulterated joy coursing through my body, up my tingling cock. He grunted like a female tennis player as he pounded my bottom unendingly, plundered my sex hole with his sword. And just when I began to think that the well-hung, well-built young stallion could, in fact, go on for ever, he suddenly wailed, 'I'm coming!', and redoubled his already furious efforts.

He jammed his horse cock all the way into my butthole, let out a roar of triumph, and blasted my ass with semen. His body jerked to and fro with each and every spout of jism, his fingernails clawing at my sweat-sheened flesh as he came and came and came – as I came, coating the carpet with my superheated sperm as Barron coated my insides.

He finally collapsed on top of me, his cock wasted, his balls emptied, and then he rolled over onto his back and cradled me in his big, strong arms, his dong still securely lodged in my ass – where it belonged. It was then, in the recrimination-free sanctity of post-coital embrace, that I confessed to Barron that I'd been planning to make a play for him ever since he'd joined the firm.

'Me too,' he confessed right back. 'To be honest, you're the third partner I've fucked since I got here – and the best.'

I smiled, basking in the soothing sensation of his caressing hands on my chest, his nimble fingers rubbing and rolling my nipples. The sensual junior exec had just what it took to make it in the business world, I thought dreamily.

Road Trip

The boys would be going off to separate colleges in the fall, so they resolved to make perhaps their last summer together a memorable one. An epic road trip was in order.

Chad and Cody had been friends since their junior year in high school, when Cody's family had moved in on the same street as Chad's family. They shared many common interests, a love of adventure, a lust for learning and living. They were as close as two boys could get.

Chad was the bigger of the pair, taller, but still with the adolescent thinness of an 18-year-old. He'd grown four inches over the summer before. His brown hair was always neatly parted and glossy from brushing, his bright brown eyes open to the possibilities all around him, his smooth, fuzzed skin tanned brown from hours in the sun out in the open.

Cody was just as tanned, just as slender, but about three inches shorter, with sandy-blond hair and sparkling blue eyes, a lush, red mouth that could become petulant on occasion. He was the quieter of the two, but just as exuberant when it came to fun and games as his friend, the same age.

They loaded up the beater they'd bought specifically for the trip, bid goodbye to their parents, and hit the open road, three weeks of unbridled excitement and exploration at their fingertips. They sang along to the tunes blasting out of Cody's boombox up on the dashboard, as they motored down the highway.

Their first destination lay 100 kilometres to the west – Lake Wassego and its famous sugar beach. They made it in just under two hours, quickly finding out that the late-model Buick couldn't be pushed over 80 kilometres an hour.

They stripped off their T-shirts and jeans, revealing their Speedo swimsuits underneath, and ran laughing across the hot, fine sand and plunged into the blue, sun-heated lake waters.

They swam and splashed around for over an hour, dodging kids on inflatable everythings and older people floating out from the beach on their backs. Then they raced out of the water and flung themselves onto their beach towels, panting with exertion.

'Pretty lady at nine o'clock,' Chad said out of the side of his mouth.

His friend raised up on an elbow and stared at the bikini-clad redhead strolling past them with her breasts almost spilling out of her bulging top. 'Little too mature for this guy,' Cody commented.

'Oh yeah, I forgot. You like 'em young – our age or below, right?'

'That's right,' Cody replied, rolling onto his stomach and stretching out. 'Got my back, bud?'

'Huh?'

'Oil me, brother. This sun's beating down something fierce.'

'Right.' Chad dug a tube of suntan lotion out of the bag they'd brought with them, crawled over and jumped onto Cody's thinly-clad bottom.

'Oof!' Cody exhaled. 'Easy!'

Chad bounced up and down on the boy's mounded bum, mock-riding him. Then he jolted his friend a second time, with a cool dollop of tanning cream.

He rubbed the white lotion into Cody's shoulders, the boy's back, smoothing his hands over the hot, brown flesh, kneading the cream into Cody's muscles. And as he rubbed the glistening skin, he bobbed up and down on his friend's butt, his groin rubbing against Spandex-stretched butt cheeks.

Chad swallowed, feeling his cock suddenly tingle, harden in the light, tight material of his trunks. It was all the rubbing, his groin against Cody's bum, the feel of the boy's soft, warm, gleaming skin, that was doing it, he figured. His friend had a butt like a girl's, just as pert and taut; flesh silky smooth and hairless, also like a girl's.

'Ah, that feels good,' Cody breathed.

'Huh?' Chad mouthed, unable to control the surge in his cock. It was stretching out his swimsuit, cap almost boiling out of the elasticized waistband. As he rubbed, and got rubbed. His face burned hotter than the sun, his body buzzing.

He took a quick glance around, then fully straddled his friend's rump and gently pumped his cock, in the cleft between Cody's cheeks.

'What are you doing?' Cody asked sleepily.

'Huh? Nothing!' Chad gulped. 'Your back is covered. You're good to tan.' He hastily rolled off Cody and onto his own towel, flat on his stomach. His hard cock pressed down into the hot sand.

They spent the day at the lake, the next day back on the road, headed for a national park that boasted some bitchin' hiking trails. It was hot again, and the two teenagers were wearing just shorts and sandals, their shirts off in the car.

Cody toed off his sandals and stretched his caramel-coloured legs out, crossing them up on the dashboard as he slumped down in his seat.

'Hey, I don't want to smell feet for the next 200 klics,' Chad protested, despite the wind rushing in the open windows.

Cody grinned. He uncrossed his legs and poked his left foot over into Chad's face. 'There's no smell, buddy.

164

They're fresh as daises. Take a whiff.'

Chad tried to brush the slim, arched foot away, but Cody persisted. So, gripping the steering wheel, Chad turned his head and opened up his mouth and captured one of Cody's slender toes between his teeth.

'Hey!' It was Cody's turn to protest.

Chad grinned at his friend, sealing his lips around the bulb-headed foot-digit and tugging on it. The toe was plump and soft and meaty at the top, thin-stemmed, Cody's brown leg stretching out before Chad's eyes. He sucked gently on the toe, staring at that tanned expanse of flesh over the delicately-constructed foot.

And something stirred again between Chad's legs, as his lips worked, his tongue brushing against the curved underside of Cody's toe. The guy really did have small, shapely little girl's feet, and that toe tasted nice, filling his mouth, wiggling cutely, alive.

Chad's eyes glazed, his knuckles whitening on the forgotten steering wheel. His lips and tongue worked, mouth sucking on the luscious foot-digit, his cock and balls swelling with that delightfully tingling sensation. His gaze travelled down the length of Cody's leg, into Cody's soft blue eyes. They were hooded, the boy's mouth broken open, his plush, red lips shining with moisture.

'Hey, watch the road, toady!'

Chad jumped, jerking his head around. An 18-wheeler roared by in the opposite lane with only a foot to spare.

'Quit distracting me, then!' he rasped, running a damp, shaking hand through his lustrous hair.

'Is that what I was doing?' Cody breathed. He carefully crossed his feet back up on the dashboard again, his left big toe gleaming with his friend's saliva.

The pair spent that evening hiking some of the shorter trails in the park. And after a good night's rest, they set off early the next morning, intent on some serious hiking.

They had covered a number of the park's longer trails by noon. By late-afternoon, they were in the farthest reaches of the park, not another soul in sight. Just them and the clear blue sky and fresh south wind and thousands and thousands of hectares of emerald green forest.

They walked out the end of a trail and onto a rocky promontory that provided a spectacular view of the park. Chad slipped off his light backpack and walked closer to the edge of the 500-metre elevation.

Whereupon Cody gave out a whoop and jumped up onto his friend's back. 'Take me over the edge, pack mule!' he yelped, digging his heels into Chad's thighs, his arms wrapped around his friend's neck.

Chad didn't even stagger under the load. Cody was as light as a feather, Chad's own thigh muscles strong after years and years of hiking. He casually walked to the very edge of the ledge, then spun around and pretended to try to shuck Cody off his back and out into the wild blue yonder.

'Hey!' Cody cried, holding on tighter with his hands and heels. 'This isn't lover's leap, boyfriend! And I ain't Susan Bucholz!'

Chad and Susan – a petite, quiet, pretty brunette – had dated briefly in the 11th grade. 'That's for sure!' Chad responded exuberantly. 'Susan knew how to put out!'

He jumped forward and spun Cody around on his upper body, collapsed to the ground on top of the teenager. The boys' perspiration-dewed bodies pressed together.

'You mean like this!' Cody cried, puckering his lips and pecking away at Chad's face.

Chad laughed, pulling his head back just a bit. 'No, like this!' He pumped his hips, grinding his cock in his shorts into Cody's shorts.

Cody laughed and clawed at Chad's back. 'Oh, yes, you big, strong brute! Make love to me! Oh, gosh, please!' He bobbed his head up and smacked his wet mouth against Chad's open mouth, spurring his heels into Chad's pumping

166

buttocks.

The boisterous grin abruptly left Chad's face, as he felt his shifting cock surge hard against Cody's cock, his head spinning and heart beating with the sweet, moist taste of Cody's lips. He grabbed onto his friend's blond head and hungrily kissed the teen, thumping his cock against Cody's cock.

Cody's arms fell away from Chad's neck, his legs away from the boy's waist. He lay back on the soft bed of moss, smothered by Chad's mouth and cock. Making no attempt to break free.

Chad pulled his head back, though, breaking the kiss himself, gasping for air. He stared down into Cody's glittering blue eyes, the boy's body hot and soft beneath him. He undulated his cock against Cody's cock, scared now, reality rushing back in on him.

Cody didn't say a word, didn't move.

Chad stopped his pumping. His body was on fire, his cock blazing steel-hard, brain reeling. 'Y–yeah,' he gulped, 'that's Susan all right. G–good imitation.'

Cody smiled. And Chad climbed off his friend, helped the boy to his feet, doing his best to conceal the enormous erection tenting the front of his shorts.

The pair spent most of the following day racing ATVs across the sand dunes in the park. It was hot, gritty fun, and when they finally returned to their motel room that night, they wanted nothing more than to hit the shower and then their beds.

There was only one shower, however. They both called dibs and made a dash for it, pushing and shoving, yelling and laughing, stripping off their dirty, sweaty clothes. They jumped over the ledge of the tub and into the shower at the same time.

Chad scooped up the tiny bar of soap, while Cody had hold of the lone facecloth. It was crowded in the small enclosure, the boys naked, their shiny brown bodies brushing against one another.

'I'll only be an hour or so,' Chad said, twisting the knobs. Hot water sprayed down on him. 'Hopefully, they'll be enough water left for you.' He crowded up close to the showerhead, taking the delicious needle-spray on his face and chest, rubbing his chest with the soap.

Cody tried to squirm past his friend, his arms reaching around, loins pressing into Chad's clenched buttocks. But there wasn't enough room. So he fell back and started rubbing Chad's neck with the facecloth. 'Share and share alike, I say. That's life on the road.'

Chad laughed, nervously. He shivered, despite the steam rising all around them, the hot water sheeting down his body. Cody was massaging his neck with the facecloth, slowly and sensuously, the boy's other hand on Chad's hip.

Chad felt that strange, warm tingling sensation all over again, his cock rising up in the spray, engorging with blood. He couldn't control it, Cody's rubbing, the touch of the boy's warm fingers on Chad's bare skin, feeling so very good.

He slid the bar of soap down lower, over his stomach, his lower abdomen, onto his cock. He jerked, as he touched his fully-erect penis.

'Rub you the wrong way?' Cody asked.

'N–no! Go ahead ... keep doing it.'

Cody rubbed down Chad's back, and Chad groaned, his head spinning, the bar of soap scrubbing his cock now. The facecloth moved onto his lower back, onto his buttocks, swirling over his shimmering skin – rubbing him the exact *right* way like he was rubbing his pulsing cock.

Chad shuddered, as Cody's left hand gripped one of his butt cheeks, Cody's right hand caressing his other cheek with the facecloth. And then the boy full-out spasmed, as his cock suddenly boiled out of control in his soapy, shunting hand. Semen burst out of the tip of his over-stimulated organ and sprayed against the tiled wall of the shower.

Chad could hardly believe it. It had all happened so fast. He tried his best to hide his excitement, his body flooding with heat, cock pumping out joy in his hand. His buttocks quivered uncontrollably under Cody's rubbing, clutching hands.

It was over as quickly as it had started, a summer storm welled up out of nowhere, unleashing a torrent, then dissipating again. Leaving one embarrassed, shaken young man.

Chad dropped the bar of soap and jumped out of the shower, mumbling, 'That's good enough for me!' He ran out of the steamy bathroom.

After filling their stomachs at a local restaurant, the two friends stretched out on their motel beds to watch TV. But they could barely keep their eyes open. Cody hadn't said anything about the incident in the shower, and Chad figured he must've not noticed.

'Why don't you watch over here,' Cody spoke up suddenly, rousing Chad from a doze. 'You can see the TV better.'

Cody's bed *was* at a better angle to the tiny, bolted-down television set. Chad got up and Cody squirmed over on the bed, making room for his friend. Both boys were wearing only clean pairs of white underwear, their smooth bodies gleaming bronze under the subdued lights. Night had fully fallen, and the motel and park were quiet.

Chad stretched out his lanky frame, leaning back against the headboard and folding his hands in behind his head, crossing his ankles. Cody lay on his side, his head propped up by his right hand.

Ten minutes later, Cody was fast asleep next to his friend, laid-out flat on his back, head cushioned on a pillow. Chad was wide-awake now, staring at Cody's caramel body, the teenager's darker-brown nipples, the outline of the boy's cock in his briefs.

The TV show was long-forgotten, Chad's field of vision filled by his slumbering companion. And before he fully realised what he was doing, he'd slid down on the bed next to Cody, mesmerized by all that lovely bare skin, the smooth lines of Cody's body, the bulge in the boy's underwear.

He swallowed, hard, not thinking of the consequences, reaching out and brushing one of Cody's tan nipples with his fingers. Then he jerked his hand back, when he felt the nipple instantly stiffen against his soft, curious fingertips.

Chad licked his lips, feeling the heat from Cody's nearly-nude body so close. He brushed the nipple again, the boy's other nipple, thrilling at the surge his fingers elicited in his friend's buds. He watched the nipples thicken and swell higher, and then he bent his head over one and kissed it.

Cody smacked his lips, but his eyes stayed closed. Chad looked back down to his friend's chest, and kissed Cody's other nipple, tasting the rubbery texture, the pebbled areola surrounding the blossomed buds. And then he looked down at Cody's groin, and saw that his friend's cock was really stretching the thin fabric of his briefs, significantly larger and longer than it had been just a moment before – before Chad had kissed Cody's nipples.

Chad trailed the fingers of his right hand down Cody's stomach, up onto the bulging curvature of the boy's cock. Cody moaned, thrusting upwards, pressing his cock against Chad's fingers.

Chad gripped the erection, acting on impulse. It beat in his palm, pulsating larger and larger. Until ... Cody abruptly rolled over onto his side, facing away from Chad.

But there was no stopping the aroused young man now. His own cock was a molten length of steel in his briefs. He stared at Cody curled up next to him, at the boy's rounded bottom. Then he pulled his underwear down, freeing his throbbing cock, pulled Cody's briefs down, exposing his friend's taut, tanlined butt cheeks. Chad was ablaze with emotion. He crowded in close to Cody on the bed, spooning against the boy.

'Jesus!' he gasped, shuddering with the heated impact of his bare cock against Cody's bare bum. His friend's body burned as hot as his own, and he thrust his cock in between Cody's ripe cheeks, gently pumping silky-smooth crack.

Chad wrapped his arms around Cody, urgently pumping his cock into the boy's butt cleavage. He was already close to coming, the wicked intimacy, the weird, wonderful sensations, overwhelming the boy.

'Fuck me, Chad,' Cody whispered, shocking his friend.

Cody reached into the drawer of the bedstand and brought out a small bottle of lubricant, handed it back to Chad. Then he snuggled back down onto the sheet and pressed his bum into Chad's cock. 'Please, fuck me. I've wanted you to for so long.'

Chad couldn't believe what he was hearing. He shook with joy, acting on instinct, lubing his iron erection, scrubbing in between Cody's hot cheeks with a pair of slippery fingers. Cody whimpered, then moaned, as Chad quickly replaced fingers with cock, thrusting his cap against his friend's bumhole.

He didn't waste any time. Any hesitation could cost them this beautiful moment. He gritted his teeth and gripped his cock and pushed his cap into Cody's rosebud. He burst through, his cockhead swelling Cody's gripping ring. He speared shaft inside, sinking almost his entire length into Cody's hot, tight anus.

'Jesus!' Chad gulped, Cody thrusting his bottom back against Chad, cock filling chute.

Chad trembled wildly. It felt so good, so bad, his cock buried inside Cody. His cock fucking Cody, as he pumped his hips, sliding his penis back and forth in his friend's – his lover's ass.

He reached around and grabbed onto Cody's vibrating

cock, pumping Cody's cock as he pumped Cody's ass. The boys moved together, faster and faster, their breath coming in gasps, their bodies melding together in the blast-furnace heat of their lust. The bed creaked, flesh smacking against flesh, ass getting churned, cock getting jacked.

'Oh God, Chad, yes!' Cody wailed, his cock jumping in Chad's hand. Semen spouted out of the tip, Chad feeling every frantic convulsion of his lover, Cody's bum gripping his pistoning cock even tighter.

Then Chad spasmed and cried out. His cock exploded in Cody's anus, searing the boy's chute with sperm. Chad flung his legs straight out, thrusting, shuddering, emptying himself inside Cody in long, spectacular bursts.

It was the best summer the boys ever spent together. The best summer, period. And come fall, they were enrolled in the same college, staying in the same dorm room, sharing everything now. Like they'd learnt to do on the road.

Dark Journey

IT WAS THE URBAN shithole, the devastated core of the city, a wasteland of rubbled buildings and burned-out cars. No place for a white guy driving a taxicab. But I'm like Travis Bickle – anytime, anywhere. And I do so love the dark meat.

A kid was walking down Front Street. He had a backpack strapped to his back, was wearing white high-tops and black gym pants and a red mesh shirt. His hair was dread-locked short, with a cap over it on sideways. His black velvet skin gleamed night under the hot sun.

I slowed the cab up alongside, thumbed down the passenger window, said, 'Want a lift?'

He stopped in his tracks and stared at me, big brown eyes narrowing, face shining. 'I can't afford no cab, man.'

'This one's on the house. I'll take you as far as you want to go.'

He looked up and down the desolate street. A couple of winos stirred in the shade of some weeds in an empty lot. 'Man, I'm getting the hell out of here. All the way out.'

I reached over and pushed the door open. 'Then let's ride.'

He shrugged, took one last look around, and then slid inside the cab. As I got out the other side and went around. 'You drive,' I said, urging him over in under the wheel on the bench seat. 'Long shift. I'm tired.'

He was only 18 or so, with high cheekbones and a high forehead and thick lips and thin limbs, long fingers. He was seriously headed anywhere but where he was, and as he pulled the cab away from the curb, I hit him up with the fare.

'You can drive as far as you can hold off coming,' I told him, reaching over and placing my hand on the crotch of his baggy pants and looking him in the eyes.

'Aw ... shit,' he breathed, his hands trembling on the wheel. But he pressed down on the accelerator, and we were off.

I found his cock buried in the folds of his pants and underwear, rubbed it. He was swelling hard in a minute, full-blown erect by the time we hit First Street. I reached over with my other hand and tugged at his waistband, and he arched his butt off the seat and let me slide his pants down. His blue plaid shorts bulged with cock.

I licked my lips, gripped his mighty erection. He jerked, the cab leaping forward almost right through a red light. My fingers could barely encircle the engorged girth of his cock through the cotton material of his shorts. The kid was packing some serious meat – dark meat. I just had to see it.

Another car pulled up alongside us, two hookers out for a morning joyride in their pimp's wheels, by the look of it. They whistled and cheered, as I dug into the kid's shorts and pulled his long, hard, ebony cock out into the open. I swallowed, hard, silently cheering like those whores, staring at the tall, thick, night-shaded pipe, feeling it pulse thumping hot against my pressing palm.

'What's your name, big guy?' I asked, gently tugging on his cock, swirling my hand up and down its smooth, inky length.

'B–Brandon,' he gulped, jerking the cab forward, through the intersection and away from the waving prostitutes.

'Nice cock, Brandon,' I said, leaning over and gripping his pube-pebbled balls with my other hand, stroking his snake.

He held on tight to the steering wheel, staring straight

174

ahead. It was Sunday, hardly any traffic. I squeezed Brandon's packed nut sac, twisting my other hand up around his hood, bathing the bloated, blue-black cap with my smooth, warm palm.

My hands couldn't contain my lust. I leaned down, slid my red lips over the young man's knob. 'Fuck!' he yelped, bucking up into my mouth, filling me with edible cap.

I clenched his balls, keeping that liquorice stick pointed high in the air, hood in my mouth, lips tugging. Brandon's lean body quivered, his cock jumping, seeking to drive deeper into my mouth.

I pulled my head up, my mouth off the swollen tip of his dick, then tongued around and around it. 'Tell you what,' I said, 'if you can make it to the city limits, you can ride for free far as you want to go.'

He looked down at me breathing all over his glistening crown. 'What'd you mean "make it to the city limits"?'

'Without coming in my mouth,' I answered. Then sucked up his hood again, plunged my mouth halfway down his towering cock.

He was game for the challenge, built for blowjobs. He pressed down hard on the accelerator, sweat popping his forehead, cockhead bumping the back of my throat. We blew past Third – Fifteenth Streets in a blur. As I clenched his nuts and bobbed my head up and down on his cock, sucking quick and tight on that luscious black dong.

Brandon's mouth hung open, his pink tongue out. He squinted the sweat out of his eyes, concentrating, concentrating on the road, trying to ignore the heated, wet tug of my mouth on his cock, the playful fondling of my fingers all over his balls. We were past the numbers and into the suburbs where streets rated names. There was more traffic, families going to church, out for brunch. The last thing they were looking for was a black teenager at the wheel of a cab, getting openly blown by a white man in his lap.

Brandon slammed on the brakes and we fishtailed to a stop at a red light. I sucked up the kid's cock, really dragging my tongue and lips, drawing out every silky dark inch of the man. Then I popped my mouth off his knob and stared over at Mom and Dad in the mini-van next to us. I smiled, stuck out my tongue, twirled it all around Brandon's cap.

A couple of kids squeezed their faces up against the window in behind their red-faced parents, trying to get a better look. I tapped Brandon's slit with the tip of my tongue, caught a drop of pearl-white pre-come that bubbled up, stretched it out into a long, sticky rope.

The mini-van shot forward, right through the red light, barely missing a couple in a convertible craning their necks to get a better look at Brandon and I. The kid's slickened cock jutted higher than the dashboard. 'Oh, Jesus! Jesus!' Brandon moaned. As I poured my lips back over his hood and flowed my mouth down almost the entire length of his prong, his balls nestled damp in my hand.

The light turned green. The cab roared through the intersection, the city limits almost within sight now.

I bobbed faster, sucking tighter and harder on the kid's cock. Then slower, more sensually, sucking deep and languorous and immensely erotic. I inhaled every delicious inch that I could and then pulled back up right to the curved tip, sinking my teeth into soft, chewy cap before I lost contact. Brandon's body quivered, his cock vibrating, more and more pre-come surging out of his slit and into my mouth. I swallowed loudly.

'Almost there,' I said, letting my voice tremor his glistening dong from the hood on down. The city limits were in sight now, just a mile away according to the fast-passing sign.

I looked up at the sweating, shaking kid, grinning from around the mushroomed tip of his cock, white teeth sunk into black meat. His knuckles blazed almost as white as my teeth, his hips moving unconsciously, trying to fuck my mouth. He was being pulled in two different directions. I added a third.

I noosed his cock at the base with my forefinger and thumb, then glided the pair of digits up and down the lower half of his shaft, as I sucked on the upper half. I had the perfect rhythm in seconds, ebony and ivory tuned to sexual perfection.

It was too much for Brandon. His dong jumped, swelling come-hard in my vaccing mouth and between my jerking fingers. He bit his lip and whimpered, staring through tear-welled eyes at the sign that read "City Limits" only 100 yards further down the road. And then he bucked, and blasted, his cock exploding under my oral and digit onslaught, hot semen spurting into my mouth.

I'd timed it just right, and I drank in my victory – in deep, satisfied, hot salty gulps. I sucked and pumped and swallowed, Brandon uncontrollably shooting sheer heated joy into my mouth and throat.

The cab swerved off the road and onto the gravel shoulder, almost right into the grassy ditch. Brandon stared down at me, humping up into my mouth, spurting his ecstasy again and again and again.

I milked every last drop out of his darkened hose, then licked the gaping slit for what was left. 'Almost made it,' I said, smacking my smeared lips with satisfaction. I gave him one final affectionate tug, then sent him packing.

If he hung that horse-cock of his out with his thumb, he wouldn't have any trouble finding the long-distance ride he was looking for.

I drove on down the highway, keeping my eyes peeled to the sides of the road as much as the middle. This was hitchhikers' alley, off the Interstate, and there was no shortage of people looking to bum a free ride.

I blew past one after another. This cab didn't stop for

177

whites or women, not when it was off-duty.

Finally, I spotted what I was looking for, times two. A pair of young black men, long and lean and looking like brothers, in both senses of the word. I roared off the asphalt and onto the gravel, skidding to a stop just ahead of them.

They ran over to the cab, as I watched them in the rearview mirrors. One of them was wearing a tight, striped shirt and a pair of tan shorts. His name was Latrell. His limbs were long and wiry, lushly dark. He had a shaved head and a pair of gold earrings, a long, hungry-looking face.

The other guy was named Arkee. He was slightly shorter than his friend, more thickly muscled. He was wearing a white T-shirt and black jeans, butt bulging the jeans, chest and shoulders the tee. His hair was trimmed short, his head just about as square as his jaw, his eyes wide-set and green in the pitch-black canvas of his face.

They dumped their gear in the backseat, along with themselves. We made small talk for a couple of miles. They were headed cross-country, to a friend's place out in San Francisco. They were my kind of people.

'I'm going to pull into this rest stop up ahead, OK?'

They looked at each other and shrugged their shoulders. They'd only been riding for five minutes, but what could they do?

'I'll tell you what, guys. I'm tired, this cab's tired.' It *was* an old cab. 'If you do something for me, you can take the cab and drive it out to 'Frisco. How 'bout it?'

They looked at each other again. Arkee said, 'What'd we gotta do?'

I grinned sheepishly into the rearview mirror. 'Fuck me in the ass and the mouth at the same time?'

We found a nice, sun-drenched strip of grass in some bushes, started taking off our clothes. I watched the men, slowly removing my own T-shirt and jeans and shoes and socks. This was going to be *au naturel* all the way.

They were shirtless in no time. I admired their dusky chests, their deeper, darker nipples. Arkee's were taut as twin chocolate eraser heads, while Latrell's were thicker and puffier.

Then the jeans and shorts came off, and the real show began. Both men were wearing tight, white briefs, the brightness of the stretched cotton material highlighting the blackness of their skin.

Arkee slid his briefs down, and his cock dropped out a goodly length along his thighs, huge and turgid even semi-erect. I licked my lips, staring at the snake; then over at Latrell's equally impressive dong, as he skinned down his briefs. His cock rose up and sniffed at the heated air, excited to be free, swelling up quicker than any cock I'd ever seen before.

We were all naked. I walked over to the men and grabbed onto their cocks, pulling all three of us together in a wet, warm, sloppy kiss. Their dongs filled my palms, throbbing me full of sexual energy, as we swirled our tongues together, the men's neon-pink stickers jumping out of their mouths and into mine.

I dropped to my knees in the soft grass, level with their jutting cocks. I blew on one swollen hood, the other, the deep purple caps expanding under my breath. They each flung an arm around the other's shoulder, crowding closer, their pricks twitching and sliding together.

It was a hell of a lot of dark meat for one man to handle. But they had the right man, and I had the right meat. I sucked Arkee's pipe into my mouth, consuming his hood and most of his shaft. He grunted and thrust out his hips, jamming his dick deeper into my mouth.

I pulled back, sucked up Latrell's cock. He groaned and pumped, his dong filling my mouth. My cheeks bulged and throat swelled. I breathed through my nostrils, feeling that dong wildly pulse in between my stretched lips, pumping my hand up and down Arkee's slickened length. Arkee was

179

longer and smoother; Latrell thicker and veinier.

I moved my head back and forth between the two heavy hoses, sucking, tugging, mouth and lips and hands. The men gripped each other's shoulders and pumped their hips in rhythm, cock spearing into my palm, into my throat. I shifted into another position, anxious to get even more.

The men lay down on the bed of grass on their backs, close together, Arkee's right leg thrown over Latrell's left leg. I straddled their charcoal bodies on all-fours, at the groin ends, gripping their pipes and gathering them up, rubbing them together. They groaned, lashing their tongues at my hanging erection.

It was a three-man 69, me the lustful recipient of two black cocks to play with. I crammed both hoods into my mouth and sucked on them at the same time. They bobbed their heads up at my hood, capturing it with one set of lips and tugging, the other set of lips. I groaned through my full mouth, feeling the wet, wonderful pulls all through me.

I broke the pair of cocks apart and swallowed drool. Then I inhaled Arkee's cap, dropped my mouth down his shaft almost right to his balls. His cock quivered in my maw, locked down in the stunning steam bath. Someone sucked up half of my dangling prick, giving me a wicked taste of my own erotic medicine.

I pumped my head up and down, hoovering Arkee's cock; as I tugged on Latrell's dong with my hand. My own cock was passed from one mouth to the other, fingers finding and stretching my asshole, probing inside.

I jerked, on fire with sensation. I pulled Latrell's cock closer, mouthed it. The man groaned from around my pulsating dick, Arkee flat-out finger-fucking my ass. The boys were getting ahead of themselves. Latrell was leaking pre-come out of the tip of his prick.

I kept my all-fours animal position, while Latrell got in behind, Arkee up front. My ass was lubed, like Latrell's cock. His long, slippery fingers scrubbed at my crack, making me sing with desire, squeal with delight when he dove two digits three knuckles deep into my chute. He pumped me in prelude to cocking me. I opened my mouth wide and Arkee jammed his dong home, stuffing me full.

He gripped my hair and pumped his hips, fucking my face in slow, measured strokes. Latrell withdrew his fingers and inserted his hood, bulging my ring, then bursting through, sinking shaft into my anus. One black man churning my mouth, his balls bouncing off my thrust-out tongue; another black man churning my ass, thighs cracking off my rippling cheeks.

Dongs sawed at me from both ends, plugging my throat and chute. The men moved in rhythm, fucking me faster and faster. Manly grunts and groans filled the heated air, along with the sharp, sweaty smack of flesh against flesh. My anus and throat burned raw, spit spilling out of the corners of my stretched mouth, ass split wide.

The frenzy built and built. I was rocked back and forth, pistoned mouth and anus. I grabbed onto my own numb-hard cock and stroked, and instantly came. Come blasted out of my cap, shaking me from the inside out. Just as Arkee shouted and spasmed and shot jizz straight down my throat.

Latrell frantically slammed my gyrating ass. Then yelled out his own ecstasy, rocketing sizzling semen deep into my bowels. I overflowed with sperm, back and front and pouring out of my own cock. The two black men brutally fucked this white boy, emptying out their balls and mine at the same time.

I gave them the cab, and they drove off down the highway. The vehicle was stolen, anyway. I crossed to the other side of the road and stuck out my thumb, hoping for a Sunday driver to pick me up. A nice, hung, dark Sunday driver.

Rear Guard

EVERYONE HAD A GOOD gut laugh when they handed me the "shit" job – guarding the washrooms of the largest city park against unauthorised penal and anal activity. Apparently, there'd been a spate of reports from indignant citizens and irate squirrels of guys coming together in the shelter of the city cans, coming all over and within each other.

'It's a dirty job, but somebody's got to do it,' I cracked wise, accepting the ribbing with a shrug. Then I headed out to my patrol car, bound for the glory that was allegedly taking place in those not-for-public-consumption glory holes.

It was a rainy day, kind of cool. The sprawling green acres and gardens were all but deserted as a result, the zoo boasting more four-legged animals than two-legged. I drove into the parking lot at the south entrance and surveilled the brown-slatted men and women's washroom building located in the far corner of the lot. The rain drummed a humdrum tattoo on the metal roof of my spy vehicle, to go with the lack of illicit action I was observing.

There were only 20 or so cars sprinkled about the huge asphalt vehicle pad, all of them empty, no one moving around, making for the forlorn washroom in the mist. It went on like that for half-an-hour, before I finally exited the car and wandered on over to the public john, to frisk the interior for any ribald gaiety. Never let it be said that I don't do a thorough job, despite the pittance they pay me, and the low-profile work they assign me.

I slipped through the swinging door and slunk down the cement hall, peeked around the blunt corner. And saw one barren bathroom facility. Not even a duck was in there getting dry out of the rain, rustling his tail feathers at some other queer quacker. I strode on in and checked the three stalls. They were as empty of cock as the three shining wall urinals.

I grimaced and headed back out into the lonely early evening.

The washrooms on the west and north sides of the park were equally innocuous. One old guy desperately trying to squeeze one out in the north country cans, and that was about it. By the time I pulled into the east side parking lot, it was getting darker, raining harder, Day One on the dick patrol looking like a complete washout.

Until a red Sentra pulled into the lot and drove right up to one of the concrete curbs in front of the small washroom building, parked. A man got out – a tall, angular black guy with close-cropped hair, wearing a blue jacket and black pants, a furtive expression. I ogled all that through my mini-binoculars from the other side of the lot, parked next to an empty service vehicle. The guy took a quick glance around, at his watch, then covered his head and ran for the can, barged in.

It was only two minutes later by my Casio that another car pulled into the lot, parked near the public crappers. This gent was shorter, even darker, with a wild-looking 'fro, wearing a poncho and pair of dungarees. He, too, glanced around after hairing his huge shades. But he didn't have a watch to check the time with, just a cellphone, which he casually filed away in his back pocket as he advanced on and into the restroom facility.

The bees were gathering at the honey pot.

A Jaguar pulled into the lot, parked near the two other cars. This man was medium-height, muscular build, swarthy-looking. He was wearing a dark-blue suit and bright

183

magenta tie, a pair of shoes whose shine blinded my eyes even from a hundred yards away. He ran a hand over his curly hair and didn't bother checking anything else, just strode on over to the building housing three urinals and toilets, and two men, and added to the collection.

It looked to me like either a drug deal or city paving contract was going down, or some of that aforementioned homo-sex was about to take place on my watch. I desired a closer look-see.

I slid out of the car without closing the door and ran through the rain, hugged the side of the building. I didn't hear a thing, just the pitter-patter of God's sweet nectar. So I moved around the side, eased the door open enough to slip my six-foot-three, 220-pound frame through, tip-toed down the concrete and peered around the corner.

The three men were all in there, all right. There was no backdoor to the place, the only other exits being straight down the pipes and into the river. But these guys weren't sucking up a storm or fucking up a deluge. They were merely standing around by the sinks talking to one another, about the zoo expansion that was underway. My ears got bored and legs tired just listening to them.

It was time to put it on the line, go from covert to overt.

I walked in on the trio, swaying my hips just a little in my Dockers, shuddering my butt cheeks just a little more in my Jockeys. I got their attention. They nodded at me; but nothing more. They went back to their yammering.

I pulled up at a urinal and straddled it, undeterred by their apparent indifference. Some perps you can lead to water, some you've got to shove their heads right into the toilet. I unzipped my fly slow and loud, drew my cock out of the folds of my clinging underwear and pants, unfolded it in front of the urinal.

I'd come armed, my rod semi-erect, thick and turgid in my hand. I pumped it up harder, longer, pointing at the porcelain and groaning slightly, glancing over at the men.

'You all right?' the short guy with the big hair finally asked.

I sort of grunted, pumping faster, my dick hidden from view by my arm and the urinal. The guy looked at his friends and then walked over closer to me, repeated his question. Flies to the flypaper, I thought, grinning.

When the man was right next to me, I suddenly half-turned around, showing him my now fully-erect dong. Showing all of them my eight inches of vein-ribboned meat. Showing them I meant business.

Then telling them. 'Yeah, my cock seems to have swelled up all on its own. Know any way to get it back down again?'

The man closest stared at my dick. Then he shrugged his shoulders, said, 'Sorry, man.'

Sweet street justice, but these guys were cautious to the point of ignoring a cocktease! I gritted my teeth in frustration.

Then I escalated the situation, telling them my name was Cap, getting them to introduce themselves as Len, Tyrese, and Tony. And when we were all on a first-name basis, I blatantly introduced Len to my cock, pushing gently down on his shoulders until he was on his knees, in front of my boner.

He looked up at me, whites of his eyes showing whiter. If it took a force-feeding, I'd give it to him, I was that fired-up.

I sifted my fingers into his afro and pulled his head close, his thick, warm lips bumping against the yawning chasm of my slit. I jerked, and grunted, and merciful man-eaters, but lo and behold Len finally took the bait, blossoming his lips open and blooming them over my hood.

The dance of seduction was over, the dirty dancing begun. Tyrese and Tony walked over and got down on their knees, watching up-close as Len gripped my dangling balls in his warm, pale palm and sucked more of my prong into

185

his hot, wet, red mouth.

My fingers curled in his hair, grabbing on tight. As the guy twisted my sac and inhaled my pipe almost right down to the furline. He bobbed his head back, forward, sucking hard and tight and long on my dong.

But he wasn't the greedy type, because after just a few pulls he handed me over to Tyrese on his right. And then that ebony man's man widened his mouth and mouthed my hood, glided his lips down my shaft. I jerked and groaned, grabbing onto the short hairs on his head.

Tyrese tugged up and down on my prick with his mouth and lips, tongue bathing the underside of my shaft, as Len kept up with the ballwork, squeezing my sac with his hand, then his mouth. He sucked my nuts right up and pulled on the tingling, tightened pouch, while Tyrese glided back and forth on my rod, wet-vaccing me wild.

It was Tony's turn. The muscleman cranked my slickened length with his heavy hand, before sucking me rugged and raunchy. His teeth scraped my shaft, my hood bumping the back of his throat. Tyrese sucked on my balls, Len strangling and stroking the base of my cock with two noosing fingers.

My throbber went up and down the line, passed from one eager man to the next like a sexual baton. It was awe-inspiring, all that oral gamesmanship. Problem was, I wasn't built for the distance events. My balls were boiling out of control after just a couple of laps around the guys' lips.

I got them up on their feet. We exchanged intimate pleasantries, kissing, frenching. I sucked on Len's long, neon-pink tongue like he'd sucked on my cock, Tony and Tyrese deep-kissing in each other's arms. We all came together at the mouth, a four-man snog, our tongues flapping against one another's, swapping drool.

And then, finally, we really got together, pulling a quad-train in that public washroom.

We stripped off our clothes in no time at all. Tyrese and

Len's cocks were smooth and long and liquorice-black, their mushroomed hoods almost purple. Tony's cock was shorter, thicker, tan in colour, marbled with veins.

We didn't waste any time – who knew when some "stranger" might bust in on us and spoil the fun. The three guys all came armed with lube, and we all used it in copious quantities, greasing our meat and nightsticks. Then Len, being the smallest, assumed the position against one of the sinks, Tony in behind, Tyrese in behind him, me bringing up Tyrese's rear.

Len gripped the porcelain with whitened knuckles, as Tony scrubbed the man's crack with his slippery fingers, then jammed his cock in between those taut back-pillows. Len grunted, taking Tony full-length up the chute.

It was Tyrese's turn – to stick Tony. He rubbed the man's butt cleavage and hole nice and slippery, then guided his dong in between the guy's quivering buttocks. He knocked on heaven's door with his hood, burst into the Promised Land, filling Tony's ass with his cock.

It was up to me to complete the hook-up. I was up for the task. I slid two slick digits in between Tyrese's clenched cheeks and along his smooth crack. I parked the tips of those digits on his butthole, pressed them on through. He shivered on the ends of my fingers, as I delved deeper into his hot, tight chute, right up to the last knuckle.

I pumped him a couple of times, gently rocking the trio of men. Then I pulled out, plugged in with the big show, popping his ring with my cap and sinking shaft into his anus. I went hard and long, slow and sensual, until my balls kissed up against his dark moons, cock totally and utterly erotically buried.

I started the chain-reaction, fucking the guy's ripe, mounded ass. The men easily caught onto the rhythm, churning each other at the pace I'd set. The searing sight of the scene, the scorching, shifting heat of my cock in Tyrese's ass, set me ablaze. My blood boiled along with my balls. I moved faster, thrusting harder, banging the man in front of me who banged the man in front of him who banged Len up against the sink, the four of us humping like a caterpillar anxious to get out of the rain.

I gripped Tyrese's bladed shoulders and full-out rammed his ass, my thighs smacking into his clenching butt cheeks, cock pistoning his sucking anus. It went up and down the line like that, the frenzy building and building, men grunting, groaning, the thunderous crack of flesh against flesh filling the building. The sink grated, was almost torn out of the wall by the sheer force of four men fucking each other at the same time.

It was too hot to handle for too long. I bit into Tyrese's long neck, reaming his asshole. My cock seemed to swell in his rear, then jump. 'Man coming!' I growled, jerking, jetting.

I was jolted over and over, raw, blistering orgasm blasting through my body and blowing out my balls, filling Tyrese's chute to overflowing. My ecstasy triggered their ecstasy, the chain-reaction going nuclear. Tyrese tilted his head back and howled and spasmed hot sperm into Tony's ass; Tony grunting and shunting and shooting Len full; Len cranking his own cock, spraying against the sink and the wall, coming with the cataclysmic impact off all three of us behind him.

I didn't bust the boys, in the legal sense of the word. They went their way, and I went mine.

See, I'm queer as folk; something the geniuses downtown didn't figure on when they handed me the "shit" patrol. And with the slim pay pickings I get as a security guard, I take my pleasure wherever I can find it, preferably on the company's dime.

Dick Work

I WAS SIPPING MUD with my dogs up on my desk, when the Captain came around, tossed a slip of paper down into my lap. 'This should be right up your "alley", Hershbeck,' he grated, garnering some off-colour guffaws from the other flatfoots hanging about. 'A guy says his sex toy collection was stolen.'

'TS,' I responded, not entirely unsympathetically. 'That can put a real hole in a man's social life, all right.'

'Get off your ass and follow it up!'

I swung around in my swivel, planted my dogs on the floor, my coffee cup on the desk, climbed erect. 'I'm hard on the case, Captain.'

The man glared at me, as I walked across the Robbery Detail room.

'Hey, Hershbeck,' Frankie Grinnell called before I could exit. 'When you find the guy's sex toys, don't keep 'em for yourself, huh.'

He horked out a horse laugh. I held the frosted glass door open for a parting shot. 'What do I need with sex toys, Grinnell,' I delivered, 'when I've got your wife?'

I sauntered on out of the stationhouse, to my unmarked, drove to the address listed on the slip of paper. It was a 22-storey apartment tower in a trendy part of town. I double-parked my wagon and hoofed it on into the lobby, pushed the buzzer on 1905.

I went through a routine of 20 questions with the occupant of that sky-high abode, showed him my badge via

189

the closed circuit camera. Finally satisfied with my credentials like he obviously wasn't sexually any more, he unlatched me inside. Whereupon the doorman proceeded to treat me as an undesirable, frisking the truth clean out of me.

I came away with fingerprints all over my sackcloth and the conviction that the sex toy theft was an inside job, if you'll pardon the pun. I didn't see how anyone from the outside could've gotten into the building without a M1-A2 Abrams tank and the know-how to use it.

Chev Toole was waiting at the finely-crafted door of his flop to greet me. 'Come in, officer!' he panted. 'Isn't it just dreadful – someone stole almost all of my sex toys! What am I to do?'

'Grow some vegetables and go organic?' I suggested.

Chev was a small, tightly-wound brunette with big brown eyes and a perpetual puppy dog expression. He was wearing a tight white T-shirt and an even tighter pair of torn and faded blue jeans. His body was as animated as his face, as he led me down the hall and into his boudoir.

He pulled a three-inch thick photo album out of a funky bureau drawer and opened it, began regaling me with tales of his stolen sex toys. 'That's Big Red,' he chirped, pointing to the full-colour picture of a huge, red jelly dong. 'And that's Smooth Blue,' he added, pointing out the posed, contoured deep-blue dildo on the opposite page.

He had a name for nearly everything, the date he'd bought the devices of pleasure carefully documented. It was on album number two, page 53, that he came to the crown jewel in his collection of dongs, dildos, butt plugs, vibrators, ball cosies, cock rings, nipple clamps, anal implants and sphincter splitters.

'That's Black Beauty,' he gushed, his finger trembling, tears clogging his eyes and choking his throat.

I grabbed the album and took a closer gander. Black Beauty was a gleaming, foot-and-a-half-long, two-headed ebony dong of rather remarkable girth and chiselled likeness to a certain appendage of the male anatomy. 'Nice craftsmanship,' I had to admit. 'Kind of big, though – for one man, isn't it?'

Chev amazed me by blushing. 'Oh, it's meant for two men, officer. One at each end. Only a fool would tackle Black Beauty all by himself.' His eyes grew even mistier with memory. 'It's fully-functional – vibrates and rotates and undulates. It cost me a fortune!'

'Uh-huh.' I set the album down. 'So, the thief or thieves stole your entire collection of sex toys, did they?'

'Oh, no, officer,' Chev responded. He swished over to a closet door, opened it, pointed down at a brimming cardboard box. 'He left these ones behind. My less valuable and least used pieces.'

I went over, bent down, picked a flesh-tinted, vein-scrolled dildo out of the box. It had a suction cup where balls would normally be located. 'How does this thing work?'

Chev snatched the sex toy out of my hand. 'Well, you stick it to a wall, or the floor, or the tub and ...'

'Can you show me?'

He smiled uneasily. 'Uh ...'

'It might help me break the case.' I shrugged, popping a goofy grin. 'I'm not too familiar with all this ... apparatus, you see.'

The man needed just that little bit of encouragement.

He rolled down his pants, revealing more smooth, tanned flesh, a semi-erection dangling out of trim and curly brown pubes. He smacked the dildo-base against the wall, and it stuck, twitching for something to bury its head and shaft in. Chev lubed the silicon hard-on, his crack, jumping with joy when his fingers touched heated rosebud.

'How 'bout this other stuff?' I stopped him before insertion, holding up a pair of nipple clamps and a cock ring. 'Can you show me how these work, too?'

The shirt came off, revealing a tanned, shaven chest and

pair of ripe, puffy nipples. The clamps were fastened onto the nipples with a delighted squeal, the cock ring around the rapidly expanding cock. Then Chev backed up to the wall-mounted dildo, worked the swollen head in between his taut brown cheeks, when I strapped a ball gag onto his head and into his mouth.

'Like that?' I asked, as if eager to learn.

He nodded, not being able to speak any more. His cock speared out from the ring, his nipples trembling in the clamps, as I gave him the all-clear and he resumed his backwards progress on the dildo.

Hood popped pucker and shaft entered anus, slow and easy, inch by textured inch. Chev's eyelids fluttered and his butt cheeks quivered, as he took the entire ten inches or so of that fuck-stick right up his ass. Until his buttocks splatted flat against the wall, the dildo anally consumed.

He started bouncing back and forth, impaling himself on the rod. It held tight to the wall, to his ass. Chev played with the clamps on his nipples, clutched and stroked his bloated cock in its squeezing ring, shuddering up against the wall.

I darted my hand in between his butt and the plasterboard and laced my fingers around the base of the dildo, pulling it out. 'I guess this thing can be operated by hand, too, huh?'

Chev stared back at me from his bent-over position, his eyes glazed. I pushed his ass forward a bit with the embedded poop-chute pole, then got in behind him and started plugging his butt on my own.

He groaned from around the ball gag, bending his knees and arching his back, fisting his dick. I churned his rear tunnel with the ass-pleaser, pumping hard and fast and even, my fist splashing up against his rippling cheeks. His whole body shook, as I reamed the guy, ramming his ass with a human touch.

Then he jerked, and jumped, semen spurting out of his mitt-cranked cock and spraying down onto his bed two

192

metres away. I kept on plunging away with the dildo, though his convulsing ass walls added to the gripping pressure. And he kept on coming, choking his chicken and tearing at his clamps.

He collapsed in a pool of his own sweat and semen, the dildo still sticking out of his caramel-coloured rump.

'I take it other people knew about your collection?' I queried, hefting the photo albums again.

Chev weakly nodded his head, popping the dripping ball gag out of his mouth. 'Yes! Yes! I've had a few complaints from the neighbours – about the noise.'

I nodded and made tracks, leaving the man to recover his drained strength.

I slowed my pace in the hallway, listening for any noise coming from those neighbours of Chev's. A particular type of noise I was listening for, made by a man or a woman or man and man or woman and man or any other combination and permutation permitted by the Charter of Rights and Freedoms; someone putting their newly acquired bounty to the wicked use it was intended, in other words.

I busted in on an old guy jerking off to a *Golden Girls* repeat, a kid giving an inflatable Jenna Jameson one hellacious workout. But no bevy of high-priced sex toys.

I went back to the stationhouse, reported my findings to the Captain in intimate detail. He filled his wastepaper basket with vomit, as I filled him in.

Then I gave it a day, was parked outside Chev's building the next morning. I still figured it as an inside job, someone living within the high-security apartment building itself. I also figured this robbery was more for personal reasons than professional, usage rather than resale. So after a day and night playing with the impressive collection, I thought I might just be able to spot the sex toy sneak thief.

People streamed out of the building, men, women, kids, and pets, headed for work or school or the next available fire hydrant. I studied them all, didn't see anything hinky, let alone kinky.

And then just around 9:32, a tall, slender, well-groomed blond came through the glass doors, glanced up and down the street. He was carrying a bulging leather briefcase, an air of furtiveness about him, dressed in a pinstriped suit; looking for all the world like just another high-priced lawyer, accountant or government receptionist. But when he started walking down the sidewalk, I knew I had my man.

I caught up with him halfway down the block, shoved him into an alley, up against the wall.

'What's the meaning of this?!' he wailed.

'Copper,' I grunted, holding tight to his collar with one hand, frisking his athletic physique with the other. My fingers arrived at his butt mounds, explored, in between. Things were a little loose in the caboose, all right.

'You didn't think you could get away with it, did you?' I rasped.

'Get away ... I don't know what you're talking about.'

'Save the pleas of innocence for the prison shower room,' I countered. 'Your stroll was your tell. This ain't a Monty Python sketch, friend. That funny walk of yours could mean only one thing – you've been playing in the dirtbox with a spade of two-man-sized proportions.'

He tried to give me some more guff. Then his whining turned to whimpering, when I unlatched his belt and yanked his trousers and underwear down, explored the gap in his ass skin-on-skin.

'What's your name?'

'Clive ... Burrow!' he gasped, as my digits sunk into his bum with no need for a shoehorn. He'd been gaped, just as I'd suspected.

'Why'd you steal Chev's toys?'

He turned his head, trying to see, as well as feel, what I was doing to his butt. 'I–I got tired of hearing him brag about his collection. Tired of hearing him use his collection.

194

You know, he never once invited me to one of his toy parties?'

'That's tough,' I growled, poking back and forth in his less-than-gripping bung. 'So where are they?'

'Well, uh, Black Beauty is in my briefcase,' he confessed. 'I was planning to give him another workout at lunch.' His voice changed, turning hopeful, his bright blue eyes beaming back at me. 'Unless ... you'd like to try him out yourself, officer. On me ... or–'

'Thanks, anyway. But I'm already packing.'

I unzipped my fly, pulled out the enormous erection that had sprung up between my legs thanks to my fleshy fondling, the sight of Clive's tight, tanlined butt. He grinned back at me, as I greased my super-rod with the lube I keep as standard equipment. Then he grimaced, gripping the alley wall, as I probed the mushroomed tip of my tool into his manhole. Even with an evening of loosening, it was still a tight fit.

I took a last look around, hooked to the guy's ring by the hood. No one about, the alley empty. I grasped my shaft at the base and eased the rest of the massive inches into Clive's bum, sticking him nice and slow and deep. This was the type of rubber-hosing cop and perp could both get on board with.

I drove right up to my clutching hand, burying my meat in the enveloping heat of the man's chute. He writhed, moaned, Black Beauty clearing the track for me.

I let go of his collar and grabbed onto his hips. He rotated his butt on my cock, allowing the both of us to rut. It felt good, it felt right. Street-level justice. An open and shut case.

I pumped my hips, fucking the blond's ass. My cock glided back and forth in his chute with sexual precision, making my face and body burn and my meat surge molten. Clive pushed back at me, matching my rhythm. His buttocks bounced and danced, his legs shaking almost as badly as mine.

It was taking a risk, sure, climbing all over the ass of a perp in public. But police work is all about taking risks, like online stock trading is all about taking gambles. Sometimes they pay off big-time and sometimes they crap out, like this time. It made living on the thin blue edge worth it.

'Fuck me! Fuck my ass!' Clive shouted, talking up a storm now.

I banged hard and heavy, using every raging inch I had in my arsenal, and his, my balls flapping against his buttocks. Sweat gripped my forehead and my fingernails bit into his hips, rocking away in a frenzy, the raw smack of flesh and squish of cock echoing off the bare alley walls.

I was ready to spill my beans, and I said so.

'Come in my mouth! Shoot in my mouth, officer!' Clive pleaded.

I'd given him so much, why not a little more?

I pulled my granite schlong out of his ass, and he spun around and dropped to his knees. The velvety wet heat of his lips consumed my glistening knob, just as orgasm knocked me back on my heels. I blasted away, coming in great, chugging gushes in the man's desperately gulping mouth.

It left me drained, another day on the beat.

'You just found them in an alley?' Chev piped, finding it all a little hard to swallow. But delighted at getting back his sex toys, nonetheless. He cradled Black Beauty in his arms like he'd given birth to the beast.

'Yeah,' I grunted. 'I guess whoever stole them just wanted to get back at you – temporarily. He obviously knew how much they meant to you.'

The guy kissed one swollen tip of his monster-dong, the other, cooed, 'Well, it's still–'

'Maybe you should be a bit more accommodating with your neighbours. Invite them all to your parties from now on.'

He looked up at me and grinned. 'OK.'

'And maybe let me know when you're having one of those parties, too, huh? I wouldn't mind following up on this case. Make sure you got everything back in good working order.'

His grin spread even wider, top and bottom.

I exited the building, the climax of another successful investigation under my belt.

Hazard Pay-off

I TIPPED THE PAVING stone-loaded dolly back, walked it ahead a few feet. Then I hit a rock on the half-completed driveway and the bricks shifted, pulling me and the dolly forward. I struggled to keep the stack upright, running now. And I clipped the dolly with a steel-toed boot and sent the whole thing flying over, pavers spilling everywhere. Right into the back of my foreman where he was kneeling on the driveway.

Once the dust had settled, Blake pushed a couple of pavers away from his backside and got to his feet. I sheepishly grinned at him. He shook his head. 'Hazard, try not to live up to your name, huh? For the good of the health of me and the crew.'

I nodded, amazed and gratified that the guy hadn't fired me on the spot. I'd only been on the job an hour, and this was already my second dolly wreck.

Actually, not a bad hour for a guy with my safety record. That's why they call me Hazard. I'd lost my previous three summer jobs when I'd: (1) accidentally pulled the ladder out from under a residential window-washing colleague, (2) smacked three guys in the head with a sheet of drywall at a house construction site, and (3) spilled boiling grease all over the brand-new shoes of my boss at a fast-food fry job. My placement counsellor at the student employment office even called me Hazard.

But I kept applying, because I needed tuition money for my first year of college in the fall. And I kept getting hired, because the skyrocketing price of base metals had turned the northern mining town into a boomtown.

Blake crouched back down, started once again picking up and placing the pavers into their interlocking pattern, building a driveway to last a lifetime. While I started restacking another load onto the dolly from the pallets at the end of the driveway. That was my job: delivering the stones to Blake who then fit them together in the sandy jigsaw puzzle. Ideally, delivering them smoothly right next to the guy, rather than catapulting them onto his back.

It was hard, hot, muscle-straining and forearm-scraping work. But the job had its good parts: all on Blake.

He was in his mid-20s, with short black hair and warm brown eyes, muscular all over from lifting and planting and stamping pavers for a living. He filled his faded jeans tight and taut, round in all the right places, his cheeks looking hard as the stones he was setting down. And since it was so hot, the work so heavy, he had his shirt off, his chiselled torso gleaming smooth and pumped in the sunshine. The guy was actually a good half-foot shorter than I was, but then I'm a carrot-topped beanpole.

I ogled my boss's rock-hard, glistening body constantly, my mouth hanging open and eating dust, craving to lick the salty sweat from his muscle-humped chest and rigid nipples. I strangled the handles on the dolly, yearning to finger the soft, perspiration-slick crack of his apple ass. And what with all my sweating and drooling, I was soon parched with thirst.

'Uh, is there anywhere I can get a drink of water?' I croaked, towering over Blake's broad, muscle-bunched back like a loving shade tree. The rest of the crew had gone on their dinner break, so it was just me and the boss.

He turned his head and squinted up at me. Making sure I wasn't holding anything that could fall on him, no doubt. 'Yeah, sure. The people who own the house are gone for the weekend, so it's locked up, but there's a hose in the

199

backyard they said we could use.' He grinned, adding, 'Don't flood the basement or anything, OK?'

I grinned back, said, 'OK.' Then tripped over the heel of his boot and went sprawling onto the front lawn, as I tried to move around him.

I managed to make it through the wooden gate that led into the backyard with only a slight tear to my T-shirt from a snagging nail, and spotted the hose hooked up to a faucet at the rear of the house. And as I was cranking the handle, getting the water to flow (after lifting my big feet off the hose), I heard some yelling and splashing coming from the house next door. So I walked farther into the yard, past the garage that blocked my view, playing out the hose and sucking sweet, cool water from the spout.

A six-foot-high plank fence surrounded the entire backyard, but that was no eyeball obstacle for a galoot like me. And when I peeked past the garage and over the fence, I choked on the water and just about swallowed the hose.

There was a swimming pool next door, two guys waist-deep in the middle of it, in each other's arms, in the midst of a hard, hot, passionate kiss!

I gaped at the men blatantly sucking face. They were really feeding on one another, lips chewing, tongues flailing, arms octopussing all over each other's backs, locked together so tight not even a sliver of light showed between their suntanned and water-washed bodies.

One guy had blond hair, the other a shaved head. And Blondie pulled back from Baldy's ravenous mouth and sealed his lips around the guy's tongue, sucked on it, the bald dude groaning his encouragement. I openly watched them go at it in that neighbouring dunk tank, dropping the waterhose and wrapping my fingers around my own hose, which had filled with something other than water in my jeans. I squeezed and rubbed my cock, eating up the erotic aquatic action next door, the two watersports too wrapped up in each other to notice my jughead floating over the fence.

Baldy reeled his sucked-dry tongue back in and dropped his head down to Blondie's chest, started licking the guy's protruding nipples. He swirled his chunky pink tongue all around the slick, tan buds, Blondie tilting his head back and moaning, gripping his lover's cinderblock shoulders.

The dude with the high-polish chrome dome vigorously sucked on Blondie's nipples, bit into them, tugged on them with his shiny white teeth. Like I was tugging on my pulsing prick through my jeans, my body burning with a heat more than sun and work-related. This was the kind of manual labour I could really get into.

And after working over his tub-buddy's boyish chest for a good, long while, Baldy steamed the guy through the water and up against the side of the pool. He lifted the sleek little blond out of the water with the greatest of ease and plunked him down on the pool's edge. Which is when I gleefully noticed that the guy was totally naked, his hard, all-man cock bobbing like an inflatable beach toy as he splashed down on the rim of the water bin.

Baldy quickly swum in between Blondie's legs, latching onto the guy's lean thighs and capturing and swallowing glistening cockhead. Blondie groaned, sprawling his hands back to hold himself up under the muscle-stud's onslaught, Baldy's head diving down between his quivering legs. My hand froze on my bulging cock, as I witnessed the dick-defying sword-swallowing. Baldy consumed his buddy's entire prick like it was nothing, and everything.

I held my breath, along with my writhing neighbour. Until finally, Baldy pulled his head back and gleaming meat oozed out from between his thick lips, like a greased snake. When he got to the cap, he bit into it, then inhaled the whole shaft again, his tongue shooting out to lick at Blondie's blond balls.

I started squeezing, rubbing again, singing the bald man's deep-throating praises with the palm of my hand. As

201

the shaven muscleman gripped his buddy's legs and bobbed his head up and down, earnestly sucking cock. Blondie rode his lover's cranium with one of his hands, his lithe body quivering with the wicked vacuum power of the awesome blowjob.

'You workin' or jerkin'?' a voice exploded in my ear.

I twisted my head around, and saw Blake lounging in the open fence gate. He was looking at me, at where my sweaty paw clutched my thread-straining cock. 'Uuuhh ...' I stammered, my face going even redder than my sunburn.

He walked over to me, then went up onto his top-toes and peered over the fence, taking in the erotic sights. 'Not bad technique. You might actually learn something,' he casually commented. 'Wanna give it a try, Hazard?'

I stared at the stud, hardly believing my burning ears. He just smiled and placed his warm hand over mine on my throbbing cock. And I just about jumped out of my work boots.

Blake unfastened his belt and unzipped his jeans, as I sank to my knees in the grass, ready and willing and eager to worship. He pushed his pants and briefs down, and his cock flopped out into the sunlight, big and getting bigger. I trembled with delight, inhaling the musky, ball-sweated scent of the man, watching his beautiful vein-ribboned tool rise up and up and expand and point at my face. Here was finally something I could truly handle on-the-job, the best job in the world.

'Suck it, Hazard,' Blake rasped. And I went to work.

I seized his thick dong with just my forefinger and thumb, forming a ring that I rode up and down his pink, pulsating length. Quick and light and teasing. He grunted, urging me to grab on and fist him. But I O-ringed his cut cock from balls to cap, sailing up and down his bumpy shaft with my circle jerk, neat and clean and tantalizing. I might be all thumbs in the workplace, but in the sexplace I consider myself a bit of a master craftsman.

Blake groaned and grabbed at my hair, as I pumped him fast, then slow, then fast again, tickling his tight, shaven nut sac with my other hand. Moans and groans from across the fence mingled and merged with Blake's gasps of lust in the superheated air. Until the guy just couldn't take my sexual taunting any more. He yanked my head into his groin, begging me to suck him.

But I didn't suck him, at first. Instead, I noosed his hood, pressed it into his grated abs, and licked at his meat, up from his tightened balls and along his pulsing shaft in one smooth, wet, tongue-beaded motion. He clawed at my hair, his legs shaking, as I sensuously painted his pipe – delicate and bold tongue-strokes that left him drenched in saliva and sweat, my fingers sticky with pre-come.

Then I dropped his cock. It strained in the still, electrified air, sniffing at my lips. I breathed all over it, steaming it raw, driving the man wild, before clipping the jumping cap with my teeth, causing Blake to cry out his sweet torture.

I sank my teeth into his meaty cockhead and slowly chewed it into my mouth, until I tasted shaft. At which point I shot my head forward and swallowed the guy right down to the balls. Then bounced back up again.

'Fuck!' he gasped, stunned. He stared down at me, unsure if what'd just happened had actually happened.

I proved that it had, sealing his cap between my lips and dive-bombing his shaft again, hands-free and balls-deep, over and over. Blake dug his fingernails into my scalp and hung on, growling, his cock filling my mouth, bouncing off the back of my throat and beyond.

Then I took a page out of Baldy's X-rated book, quick-downing my man's cock and holding it. And holding it. Nose pressing into his abdomen, chin pushing into his balls, I locked him down tight and wet and let the superheated, vice-like pressure build to outrageous proportions. Fortunately for the both of us, my gag reflex is like the rest

203

of my reflexes – virtually non-existent.

'Holy shit!' Blake cried, pulling on my ears, banging on my head. His watery brown eyes were frantic, his pressure-packed cock gone from his sight for an excruciating minute and counting.

The tension tightened like a wrench on a bolt, sweat pattering down off Blake's agonised face and onto mine. Humid breath steamed out of my flared nostrils and bathed his stomach, my cheeks and throat bulging with meat.

Until at last he grunted and shoved me back, before his balls boiled over. His dong burst out of my mouth in a gush of saliva, a slickened spear still tied to my lips by strings of spit.

'Want me to fuck you, Blake?' I asked, breathing hard, hardly at all.

The guy nodded in amazement, and respect.

He ended up on his back on the picnic table, stark, stunningly naked, legs up and spread. Very receptive to learning a further thing or two from his work-inept apprentice.

I shoved my jeans and shorts down around my ankles and shuffled in between his legs, letting him get a good look at the fat, squat tool that was going to pound him like the compactor he used to pound the paving stones together in the sand. Then I gripped his ankles and slapped my cock against his cock. He moaned.

His legs were as gorgeously muscled as the rest of him, just as smooth, and I slid my hands down and around his clenched calves, squeezing them. Then I shouldered his legs and ran my hands along his thighs, inner and outer, digging my fingers into his big, bunched quads. His muscles twitched and his cock bounced up and down on his flat belly all on its own, as I felt him up.

'Fuck me!' he implored, playing with his golden nipples and staring up into the sun.

I could see the perverted neighbours over the fence

again. Blondie was on all-fours on the diving board, like a tawny animal, Baldy at the top of the steps gripping the steel railings and hammering the guy's upraised ass. The board quivered like the pair of them, hanging out like Blondie's tongue as his chute got reamed. I nodded my approval at the workmanship and then teased Blake's asshole with the tip of my prick.

'Yeah, fuck me!' he responded, rolling his nipples, rolling his head back and forth on the smooth-sealed slats in sexual agony.

I squatted down, his legs riding my shoulders, and dug around in my grass-level pants pocket, came up with a one-session portable packet of lube. A good worker always comes prepared, with his own tools. I greased up my dick, nice and slow for Blake's benefit, and mine. Then I oiled his crack, wriggling a couple of fingers two knuckles deep inside the hunk just to hear him squeal, see him squirm. Finally, I steered my shiny cockhead up against his smooth-as-silk asshole again.

But if he'd thought I was going to take it slow and gentle, ease my way into his tight crevice, then my cocksucking hadn't taught him anything about the way I work the body. I punched through his starfish and plunged bowels-deep inside him, buried to the hilt in an instant. He jumped on the table like he'd been electrocuted, shouting obscenities to match our neighbours.

I gripped the pale soles of his feet and thrust sure and deep, full-cock fucking the stud, out to the cap and all the way in again, over and over. He was super-tight and burning hot, smooth-riding, the sight of his prone, cock-rocked body sizzling. The firm smack of my thighs against his shuddering ass filled my ears, the sensual feel of his gripping chute milking my churning cock stoking my body with heat.

He frantically tugged on his own prick as I crammed his ass strong and steady. I tickled his feet, licked at his puckered soles, sucked on a tender toe or three, all the while pumping my hips, fucking his sweet anus with authority.

A scream sailed over the fence. Followed by another. I jerked my head up and saw Blondie shaking out-of-control on the end of Baldy's ramming cock, jacking ropes of sperm out of his own cock and onto the diving board. As Baldy tilted his head back and let out a roar, emptying his balls in the blond bottom's rippling ass.

'You're going to come all over yourself!' I instructed my boss, pumping faster. 'Right after I do!'

He groaned and flung his head from side-to-side, his sun and cock-blasted body shaking.

I grasped his armoured thighs and dug in, force-fucking the gorgeous man, brutally slamming his ass. We smashed together, my cock pistoning his chute, the wet-hot friction unbelievable. I surged with an incendiary heat, balls flapping and boiling, Blake's hand flying up and down his shaft, in rhythm to my savage fucking.

I caught fire, and my cock exploded in the stud's sucking hole. I ripped out of Blake's ass and fisted wildly, spraying white-hot semen onto his jacked-up cock, torquing his action even more. He cried, 'Fuck!', and sperm jetted out of his jizz-slick cock, splashing down onto his heaving chest and stomach in great, sticky gobs.

I still have plenty of goof-ups on the job. But it's great finally having a boss who's so forgiving. Among other things.

Cab Fare

THE CAB PULLED UP to the curb, Second and Main, skid row. A guy jerked the door open, jumped in.

'You got money for the fare?' the driver asked, glaring at the man through the rearview mirror, the plexiglass shield that partitioned back from front.

The cab was big and old, a rebuilt Checker. The driver made no move to pull it away from the curb.

'Yes, I've got money.'

The cabbie kept his eyes on the guy, sizing him up. He was small, with short brown hair and big brown eyes, a delicately-featured, pretty face, tanned. Dressed in a white T-shirt and blue jeans, white sneakers. The shirt was dirty, the faded jeans torn, the sneakers scuffed and scruffy.

'Are we going to move, or just enjoy the pleasant conversation?' the guy asked, smiling. His teeth were white, with no visible gaps.

The driver grunted and shifted into gear. The big car leapt away from the trash-strewn gutter.

It was two in the afternoon – slow time – the hot summer sun beating down on the buckled asphalt, the tired fronts of the grimy, centuries-old buildings that lined the dirty street. Traffic was light, but noisy and profane.

'John Ivanovich,' the man in the back read off the laminated plate. 'Hi, I'm Phil.'

John gripped the big black steering wheel even tighter. A talker, he thought, great. There was sweat on his lean face, the back of his long neck and the palms of his large hands; hardly any money in his wallet. He just wanted to drive, and get paid. The last hour was always the toughest.

'I said I'm Phil,' the guy persisted, amiable.

'Heard you the first time.' John pushed his lank, dark hair over to one side, eyes locked on the road, avoiding the rearview mirror and contact with his fare. 'Where to?'

'Take a right at Hollings and then keep going south. I'll tell you where to turn off after that. It's quite a ways.'

John grimaced, eyes flicking to the mirror. 'Show me the dough.'

Phil gazed back at him, studying John's clear blue eyes carefully. The cab rocked to a stop at a red light, the crumbled curb only one short lane away. Phil finally shrugged and smiled and unfastened his jeans, arched his butt off the seat and pushed his pants right down to his sneakers, grabbed onto his cock and pulled it up.

'What the fuck?' John yelped. Staring at Phil's thick, cut slab of meat, watching it grow even longer and harder in the man's stroking hand. Phil staring back at him, grinning.

The tip of John's pink tongue speared out and bathed his full, red lips, his Adam's apple bobbing. He dimly heard the irate honking behind him over the rush of blood in his reddened ears, and he pressed down on the accelerator. The cab shot forward.

They roared down Main heading for Hollings, John watching his fare in the backseat ride his small, brown hand up and down the incredible length of his jutting cock. The shaft was wrist-thick and smooth, a lighter bronze than the rest of the man, the cap big and bloated, meaty. The tremendous member now so fully engorged that it could stand on its own, Phil briefly letting it loose to wag in rhythm to the road, ten inches of solid rod.

Then Phil slumped further down on the big, black, cracked-vinyl bench seat, and his cock seemed to grow taller still, right up to his cleft chin, from John's wide-eyed perspective in the oblong mirror. He regripped and pumped, from heavy, shaven sac to mushroomed hood, his little hand barely able to contain the beefy circumference of the giant dong.

A horn bellowed obnoxiously and a driver in the next lane shook his fist at John. The stunned cabbie yanked the wheel over to the right, the car back into its own lane. His eyes darting only momentarily onto the road, then back onto the cocky fare in his rearview mirror.

Phil licked his plush lips, his fine-chiselled face tightening with pleasure, brown eyes gone dreamy. 'I like it when someone watches,' he breathed, swirling his hand up and down and around his massive erection.

John watched. Frantically blinking the stinging sweat out of his gaping eyes and strangling the steering wheel with his sodden hands. His own cock gone as hard as Phil's in his pants.

'God, that feels good!' Phil groaned, really jacking his prong, hand tugging hard and swift on the engorged length of meat. Grabbing onto his hanging balls and squeezing, juggling. Mouth open, pink and wet and inviting.

John trod on the accelerator, the cab racing down the street doing 60K. Dodging cars and pedestrians, catching Hollings on two wheels and barrelling down the avenue, sailing southbound. John's shining eyes full of the erotic cock show in the backseat, anxious to keep it going; the cabbie even more anxious to take hold of that huge, hot, pulsing appendage and really jack it himself, then take it into his hungry mouth and consume it.

'Oh, John!' Phil gasped, both hands working his dong now, rapidly pumping. 'I'm–I'm going to come, John!'

John swallowed so hard his throat clicked, dry as the yellowed grass in the city park that flew by in a blur. 'No! I mean ... can't you hang on?' His eyes were panicked in the rearview mirror.

Phil desperately shook his head, two hands urgently tugging, pulling skin and pipe, pretty face distorted with lust. 'It's too late, John! My cock's getting so hard – come-hard!'

John chomped down on his lip so hard he drew blood, knuckles blazing white on the wheel. Staring at Phil's gaping slit, the straining, overswollen, hand-swept shaft, the ominously tightened sac – seeing it all through the mirror and the plexiglass and feeling it right inside him, his own cock screaming in his pants, along with his soul.

They blew through a red light doing 70. Phil's hands pumping full-steam. John not breathing, sweat-drenched body quivering.

'Here it comes, John!' Phil cried, tugging, yanking, stretching his towering cock.

'Fuck! Jack that fucking beautiful prick!' John screamed, cab hurtling over 80.

A pearl-white drop of come appeared in Phil's slit, glistened. Followed by another, and another. A steady dribble. Then a stream. Then a geyser.

Phil moaned, white-hot semen leaping out of the tip of his handled dong. Spouting and showering onto the floor of the rumbling cab. Twice, thrice, four, five, six times. The volume of viscous come as large as the volume of cock.

John howled with every savage blast, a maniacal grin on his shining face. Fervently yearning that it were his own loving hands on that spurting, jumping snake; his flaming face taking the heated, sticky blasts of salty sperm.

'Make a left at Royal Oak Road,' Phil gasped, slowing hands squeezing the last juicy drops of satisfaction out of his twitching cock. His little body jerking with the sweet aftershocks of fully spent ecstasy. '1925 Royal Oak Road.'

When John had brought the big cab to a skidding stop on the semi-circular cement driveway in front of the two-storey, red-brick mansion, he turned around and looked at Phil. The man had his cock tucked back into his jeans by now. '*You* live *here*?'

Phil nodded. Then slid forward on the seat and pulled a

roll of money out of the front pocket of his jeans and skinned off $200 in bills. 'For the ride – and the clean-up.' His teeth flashed white in a mischievous grin, his face only inches away from John's, behind the plexiglass.

The cabbie shook his head, grinning back. 'You know your money's no good here.'

He got out of the cab and pulled the back door open, helped Phil outside. Then led the trim-figured young man around to the back of the car and gripped him by the armpits and lifted him up, dropped him down on the expansive trunk. Tall and lean, John was wiry, as well.

Phil glanced around the hushed, green, tree-lined lawns, at the big brick house drowsing in the hot afternoon sun. 'You mean ... right here, right now?'

John smiled, unbuckling the belt that held up his tan dungarees. 'You didn't seem to mind when it was my backyard.'

A matching smile spread across Phil's sunbrowned face. And then he further matched John's actions, unzipping and pushing his jeans down.

John pulled them right off the man's smooth, slender legs. Standing there on the sunbaked cement with his own pants and boxers down around his ankles, his pale, skinny legs bared, his cock rising up and sniffing the heated air.

John shuffled closer, shouldered Phil's legs. Staring at the guy's still-strong cock, the shaven balls, the puckered, pink opening to Phil's glory hole that gaped seductively between taut, brown buns. He'd taken his "road lube" out of his pants pocket before shoving them down, and now he greased his throbbing cock. Slid two fingers into Phil's cheeky ass crack and slickened cute asshole.

'Yes!' Phil groaned, his body jumping at the other man's touch.

He leaned back on the yellow metal and slid his shirt up, exposing his smooth, sunkissed chest, his stiff, burnt-sugar nipples. He gripped the rigid buds between two fingers and

211

pinched and rolled them, his cock jumping on his flat stomach as John manoeuvred closer. 'Drive me, driver!' he gritted, squinting up at the towering man.

John clutched Phil's thigh with one hand, his other hand on his own cock – pointing, steering the rigid, pink, eight-inch dong at and into Phil's winking browneye. Pushing the fat, gleaming hood up against Phil's asshole. The heated contact sending a shiver through both men.

John didn't press it, though, not yet, the meaty cap staying squished there in the groove. As he took his hand off his cock and put it on Phil's. Grasping the man's enormous erection mid-shaft and squeezing. Getting a good feel for the mammoth appendage that had aroused such passion in the pair of them, set the chain of scorching sexual events into action.

Phil's cock was just as silky-smooth and amazingly thick as John had imagined it would feel. And he revelled in the beating, engorged heat of it. Pumping it with his sweaty hand, stroking and stretching the skin, rubbing the huge, well-defined hood, making the clean-shaven balls jump.

Satisfied, for now, he unhanded the swollen snake and took up his own cock again. Pushed his cap hard against Phil's pucker. And popped through, in; vein-striated shaft gliding smooth and sensual past stretching ass ring and deep inside accommodating chute.

Both men groaned with the exquisite sensation of long, hard cock sinking into hot, tight ass, the one man's clenched thighs bumping up against the other's clenched buttocks – pulsating dick buried to the hilt in gripping anus.

'Fuck me, John! Fuck me!' Phil pleaded, rolling his head around on the hot metal. Brimming ass gloriously swelled with embedded cock.

'Play with your prick!' John hissed, gripping both of Phil's golden-brown thighs and churning his narrow hips. 'Jerk yourself off like you did in my cab!' Pumping Phil's chute, fucking the man's ass.

Phil grabbed up his dong and started urgently stroking, his small, fine-lined body getting brutally shunted to and fro by John's vigorous cock-thrusts. Sweat poured off John's face, splashing down onto the superheated sexual nexus of the two men, adding more grease to the homoerotic fire. His body rocking and hips flying back and forth, cock surging in and out of Phil's sucking asshole, clear blue eyes fixated on the writhing man's hand-cranked member.

Phil fisted his cock with one hand, felt up his tingling chest and buzzing nipples with the other. John's relentlessly pistoning rod filling him up to bursting. Setting his chute ablaze and his ass and body to shimmering with fiery joy.

'Yeah, baby! Fuck, baby!' John cried. Pumping his hips in a frenzy, pounding his cock into Phil's anus. His flapping sac bubbling and boiling, thrusting dong humming as tellingly hard as Phil's.

The wet, hot splat of corded thighs banging against shivering butt cheeks obscenely split the still, dry air. The animal grunts and groans of the two men gaining in urgency and intensity. The cock of the one jackhammering the ass of the other. Tall, standing, shaking man savagely fucking the smaller, shuddering man stretched out on the shiny trunk of the big yellow taxicab. The sun beating down on the wild men and the wild scene, exposing everything.

Phil groaned low and long, jerking on the end of John's prick. Semen jetted out of his jacked up cock, striping his face and chest with wicked orgasm. He stuck out his long, pink tongue to capture some of the leaping come, ecstatically taking it into his mouth and gulping it down.

John stared glassy-eyed at that spouting dong, sawing away at the coming man's chute. Then jerking himself, jolted by his own blistering orgasm. His cock exploded in Phil's ass and sprayed bowels and chute with such body and soul draining ferocity that it backed up and basted his own balls.

Until, at last, John collapsed on top of Phil, the two

213

steaming, gasping men kissing and frenching. John feeling Phil's thunder cock press against the slickened skin of his stomach, his own cock still buried in Phil's ass, gently pumping.

The taxi driver left his card behind, as well. He was available for pick-up anytime. Phil was just the kind of cocky fare John's kind of cabbie loved.

The Pantyhose Bandit

IT WAS ALL OVER the local newspapers and TV – the case of the "Pantyhose Bandit". Apparently, some dude was breaking into people's homes and stealing primarily worthless items while indulging in what was his primary reason for breaking-in in the first place – sniffing, fondling and dressing up in women's lingerie and high heels. In fact, according to some eyewitness accounts, the thief had broken in as a man – a pair of pantyhose over his head – and come out as a woman, dressed in ladywear everywhere including his head.

I read and watched the reports, not getting nervous like some, or giggly like others – but rather, getting very, very turned-on by it all. As I stroked my cock in front of the latest telecast of the Bandit's exploits (breaking into a house a couple of blocks over and making off with a lacy, black bra and panty set and a pair of six-inch black stilettos), I resolved to do something myself to catch the culprit. To protect the neighbourhood, yes; to get me a piece of the perverted perp, damn right!

It was all a matter of setting the right trap, I figured. I live alone, but just for the Pantyhose Bandit's sake, I made it look like I'd just taken on a female roommate – a very sexy female roommate – or become a serious cross-dresser myself.

I picked up some cheap women's high heels at the local Goodwill, set them out on my front doorstep. I dug through the trash at the rear of a lingerie shop, carried home numerous gold and red boxes, which I then prominently displayed in my own trashcans. I borrowed some bras, panties, stockings and pantyhose from various female friends, and hung them out on my clothesline. I even got a bottle of perfume and sprayed the entire contents around my yard, hoping the Pantyhose Bandit would pick up the scent, nose as well as eye-wise.

Then I darkened my home and drove off into the night; stopping three blocks over and sneaking back around inside, setting up shop in my bedroom, which now contained the final honeypot to attract the pilfering animal: a top bureau drawer over-brimming with women's lingerie.

It took three hours of patient, panting waiting, only my hard-on and visions of the heroic capture to come to keep me company. But around one o'clock, I heard the french doors that open out onto my backyard deck open up. I'd left them loosely latched, of course, just for the occasion.

I held my breath, my cock, peering out of the crack in my bedroom closet, my ears pricking and heart pounding. I heard a soft, padding sound – someone tip-toeing down the hallway carpet, coming closer. I froze, my sweating hand throttling my throbbing erection, as the stealthy steps drew nearer and nearer.

Until a shadow suddenly appeared in the bedroom, bigger and darker than any of the other shadows. I swallowed, staring, straining. A flashlight flicked on, the white beam finding the overflowing bureau drawer with uncanny accuracy. The Pantyhose Bandit was in the room with me, inside my house of games!

The mini-flashlight was secured to his head, the better for hands-free fondling and sniffing. He was wearing the pantyhose, all right, also on his head, the gossamer legs flopping down like two oversized rabbit ears. He was tall, with a nice, slender, shapely figure, clad entirely in black.

I heard him sigh as he beheld the dazzling array of cotton, nylon and silk women's undergarments. Then I saw him plunge his hands into the frothy cloud of lingerie, bring an armful up to his nose. The inhalation and exultation was something to behold for myself.

I grinned, gently stroking my dick so not even the shifting foreskin made a sound to disturb the man's reverie. He was in his element now, wallowing in it. He rubbed satiny bras and panties, silky stockings all over his pantyhosed face, sniffing loudly.

And then he put on a real show.

My cock just about knocked the shutter doors of the closet wide open, as the guy suddenly dropped his armload of undergarments and stripped off his shirt, his pants. He stood there before me in just his black sneakers and sheer black pantyhose, his cock poling out even longer than mine.

I gulped, my balls popping with seed. His body was smooth and pale, every hair on his nut-sac shaven away, butt cheeks sticking out taut and rounded, legs and arms long and lithe, like his dick. He quickly slipped into a coral-pink pair of panties, secured a matching bra across his chest. Then stepped into a pair of red stockings, the red leather pumps he'd brought with him from my front door.

It was quite a sight, one he and I both enjoyed; me through the crack in the closet doors, the dolled-up dude in front of the large mirror that sits atop my bureau. I stroked my pulsing cock, pinched and rolled my wildly tingling nipples, as the Bandit stood in silk-sheathed legs and rubbed his satin-clad cock, pulling on his nipples through the bra. He moaned softly, sexily, oblivious to committing any more crimes. It was time for me to take the law into my own hands.

I parted the shutter doors six inches or so, taking advantage of the thorough oiling I'd given the hinges just that afternoon. Then I tucked my dick in against my stomach and slipped through the opening, around in behind the posing pervert. He was so enthralled with his appearance, the feeling-up process, that he didn't even hear me, let alone see me. Until, that is, I gripped my rod and poked it against his pantied left cheek, growled, 'Put your hands up, Pantyhose!'

He jumped, the guy caught utterly off-guard. He'd gotten a little too cocky with all his recent successes; not quite cocky *enough* for me just yet, however. He shot his hands up into the air, body trembling most appealingly against my prick.

I kept it like that for a moment, enjoying the tremoring of his tush, the shape of his torso. Then I put a cap in his ass – my cap, shoving it under the panties and into his crack. He shuddered and gulped. I reached around, grabbed onto his cock in the scanties, gave it a stroke.

'We're going to do things my way from now on,' I rasped, the guy's dick filling my damp palm with a hot, pulsating need.

He nodded, keeping his hands high, his cock hard.

I pushed him down onto the bed. Then quickly secured his wrists and ankles to the bedposts with nylon and silk strands of stocking, brown and red and white and black. 'Just so you don't get away, before the cops ... come,' I said, not bothering to use the telephone on the nightstand to dial some help. Instead, I spread myself out on top of the girly-clad man, keeping his warm, beating body covered – with mine.

'What's your name?' I breathed into his face.

'N–Nevin,' he gasped through his pantyhose.

'Nevin,' I repeated, rolling it around in my mouth. Then I brought my mouth even closer, pressed it against his mouth.

We made intimate contact through his fine-threaded disguise, our lips joining warmly, then hotly. I grabbed onto his head and mashed my mouth into his through the pantyhose, grinding my cock against his cock through the panties. He shivered, straining at his sexy restraints, arching his hips so that his cock pushed harder and tighter against mine, the pair of surging appendages rubbing, squeezing, sliding together.

I thrust out my tongue, clotting his hose with my humid lust, painting his lips, pumping my cock into his cock. He moaned, writhing beneath me, pushing out his own tongue. The tip of our stickers met through the nylon and danced together, our hot breath steaming up a storm front.

I smelled sweat, the sweet, tangy stuff that sheened Nevin's exposed armpits. I licked his lips through the pantyhose again, his chin. He tilted his head back, and I lapped at his slender neck, his bobbing Adam's apple. Then I dragged my damp mouth-organ across the top of his chest and into his right armpit.

He groaned when my tongue hit the soft, moist, sensitive flesh of his shaven underarm, his cock jerking up against mine. I licked his armpit, really tasting the man, really loving the taste of the man. I scooped up some of his sweating need and carried it over to his mouth, smearing it across his lips and onto his tongue. Before diving back down and lapping at his other arm hollow, always fucking his cock with my cock.

I gripped his bra'd pecs, and squeezed. His heaving chest rose up in my hands, the bedposts creaking with the strain of his pulling arms. I pinched his nipples through the satin cups, rolled them, licked them, sucked on them. Before spilling his cups and grabbing onto his bare pecs, his naked nipples.

He gasped, body quivering beneath me. His pecs were smoothly mounded, his nipples tautly rigid. I swirled my tongue around one stiffened bud, the other, rejoicing at their rubbery, pebbled textures. Then I sealed my lips over a jutting man-teat and sucked on it.

Nevin strained against his bindings, but there was no breaking loose. I pinched up his other nipple and captured it between my lips, sucked hard on that one. I bobbed my head back and forth, sucking, licking, biting, clutching his pecs and churning his cock.

And then I dropped lower, trailing my tongue down the man's tightened stomach, pouring into his bellybutton and swirling around; dragging lower. Until my tongue touched panty, and I abruptly painted the bulging outline under the satin with a series of hard, wet strokes.

'Yes!' Nevin cried, slamming his cock against my tongue.

I gripped his narrow hips and held him down, lapping at his panty-clad cock. His swollen hood and part of his smooth shaft peeked out the elasticised top of the sexy underwear, and I tickled them with my taste appendage, getting more than a rise out of the guy. In a matter of moments, his panties were just as wet as if there'd been a woman inside.

I drew them down with my teeth, fully exposing Nevin's dick. It sprung up and kissed against my nose. I left the panties bunched at his balls and blew on his bare cock. He gasped; groaned with pleasure when I took his meaty crown into my mouth and swallowed shaft halfway down. I bobbed my head, tugging with my lips, sucking on the man's awesome cock.

He rolled his head around on the pillows, breathing hard. His dick filled my mouth and part of my throat, beating inside me. I sucked hard and tight and quick, then more slowly, sensually, pulling my lips right up to the mushroomed cap and just about off, then diving right back down shaft again, devouring meat.

I sucked on and on, making him squirm and writhe, squirt pre-come. I gave his dick a couple more quick pulls, then dropped it from my mouth.

I jumped off the bed and scooped up some stockings from the overflowing bureau drawer, jumped back onto the bed before Nevin could whimper too much. Then he outright howled, with joy, when I lashed his cock with the slick, supple leg garments, winding them around and around the base of his prick, trussing up his balls into a bunched mass. So that his stake stood rigidly right up in the air, straining for something to impale – like a man's hot, tight anus.

I reached past Nevin's head and pulled some lube out of a drawer in the headboard. He thrust up his head, tongued my armpit through his pantyhose. I let him get in a couple of licks, then went to work on his cock again, this time coating it with something even slipperier than my saliva. I pumped his dong with my hand, greasing it good as he groaned.

My asshole was next. I reached back and around and lubed my pucker, groaning myself at the slick touch of my fingers on my rosebud, the plunge of those same digits right into my manhole. I was wet and stretched and ready for the biggest payoff of the whole erotic evening.

I straddled Nevin's hips, spread my cheeks. Then I slowly lowered myself down on his upthrust cock. His cap squished against my starfish. I dropped lower. His hood burst through my ring, was swallowed up by my anus. I sat down, splatting my cheeks on his thighs, his cock ploughing into my chute.

We groaned, the bed shaking like our bodies. I started bouncing, fucking myself on the guy's steel pole. His cock filled my ass to bursting, sawing my anus, wicked heat shimmering all through my overwrought body. Nevin pumped his hips, fucking my bung in rhythm to my frantic rising and falling.

It was a wild, wonderful ride. I grabbed onto Nevin's bra'd pecs, undulating my bum up and down on his spear. His cock churned my chute, filling me, fucking me, making my own bobbing cock hum with erotic sensation. I gripped it and ripped it, enjoying every inch of Nevin's dick oiling back and forth in my ass.

We moved faster, stroking harder. The bed groaned with our efforts, the air full of the cracking of thighs against cheeks, the moans and groans of two men getting it on. Then Nevin jerked and cried out, jetted white-hot semen up

221

against my bowels; his cock overcoming its restraints and searing my anus with seed.

It was too much for me to withstand. My own dick went off in my fist, sperm leaping out and striping Nevin's chest and stomach. We came with jolt after jolt of ecstasy, Nevin creaming my chute, me his body.

'Well, I guess I can't hold you for ever,' I sighed afterwards.

I popped off the guy's cock and unleashed it, watched it swell even bigger with the sudden rush of blood, then tongued the last drop of semen out of its slit. And then I untied the rest of Nevin's restraints. But only with the promise that he was going to be good from now on – and only break into my place in future.

Heavies

JACKSON STEPPED OFF THE bus into the cold driving rain. Wilton; deep in the coal mining region of the state, way deep in the minor hockey league system; deep enough to bury a man permanently if he wasn't careful, suffocate his dream of ever making it to the NHL.

Jackson was 22 years old, a huge, hulking man with the scars on his face and fists already a testament to how he played the game: tough; his role in the game: enforcer.

He grimaced, ran a big, square-knuckled hand through his bright blond hair, looking up at the leaden sky, then across the street at the dilapidated, barn-like structure that was the valley city's arena. He heaved his hockey bag up onto a broad shoulder, shuddered slightly, then strode across the street, intent on making the team.

Boyd hit the deserted city limits and drove on through. There were no brass band and cheering fans there to greet him, like when he'd won the Stanley Cup as a late-season add-on one long decade earlier. There was just wet, black, winding asphalt and abandoned warehouses and mills, craggy rocks jutting out from the moon-like landscape. He shifted the GTO down, slowing, slowing, always slowing, headed down into the valley. From the pinnacle of pro sports to near absolute bottom.

Boyd was 30 years old, six-feet tall, compact, muscular. His nose had been broken so many times it wandered his face, and his knuckles were so out of alignment they'd never

223

form straight rows again no matter how much surgery he had.

He drove through the flashing yellow intersection lights along Main Street, turned off, into the parking lot of the arena. Then he snapped off the rumble of one of the last remaining toys of the glory days. He stepped out into the rain, lugged his hockey bag out of the car's trunk, stared at the 80-year-old arena.

It had come down to this, his dream of reliving the triumph that he'd tasted far too early and far too easy. The steady slide down had seemed inevitable after that, fuelled by booze and boredom and a belief in invincibility.

Boyd shuddered beneath his leather jacket, threw back his long black hair, a hard man still, but nowhere near unbeaten. His brown eyes shone with memories; and a fierce, renewed determination to give it one last shot. If he could latch on as the enforcer for the Thunder, he could begin the long climb back up. Anything beat driving a delivery truck for a living.

He caught movement out of the corner of his eye – a man walking across the street towards the arena; a big, broad, tough-looking man, striding confidently. Their burning eyes met through the pouring rain in the pre-dawn chill, and they both knew their jobs had just gotten a lot harder.

They tangled during the first practice. The coach of the Wilton Thunder was a white-haired, red-faced guy who had worshipped at the temple of Fred Shero many, many hockey moons ago. He watched with a twinkle in his milky eyes, as Jackson and Boyd dropped the gloves before a puck had even been dropped and circled each other.

They clutched uniforms, started throwing. A right bounced off Boyd's temple, a left drove into Jackson's nose. It went back and forth, punches thrown at a furious pace, some landing, most not. Until their uniforms were so tangled up and the pair so exhausted that they didn't protest when the coach yelled at two other players to break it up.

'I like the game played rough and tough!' Coach barked afterwards. 'Team tough. There's only going to be room on this squad for one goon.'

The die was cast.

The first shift of the first scrimmage, Jackson nailed Boyd into the boards with a cross-check. Boyd saw stars, then came up swinging.

They bloodied each other's noses. Boyd's lower lip was split open down the middle. The coach let that fight go on for a full minute, the other players whacking the boards and the ice with their sticks when it was finally all over.

But it wasn't all over, not by a long shot. In the small, dreary dressing room afterwards, Jackson was bending over to pick up a roll of tape, dressed just in his jock, when Boyd shoved him from behind, headfirst into the row of metal lockers.

Boyd's upper body was bare, and his muscles popped all over his arms and chest, his smooth, pale skin gleaming with perspiration under the 30-watt bulbs. 'That's for your cheap shot,' he growled at Jackson.

The other picked himself up and gave his head a shake. His wet blond hair flopped over his eyes, and he slicked it back. His tall, tanned body was thick with vein-striated muscles, his thighs flared wickedly wide from a summer school of power skating. 'You're going to get more of those before this camp is over, old-timer. If you can't take it, retire.' Jackson grinned a clean row of teeth.

Boyd's tongue inadvertently sought out the gaps in his own dental work, as his eyes roamed over Jackson's lean, handsome face and young, hard body. Then he turned as if to go, but leapt back into the fray, tackling Jackson and smashing the both of them into the lockers.

The men grappled, their semi-nude bodies pressing together, big muscles straining. Boyd head-butted Jackson,

225

momentarily stunning the younger man. Then Jackson kneed Boyd in the groin, the older man's jock only partially absorbing the blow.

They rolled onto the floor, around on the chewn-up carpet, the other players in various stages of undress scrambling to get out of the way. 'Save it for the motel room on the road, lovers!' Coach suddenly barked, putting a halt to the wrestling match.

He slapped his clipboard against his thigh. 'We're playing the Turnberry Wildcats tomorrow night, in Turnberry. Everyone gets to play. For now. Be back at the arena at six tomorrow morning. It's a five-hour ride on the iron lung, boys, one-way.'

The other players groaned.

Boyd and Jackson got to their feet, glaring at one another.

Jackson quickly discovered that he and Boyd were already sharing the same motel in Wilton, a horseshoe-shaped, two-storey structure along the highway on the west side of town. He was walking by the leaf-filled wreck of the swimming pool, headed for the ice machine to continue nursing his various bumps and bruises, when he spotted Boyd through the partially open door of Room 12. The older man was stretched out on his bed in his underwear, watching a black-and-white movie on TV. Despite the frigid temperature outside, the ancient, overheated rooms made cracking a door or window mandatory.

Jackson thought about just walking by. He thought again.

'Better get your beauty sleep, old-timer,' he said, smacking Boyd's door wide open with his free hand.

Boyd leapt off his bed and into a fighting stance. Then he saw that Jackson was wearing just a bathrobe and flip-flops, an ice bucket in his hand, and he grinned at the man's battered face. 'Soaking your head in a bucket, huh? That's where it belongs, all right.'

Jackson entered the small, dingy room, walked up to Boyd. 'Why don't you just call it quits right now, Pops? Save my knuckles some punishment.'

Boyd spat in the man's face.

The hot spit struck Jackson on his left cheek, rolled down. He spat in Boyd's face, catching the other man full in the mouth.

Boyd licked Jackson's saliva from his lips, swallowed. Then he thumped the bright purple bruise on Jackson's chest, just above the man's left nipple. He didn't hit him hard with his folded fist, just enough for Jackson to really feel it.

The blond rocked back on his heels. He slapped Boyd's face, catching the smaller, stockier man right on the stitched-up cut that decorated his left cheek like a war ribbon.

Boyd's head twisted to the side and he groaned. He put his hand up to finger the wound. Then he tore Jackson's bathrobe open, grabbed onto the man's semi-erect cock and gave it a twist.

'Fuck!' Jackson grunted, jumping up onto his toes, his cock swelling in Boyd's hot, gripping hand despite the pain. He dug his fingernails into either side of Boyd's underwear and ripped the skimpy white briefs down.

Boyd's cock flopped out into the open, huge and heavy with blood. Jackson grabbed onto it, roughly pulled it. Boyd gasped and jerked forward.

The men stared at one another, face-to-face, cocks clenched tightly in each other's hands, cocks growing as hard as their bodies and thoughts. Jackson mashed his mouth down onto Boyd's mouth, savagely kissing the man. Boyd fought back with his tongue, shooting it into the younger man's wet, open mouth and slamming it up against Jackson's tongue.

They wildly frenched, their cheeks bulging with each

other's tongues, their hands clasping and pulling on each other's cocks; their hard, fully-engorged cocks, filling the squeezing hands with pulsating meat.

Boyd pulled his head back and attacked one of Jackson's taut, tan nipples. He bit into the rubbery bud, pulled on it, stretching it almost right off the groaning man's chest. Jackson grabbed Boyd's big, hairy balls with his other hand and gave them a ruthless jerk. Boyd groaned, but didn't let go with his teeth.

Jackson tugged on Boyd's prick, twisted the man's sac. As Boyd left his teeth marks behind on Jackson's one nipple, swirled his wet, red tongue all around the other. The blond grunted and shivered, sticking out his muscle-humped chest, spearing his cock deeper into Boyd's hand.

Boyd grasped Jackson's blond-dusted balls and gouged them with his fingers, digging into the testicles, separating and squeezing them individually. As Jackson sunk his fingernails into the veiny shaft of Boyd's cock and scratched all along its rigid length. The men panted, straining against one another, their big, heated, naked bodies close together.

Then Boyd suddenly pulled his hand off Jackson's swollen prick and slammed the man on the side of the shoulder, sending him toppling over onto the bed. He quickly joined his teammate there, the two men wrapping into a sideways 69, legs upraised for easy access to cocks and balls and asses.

Boyd inhaled Jackson's smooth, sculpted hood, sent his mouth and lips sailing down Jackson's clean-cut shaft. The blond followed suit, blossoming his red lips over Boyd's bloated cap and pouring his mouth down the brunette's bumpy shaft. The two men clutched at each other's muscular butt cheeks, joined at the mouth and cock.

Boyd moved his head back and forth, sucking Jackson's prick. He didn't go easy, though, giving the young man another rough ride, teeth scraping shaft, biting into hood. Jackson reciprocated, giving inches, and taking them, biting into Boyd's shaft, chewing on the man's cap.

The bed groaned with their heated movements, straining to contain the heavy pair of lusty he-man. The men sucked hard and fast on one another's cocks, cramming their mouths and throats full of throbbing meat, neither backing down from the challenge.

Boyd pulled his mouth off Jackson's cock only long enough to spit on two of his fingers, suck on the pair of digits. Then he swallowed the blond's pipe again, and hooked his slickened fingers in between Jackson's quivering butt cheeks and down into the man's asshole, busting pucker and plunging two knuckles deep.

Jackson groaned around Boyd's cock, his body jumping with the erotic intrusion of the fingers up his ass. He fought back with his own digits, rapidly wettening three and ramming them into Boyd's manhole.

The brunette gasped, gagging on Jackson's cock, the man's long fingers diving full-length into his chute. The two men shimmered all over, ablaze with emotion, cocks jammed deep into mouths, fingers plugged deep into asses. And then the fucking began.

Neither man would give ground in the battle for supremacy, in the bedroom as it was on the ice. So neither would allow the other to top him, stick cock in ass and fuck bottom. So they pumped their hips, and fingers, fucking one another's mouths and throats and asses.

Jackson churned Boyd's wet-cauldron of a mouth with his cock, as he slammed his fingers back and forth in Boyd's chute. And Boyd did the same, driving his dick into Jackson's mouth, fucking the man's face, as he hammered ass with his fingers, reaming Jackson's anus.

The temperature in the tiny, stifling room skyrocketed, the air thick and heavy with the funk of sex and sweat, the muffled groans of the two men fucking and getting fucked. Neither would let up, pumping mouths, pumping asses. Their bare bodies shone with perspiration, their big muscles straining, buttocks clenching.

On and on it went, cocks and fingers pistoning, throats and butts getting ravaged raw. Until, at last, Boyd jerked, Jackson jerked, the blistering sexual pressure built to the blow-off point, no stopping it.

Boyd exploded in Jackson's mouth, blasting white-hot semen down the man's throat, in fearsome rhythm to the fingers sawing his chute. His cry of ecstasy was drowned in a shooting sea of Jackson's sperm, the blond's cock rupturing in Boyd's mouth and rocketing salty come, Boyd's driving fingers spurring on the heady gouts of ecstasy.

The men shuddered and jetted and pumped and swallowed, over and over again. They blew out everything they had in their balls, even in their joy each trying to outdo the other in volume and intensity and repetition.

Finally, when the last tremors of all-out orgasm had rippled through their muscular bodies, they shifted around face-to-face on the bed. They kissed, giving back as good as they'd gotten, swirling each other's warm, rubbery sperm around in their mouths. They crossed tongues again in the gooey mess, their cocks pressed tight together like their bodies, clutching one another in their arms.

They fought the Turnberry Wildcats to a draw, Boyd and Jackson both scoring a pair of kayos. Then the two men fought each other in their motel bedroom that night, on the ice at practice the following day, after the long, exhausting bus ride back to Wilton.

A week in, even the jaded old coach was shaking his head in amazement. He'd never seen such consistent ferocity, a burning hatred so passionate. He wanted to keep both men, but the GM overruled him, trading Boyd away just before the start of the grinding 84 game minor league season – to a rival team in the same division.

The men fucked and sucked like wild animals in Jackson's motel room that night. Then Boyd jumped in his car and keyed the engine to life, roared off into the chilly, rain-streaked night with Jackson's warning that he'd kick his ass the next time they met – as opponents – ringing in his ears.

More titles from Xcite Books

9781907016097
£7.99 $11.99

9781907761522
£7.99 $11.99

9781907761638
£7.99 $11.99

Xcite Books are also available as ebook downloads on
iTunes, Kindle and www.xcitebooks.com

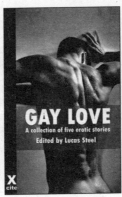